THREE FACED DOLL

SUZI BAMBLETT

Broodleroo

First Published by Broodleroo 2021
Copyright © 2021 by Suzi Bamblett

Suzi Bamblett asserts the moral right to be identified as the author of this work.

First edition
Paperback ISBN: 978-1-8382550-1-5

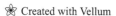 Created with Vellum

To my sister, Pauline.
Love you.

PROLOGUE

It's funny isn't it, the things people consider suitable for children. You remember that doll? A hand-me-down bequeathed to our mother by a well-meaning maiden aunt. By the time the doll came to live with us, her pink satin dress was faded, her lace bonnet yellowed and torn.

The bonnet concealed a secret. Twisting the hidden knob on top of the doll's bisque head revealed three faces. The first, a lifeless mask of a sleeping face. One rotation revealed a grotesque crying face with puckered eyebrows, tearstained cheeks and a mouth contorted in pain. Another turn exposed the third face, lips curled in a hideous sneer and knowing eyes following our every move.

That smiling face. So creepy and clown-like. Almost as though she could see right through us.

CHAPTER ONE

We hide behind the airing cupboard door, hardly daring to breathe. 'Is she sleeping, Mummy?'

Mummy reaches up to lift the doll, source of our childhood nightmares, from the pile of stacked towels on the top shelf. Following our familiar bedtime routine, Mummy cradles the doll to check her eyes are closed and her mouth forms a sweet rosebud. 'Fast asleep.' Mummy stows the doll back in the airing cupboard and claps her hands. 'Now, off to bed.'

Squealing, we run into the bedroom and jump onto Khalu's bed.

Daddy follows, loosening his tie. 'Have you chosen a bedtime story yet, girls?' He unfastens his top button and rolls up his sleeves.

'This one.' Khalu passes him *The Big Book of Fairy Stories*.

'No.' I dive under the quilt. 'Not that one. The lady's too scary.'

Daddy sits on the bed and turns the book to look at the

cover. 'You don't need to be frightened of this old lady. Isn't she Red Riding Hood's granny?'

'It's Old Mother Goose,' Mummy calls from the landing.

I peek out to look at the book.

'She's a witch,' whispers Maya. 'She'll put a spell on us.'

'Well, I want the troll story' – Khalu flicks through the pages – 'and it's my turn to choose.'

'It's always your turn,' grumbles Maya. I giggle.

Daddy leans back against the headboard and begins to read. 'Once upon a time, there were three Billy Goats Gruff…'

We snuggle up while Daddy does the voices, joining in with the trip-trapping. When the troll says, 'I'm going to eat you,' Daddy pretends to gobble us up. We wriggle and squeal.

'Don't get them all wound up,' calls Mummy, but we know she's listening to the story too.

'And the goats gobble all the green grass and live happily ever after. And now it's time for my little goats to snuggle down in their beds. Night-night, Khalu.' Daddy gives Khalu a tickle and a kiss. She always has to be first. 'Night-night, Ilona.' He tucks Brown Bear in beside me. As he gives me a kiss and a squeeze, his prickly chin scratches my face. Maya gets the final kiss before Daddy props the door ajar, so we have light from the landing.

'Nighty-night girls.' Mummy blows us a kiss from the doorway before following Daddy downstairs.

My sisters are asleep in no time, but I lay awake, thinking about the doll in the airing cupboard. What's that scuffling noise? Is she sitting up? Turning her head around? In the half-light I make out the shape of our bookcase with Raggedy Doll and Harvey Rabbit jostling for space on top. Daddy put the book on the shelf. Now I hear it sliding back out all by itself.

Perhaps the old lady is a witch after all? I scooch down under the duvet, hugging Brown Bear tight.

Brown Bear, Charlie Dog and Monkey sit on the blue checked picnic blanket. Khalu is in charge of the red spotty teapot.

'Maya wants more tea,' I say.

Khalu frowns but pours another cup. Maya and me nibble jam sandwiches while Khalu divides Iced Gems into equal piles. As the sky darkens, big spots of rain plop onto yellow plastic plates.

Mummy runs into the garden and scoops everything up. 'Quickly, inside. Take your toys and I'll bring the picnic things.'

Safely indoors, we kneel on the window seat. Raindrops run down the windowpane and we trace them with our fingertips.

'I win,' Khalu yells.

Maya pulls a face and I shrug. There's a flash of light and we count together – 'one, two, three…' When the thunder comes, its rumble is deep and angry. We squeal as the glass rattles in the window frames.

'Let's play shops,' Khalu says. 'Go and get people to buy stuff.'

Maya and me run upstairs to fetch Raggedy Doll and Harvey Rabbit. When we get back, Khalu's already set out the till and Mummy's given her cans and packets from the kitchen to sell. We help by arranging the food along the settee.

'Not there,' Khalu says, moving everything and lining it

up on top of the sideboard. 'Go and get some other stuff for the shop.'

Maya and me race off again to find Lego and crayons. In the bedroom, I pick up a book from the floor. It's the one about a cow with no friends and there's a button to press that makes a mooing sound. We're giggling when Khalu comes to find us.

'Come on,' she says, 'everything's ready.'

Maya shakes her head.

'We don't want to play anymore,' I say.

Khalu's bottom lip quivers. 'Mummy…'

I put my hands over my ears to block out her loud wails.

Maya laughs.

Mummy runs upstairs. 'Why don't you come and play? Khalu's set everything out so beautifully.'

Maya and me bury our heads in the book.

Mummy holds out her hand. 'Come on, just for a little while.'

'Maya doesn't want to,' I say.

Mummy sits down beside us. 'You're a team, you should look out for each other.'

I pout.

Mummy sighs. 'Sometimes it's nice to play with your other sister. Maya can stay here to read the book if she wants.'

Maya's eyes are wide in panic.

'No,' I say, 'we don't want to.'

Mummy gets up from the floor. 'Okay, I'll play shops with Khalu and you can stay here.' She clomps back downstairs.

'Moo,' says Maya.

The wall hangings Mummy and Daddy brought back from Africa hang over the stairs.

'That one's my favourite,' Khalu says. 'It looks like Monkey.'

I point at the purple wall hanging. 'I like the elephant.' I love elephants. My favourite is the jewelled elephant who lives in the sitting room. I love his bright red tongue and big smiley eyes. He has thirty-two diamonds on his blanket. I know because I counted.

Maya stares at the picture of a tiger stalking through the jungle. He looks like he's going to jump right out of the frame with those green, piercing eyes.

'Let's make up stories,' Khalu says. 'I'll go first.'

'No, it's Maya's turn.'

Khalu huffs but she settles down to listen.

Maya tells the best stories. 'Once upon a time there was a beautiful princess…'

'What was her name?' Khalu interrupts.

'Princess Diana,' says Maya.

Our stories usually involve Princess Diana. Mummy told us, before we were born, a beautiful young girl called Diana married a prince and went to live in a real castle.

'…and the elephant helped Diana escape…' continues Maya

'Why didn't the tiger catch them?' Khalu says. 'He could run fastest.'

'Because he didn't want to get his feet wet,' I say.

Maya grins. 'The tiger stood on the banks of the river and roared, but he couldn't cross the water because he didn't like getting his feet wet. So Diana got home safely to the palace and lived in Africa happily ever after.'

Princess Diana often ends up in Africa. It's the place where Mummy and Daddy met when Mummy was teaching poor children and Daddy was building wells for clean water. They came home when Mummy was expecting us. 'It was like waiting for a bus,' Mummy said, 'wait ages then three come along at once.'

'Let's go and help Mummy,' I say.

We run downstairs and find Mummy in the kitchen. I love Mummy. I love her shiny brown hair with a fringe and the way she always smells of lemons. Today she's wearing her daisy skirt that goes all the way to her ankles.

'Hello.' She smiles. 'Where did you spring from?'

'We've been making up stories,' Khalu tells her.

'Maya told the best story ever,' I say.

'No, she didn't,' Khalu says.

Maya sticks out her tongue.

'No bickering,' Mummy scolds. 'Well, now you're here, you can help me get dinner ready.'

I spot the vegetables, washed and ready on the chopping board. 'Can I chop the carrots?'

'Yes.' Mummy turns the chairs around so we can kneel on them.

'Are we having lentil soup?' Khalu asks, scrambling up on a chair.

'Bean and vegetable.' Mummy's a really good cook but we don't eat meat because she says it's not kind to the animals.

'Yummy. My favourite.' I clamber up beside Maya. She scrapes the carrots and I chop them. Khalu slices potatoes.

Mummy stirs the beans in a big silver pan. 'How are those vegetables coming along?'

'Nearly done,' I say.

Khalu stares at my chopping board. 'Ilona's cut the carrots all wrong.'

'No, I haven't.'

'Yes, you have. They don't taste good in circles.'

Mummy leans across to check. 'They look fine to me.' She tips the vegetables in with the beans. 'Now, where's that lid?'

Maya climbs down from her chair. She doesn't like it when the pan gets noisy.

'Will it hiss?' I ask.

'Don't worry, it's just the valve.' Mummy fastens the lid on the pressure cooker.

'Will Daddy be home soon?' asks Khalu.

Mummy glances at the kitchen clock. 'He'll be a while yet.'

Daddy works in London where he has a big desk and draws pictures of tunnels and bridges with his sharp black pen. Mummy says Daddy's work is important because he makes the roads safe and, after the roads have been built, he makes sure the fields are put back the way they were.

Mummy slides the vegetable peelings into the compost bin. 'Why don't you go and sit at the table in the other room and do your number work?'

We don't go to school because Mummy says other children can be unkind. We learn at home instead. Mummy taught us to read and write and do sums before we were four. She buys us new exercise books each time we start a new topic. So far, we've done *Water* and *Flora and Fauna*. We've been to a reservoir and visited a Pinetum. We're starting *Castles* and this weekend we're off to Bodiam.

The man in the kiosk checks the badge on our windscreen and waves us in. Daddy parks the car and Mummy opens the boot. 'Right, everybody has to carry something.'

I grab the blanket and race after Daddy who is striding ahead in his shorts. We cross the car park and clamber up a steep bank. When we get to the top, I stand and stare. 'Does Princess Diana live here?'

'No.' Daddy shields his eyes from the sun. 'No-one has lived in this castle for a very long time. It's Fourteenth Century. Can you tell what the shape is?'

'A sort of square,' Khalu says.

'Well done, Khalu. Yes, it's a quadrangle.'

Maya puts a thumb to her nose and wiggles her fingers at Khalu.

I giggle. 'Has it got a keep? I read about keeps at the library.'

'No, it hasn't, Ilona, but that's a really good question. It has, however, got a big moat.' Daddy always asks us lots of questions and, when we answer them, he asks us more. Now he gestures towards the water. 'If we were to construct a drawbridge, what sort of design would work best?'

'We could have a swing bridge, from here.' Khalu moves closer to the water.

Maya mimes a pushing action, but I shake my head.

'Not too close, Khalu,' says Daddy. 'Yes, we could definitely have a swivel bridge. What other designs might work?'

Maya moves her hand up and down, like nodding.

I copy her. 'One like this?'

'Yes, excellent, like a see saw. We could have a single or a double leaf.' Daddy grabs my notebook. 'Like this.' He draws a diagram. 'Opens in the middle, see? Yes, that might work. Tell you what, let's sit down and have a go sketching some initial ideas. That's right. Sit here.'

We flop down on the grassy bank. I chew the end of my pencil. Mummy unpacks sandwiches and cake from her bag. Daddy plonks himself down on the grass next to

Mummy and gives her a big smacking kiss on her cheek. We giggle.

'When we've finished lunch,' says Daddy, 'we'll go up the tower. We can go right to the top. You know? Perhaps we'll make a working model of a drawbridge when we get home.' Daddy always gets very excited about making models.

Maya nibbles up to the crusts of her bread. 'I want to feed the fish.'

'When can we feed the fish?' I ask.

'Let's get these sketches finished and you can stick them in your scrapbooks.' Daddy puts the lid on the cake tin. 'We'll save Mummy's scrumptious cherry cake for after we've been up the tower.'

We've been copying pictures of drawbridges and labelling them to show Daddy. As we're walking back from the library through the park, Mummy stops to fuss over a baby in a pram. 'Oh, look at him. Such a bonny boy.'

The baby stretches out his chubby hand to tweak the toys strung on elastic across his belly. He has rosy cheeks and when he grins I see two tiny teeth.

The baby's mummy stares at us. 'What sweet little girls and what stunning locks. How old are they?'

It's always 'they', always 'we'; never 'her', never 'me'.

Khalu smiles while Maya sticks out her tongue. Mummy doesn't seem to notice. 'Five last month,' she says.

'Don't you get them mixed up?'

People always ask this. Mummy said when we were in her tummy, we curled up together like three peas in a pod.

'Why don't you go and play on the swings?' says Mummy.

'What lovely outfits,' continues the baby's mummy. 'Did you make them yourself? I wish I was that good at sewing.'

Mummy smiles. 'I like to dress them in different colours so they get to experience a little personal identity…'

We run across to the swings and practise forwards and backs while Mummy and the baby's mummy chat.

'Let's go on the slide,' says Khalu.

Maya and me don't want to leave the swings but Mummy's still talking so we follow.

'Come on,' Khalu shouts, already halfway up the ladder.

I circle one of the metal poles while Maya hangs, monkey-like, from the other. 'Maya doesn't want to,' I say.

Khalu glares down at us from the slide. I wait for Maya to untangle her legs before climbing the steps. Khalu's at the top, holding onto the bars either side. I guess what she's going to do before she does it. As I step onto the metal platform, she starts to jump. The platform creaks, bouncing up and down and I fall to my knees. Behind me, Maya pauses on the top step.

'Don't,' I say.

'Don't,' Khalu mimics, jumping even harder. The platform squeaks noisily as the rusty nuts and bolts stretch. *It's going to collapse.*

'What's the matter?' Khalu taunts. 'Gonna be sick?'

I glance down at the ground. Everything's blurry. I squeeze my eyes tightly closed.

'Stop it, Khalu.'

Did I say that or was it Maya? My ears hum and puke rises in my throat.

Something or someone brushes past me. A scream. A thud. The whole world shakes. Everything goes quiet.

I open my eyes and peer over the edge of the platform. Everyone is frozen, like in *Sleeping Beauty* when the bad fairy casts a spell. Far below us, on a worn patch of grass, Khalu's not moving.

Someone shouts. 'Oh no, oh no.' Mummy runs towards the slide, skidding to a halt on her knees. She strokes Khalu's forehead and lifts her hand, but her arms and legs are floppy like Raggedy Doll.

I look at Maya.

She holds out a hand to help me up.

'Is Khalu dead?' I whisper.

'No.' Maya puts an arm around me. 'Don't be silly.'

We watch from above. A lady runs to the phone box and, after what seems like ages, two men in blue shirts carry Khalu to an ambulance. Mummy gets in and the ambulance drives away, the blue light spinning around screaming *nee nah, nee nah*.

Mrs Wilson calls to us. 'Come on down.' Mrs Wilson lives at number sixteen and smells of talcum powder. She's old because she's got grey hair and walks curved over like she's about to bend down and pick something up. 'Don't dawdle,' she says as we head back to her house.

When we step into Mrs Wilson's sitting room, a green bird in a cage begins to squawk. 'Don't mind Jimmy.' She covers his cage with a big cloth and he stops making a noise. It smells of bird poo in here. Mrs Wilson makes us a cup of tea, but the milk tastes funny so we don't drink it. She offers us biscuits from an old tin. We bite into them. They're soft and stick to our tongues.

Mummy and Khalu don't come home. Neither does Daddy. Mrs Wilson takes us to our house and puts us to bed. 'Your sister will be fine,' she says. 'Don't you go worrying now.'

We don't have a story that night. We don't even get to check the doll.

'Did we make it happen?' I ask Maya.

'No, Khalu fell, 'says Maya. 'Go to sleep.'

But when I close my eyes, I keep seeing Khalu falling.

Daddy comes home when it's dark. He kisses me on the forehead. 'Still awake?'

'Is Khalu okay?'

'She'll be fine. Mummy's waiting for the doctor to put a plaster cast on Khalu's arm, then I'm going to pick them up. Mrs Wilson's going to stay until we get home.'

I hug Brown Bear. 'You didn't kiss Maya.'

Daddy turns at the door, rubbing his forehead with his hand. 'She's asleep.'

CHAPTER TWO

I stare at the empty bed. 'Where's Khalu?'

Maya shrugs.

I run downstairs to the kitchen. Mrs Wilson is sitting at the kitchen table, her eyes red and puffy like she's been crying. *Has something happened?*

'Where's Mummy and Daddy?' I ask.

Mrs Wilson blows her nose, making a loud noise. 'Sit down. Have some breakfast.'

'But where are my mummy and daddy?'

Mrs Wilson smiles a funny sort of smile. 'You need to eat something, dear.'

There's only one pink bowl on the table. 'What about Maya?' I ask.

'Maya?'

'Yes.' I go to the cupboard and fetch the green bowl that Maya likes. Ignoring Mrs Wilson, I tip Rice Krispies into both bowls. Maya's standing in the doorway. 'Come and eat your Krispies,' I tell her. Just then the doorbell rings.

'That will be the nice lady coming to see you.' Mrs Wilson heaves herself up and goes to answer it.

Maya and me stare at each other. *What nice lady?*

Mrs Wilson comes back with a police lady and another lady in a white mac. I slide down from my chair.

'Hello,' says the lady in the white mac. 'My name's Miss Bishop.' She has big brown hair and a mark on the front of her coat. 'Let's sit down, shall we?' She sits opposite us.

Mrs Wilson and the police lady stay standing near the door.

'I'm afraid I have some bad news. Mummy, Daddy and your sister have been in an accident.'

There's a fluttery feeling in my belly. 'But they're all right?'

'No dear.' Miss Bishop leans forward to touch my arm. 'I'm afraid they're not.'

Maya's cheeks have gone white. Mrs Wilson's making a strange sound. *Is she crying again?*

Miss Bishop stands up. 'Come on, we'll pack a few things and you can come with me. We'll sort everything out.'

Maya shakes her head. We're not supposed to go anywhere with strangers. But I don't want to stay here without Mummy and Daddy, and I don't want to go back to Mrs Wilson's house. Miss Bishop's holding her hand out like I'm meant to take it. I don't know what to do.

'Go on, dear.' Mrs Wilson smiles. 'It's okay. Miss Bishop will look after you. I must get back to my Jimmy. He'll be wondering where I am.'

The police lady nods at us. Mummy and Daddy always say we can trust the police so it must be all right. I follow Miss Bishop upstairs while Maya stays in the kitchen with Mrs Wilson and the police lady.

Miss Bishop stops on the landing. 'Do your mummy and daddy have a suitcase?'

I lead the way into Mummy and Daddy's room and point

at the suitcase on top of the wardrobe. Miss Bishop lifts it down. It's the one with stickers, a kangaroo and a dodo bird.

We go into our bedroom next. Miss Bishop lays the suitcase on my bed. Pulling open drawers, she lifts out piles of clothes and lays them in the suitcase, but she's mixing everything up.

'Those are Khalu's,' I say.

'Sorry,' says Miss Bishop. 'What about these? Are these all right?'

I nod, squeezing Brown Bear tight.

'Do you want to bring your bear?'

'Yes.' I tuck Brown Bear under my arm.

Miss Bishop closes the case and steps towards the door.

'And Charlie Dog.' I run to pick him up. Monkey's sitting on Khalu's pillow. He looks cross about being left behind. 'You're to stay here,' I tell him before following Miss Bishop downstairs.

Miss Bishop straps Maya and me into the back of her red car. White hairs are all over the seat and there's torn up newspaper on the floor.

Miss Bishop drives under the Thomas Bridge, but she doesn't say, 'Woo woo,' like Mummy and Daddy do.

I reach for Maya's hand. 'Are we nearly there?'

'I don't know,' she whispers.

After what seems like ages, Miss Bishop pulls up outside a row of red brick houses. Each one has a door, three windows and a triangle shaped roof with a chimney. Miss Bishop unbuckles us. We get out of the car and follow her through a broken gate, past two dustbins and up the path to a green front door. She rings the bell.

A fat lady with grey curly hair opens the door. She crouches down to us. 'Hello. I'm Mrs Glover. Come on in.' She stands back up and leads the way into the sitting room. There's a film on the television but it's black and white like an old photo. 'Would you like a drink? Orange squash?'

Maya grabs my arm. 'When are we going home?' she whispers.

I shake myself free. 'Yes, please.'

'One orange squash coming right up,' says Mrs Glover.

'And one for Maya,' I say.

Mrs Glover's bottom sways as she goes to fetch our drinks.

'Why don't we make ourselves comfortable?' Miss Bishop sits down and gestures to the settee opposite. 'You can sit there.'

We perch on the edge of the settee. I nudge Maya and we giggle at three blue ducks over the fireplace trying to escape out of the window.

Maya points at a wooden box full of toys standing in the corner.

'Can we play with the toys?' I ask.

'I'm sure that will be all right.' Miss Bishop reaches forward to turn down the volume on the television.

I grab Maya's hand and we rush over to the box. Rummaging around, pushing cars and skittles out of the way, I come across a green Percy engine.

Maya snatches it from me. 'Mine.'

I search again, pulling out a blue Thomas train and we kneel on the rug to construct a track.

The door opens and Mrs Glover staggers in with a tray.

Miss Bishop jumps up. 'Here, let me help.'

'No, no, it's fine.' Mrs Glover sets the tray on the coffee table in front of the settee. 'Ahhh,' she sighs, lowering herself into the other armchair. 'Two orange squashes. And there's biscuits too. Now, do you take sugar, Miss Bishop?'

We sip our orange squash and nibble the squashed fly biscuits while we carry on playing. Maya pushes Percy along the track while I build a small bridge.

'So' – Miss Bishop lowers her voice – 'you'd be willing to be temporary carer until we can sort something more permanent?'

'Of course,' says Mrs Glover. 'We're used to this sort of thing and a week or so should be fine. Although my Henry isn't as fit as he was.'

'Mr Glover is still working?' asks Miss Bishop.

'Oh yes, my Henry's been on the buses for thirty-three years.'

'A week would be brilliant, Mrs Glover.' Miss Bishop puts her cup down on the tray and stands up. 'I'll be back to see you soon.'

She's leaving us here? Maya and me follow her into the hallway.

Mrs Glover opens the door. 'Tragic. Don't bear thinking about.'

'It's reassuring to know we have somewhere to place our young charges at such short notice.' Miss Bishop buttons up her raincoat. 'We're very grateful, Mrs Glover.'

'So, it's Ilona?' says Mrs Glover. 'Funny sort of name.'

'Yes.' Miss Bishop winks. 'And Maya.'

'Yes, and Maya. Of course.'

It's almost dinner time when the key turns in the lock. We peer around the door for a sneaky look at My Henry. He takes off his hat and places it on a high shelf above the coats. It has a badge on it. *Is he a policeman?* He shrugs off his big blue jacket and hangs it over the banister.

When he unfastens his top shirt button, I whisper to Maya, 'Daddy isn't hairy like that.'

'Perhaps he's a bear?' says Maya. We giggle as we shrink back behind the door.

'Come on out.' Mrs Glover pushes us forward. 'This is Ilona.' She pauses before continuing. 'And this is Maya.'

'Would you look at that?' My Henry tousles my hair. 'Proper little carrot top.'

'Only be a week or so,' says Mrs Glover. 'Won't be no trouble.'

My Henry ambles into the sitting room and turns up the volume on the television. He sits in the shiny black chair and it goes whoosh as he sinks into it. Reaching down, he pulls a lever and the chair tilts back like at the dentists.

Mrs Glover fetches a mug of tea for My Henry and goes back out to the kitchen.

My Henry takes a pipe from his shirt pocket. Fumbling in a pouch on the side of the chair, he pulls out a square tin. When he takes off the lid, there's a horrid smell. Maya and me hold our noses. Pinching up small clumps of black, grassy stuff, he fills his pipe before putting it in his mouth and rummaging again for matches. It takes several attempts and lots of puff before a tiny stream of smoke comes out. He sits back with a sigh.

'Tea's ready,' calls Mrs Glover.

Maya wrinkles her nose as we go into the kitchen. 'What's that smell?'

Mrs Glover plonks a plate of food on the table. 'Sit down.'

'What is it?' whispers Maya.

I look at Mrs Glover.

'What's the matter?' she says. 'All children like fish fingers and chips. Come on now, eat up. They're yummy with ketchup. Here.' Mrs Glover squirts a big dollop of red sauce onto the edge of the plate, before helping herself to one of the fish fingers. She dunks it and takes a bite before putting the other half back on the plate.

We eat with our fingers, while Mrs Glover places food on a tray for My Henry and carries it into the sitting room.

After our tea, Mrs Glover runs us a bath. She pours in bubble bath and waggles her hand about to make bubbles. We climb in. The bubbles come right over our tummies. I pile bubbles on my hands and blow them at Maya. She does the same thing back. We giggle. It's like a snowball fight. Mummy says we can't have bubbles at home because they go down the drain and poison the fishes in the sea.

'Stop it.' Bubbles have gone in my eye. It stings and when I rub, it hurts more.

'Time to get out now,' says Mrs Glover.

We climb out and pat ourselves dry. The towel feels rough, not fluffy like the ones at home. After getting dry, we put on our pyjamas. When we go into the bedroom there's only one bed.

'We'll have to share,' I say to Maya.

Maya climbs in beside me.

Mrs Glover comes in. 'All right? Do you want a story?'

'Yes please,' I say.

Mrs Glover pulls a chair close to the bed. The story is about hedgehogs, but she doesn't do the voices.

Mrs Glover closes the book. 'The end.' She heads for the

door. 'Night-night. Don't let the bed bugs bite.' We listen to her heavy footsteps going down the stairs.

'Bed bugs?' Maya shudders.

'Do you want Charlie Dog?' I ask.

Maya nods. I climb out of bed and root around in the suitcase to find our special toys, then I get back into bed and curl up with Maya. She rubs my back.

'I wish Mummy and Daddy were here to give us a cuddle.' I whimper. Soon Brown Bear's face is wet from my tears.

———

I wake in the morning to the sound of someone throwing up. *Who's being sick?* I'm shivery and cold. *Perhaps I'm sick, too?* But when I move my legs, I realise. I scowl at Maya. 'You wet the bed.' As I climb out, I squeeze Brown Bear to make sure he's dry.

'I never,' Maya says as she rolls out of bed.

Mrs Glover comes into the room. 'Rise and shine.'

I point at the bed. 'Maya wet the bed.'

'Doesn't matter, dear.' Mrs Glover pulls off the wet sheets. 'You've had such a shock. It's a good job I keep a mattress cover on this bed, eh?'

'Who was being sick?' I ask.

'Sick?' Mrs Glover is puzzled for a moment, then she laughs. 'Bless you, dear, that's my Henry. He always coughs like that first thing. It's that blasted pipe.'

———

While Mrs Glover watches television, the ball of purple wool jiggles about in her lap. It looks like she's knitting but instead of needles she's using a little metal stick.

'What are you doing?' I ask.

'Crocheting,' says Mrs Glover.

'Mummy uses two needles,' I say.

'Those'll be for knitting, dear. I'm crocheting and have to use this hook.' She holds up the little stick and points out the hook on the end. 'It's much quicker. Look.'

We watch Mrs Glover wrap the wool around the hook, give it a quick twist and pull it back through the hole until a lacy bit dangles down.

'It's pretty,' I say.

'I'm making dollies.'

'Dolls?'

'Dollies, dear, for toilet rolls. Let me show you.' Mrs Glover puts her work down on the settee and groans as she pulls herself up. Staggering across the room, she opens the door of the sideboard and pulls out a plastic bag filled with brightly coloured wool. Mrs Glover sits back down and unwraps a beautiful doll. She's wearing a blue lacy princess dress and has shiny blonde hair.

'Oooh.' I clap my hands.

'She's so pretty,' says Maya.

I reach for the doll. 'Can we play with her?'

'No, dear.' Mrs Glover wraps the doll back up. 'You might get her dirty. I make them for the Women's Institute Bring and Buy. They're for poor children in Africa.'

I'm bouncing with excitement. 'Mummy and Daddy used to help poor children in Africa.'

'Did they, dear? That's nice. Right, *Blue Peter's* on soon. Why don't you watch that while I heat up some Spaghetti Hoops?'

'Won't the dolls get dirty if the poor children use them instead of toilet rolls?' I say.

Mrs Glover laughs so hard it makes her cough. 'Bless you, dear. The dollies go over spare toilet rolls. The W.I. sell them to make money for the poor children. They don't go out to Africa. Oh, bless you. Wait until I tell my Henry...' She's laughing again.

I don't like her laughing at me. Maya gives Mrs Glover one of her looks.

'When are we going home?' I ask. 'We've been here ages.'

'It's only been a couple of days.' Mrs Glover puts down the *TV Times*. She winces as she hauls herself up and shuffles across to the TV to change channels. 'There's supposed to be a musical on somewhere...'

'We're not supposed to watch too much television.'

'Why ever not? It's educational.'

'We watch *Thomas the Tank*.' I roll the wheels on the toy train. 'Daddy had the books when he was little and Mummy likes Ringo's voice.'

'You'll like this film.' Mrs Glover settles back on the settee.

I speak louder as the music gets loud. 'We like *Rainbow* too, but Mummy says it's a bit silly.'

'That's nice. Shhh now, the film's starting.'

'When's Miss Bishop coming back?'

'Crikey, you do ask a lot of questions. She's coming this afternoon as it happens. Hope she doesn't turn up during *Countdown*.'

'Will she be taking us home?'

The doorbell rings and Mrs Glover goes to open it. She comes back in with Miss Bishop.

'I'll put the kettle on,' says Mrs Glover, bustling out to the kitchen.

Miss Bishop turns the volume down on the TV. She tilts her head to one side and smiles. 'How are you?'

'Why are your trousers all hairy?' I ask.

Miss Bishop brushes them down. 'Oh dear, look at these hairs. That's my dog, Blondie. She's a Labrador and moulting.'

'Can we see a picture of her?'

'I'll bring one next time.'

'When can we go home?'

Miss Bishop clasps her hands together. 'Do you understand what has happened, Ilona?'

I shrug.

'Remember I told you about the bad car accident?' She takes my hand. 'Mummy, Daddy and Khalu won't be coming home.'

'Not ever?'

'I'm sorry, dear, but no.' Miss Bishop squeezes my hand.

Maya tugs at my sleeve.

'Maya wants to know when we can go home,' I say.

Miss Bishop takes a deep breath. 'You won't be going back to your old home. There's no-one there to look after you. In a few days we'll find you a new home.'

'Me and Maya?'

'Of course. You and Maya.'

Maya's eyes are watery. I want to join in.

'It's okay to cry,' says Miss Bishop.

I bite my bottom lip. Daddy will want me to be brave. When they're better, Mummy and Daddy and Khalu can come and live in the new home too.

Mrs Glover tucks us into bed. She picks up a book and reads a story about a rabbit. After she's finished reading the story, she closes the book and puts it back on the bookshelf. 'Now dear, it's one of our favourites on telly tonight, so you need to settle down nicely. Night-night. Don't let the bed bugs bite.' She leaves the room and closes the door.

I finger Brown Bear's ear and think about Daddy tickles.

Maya pinches my arm.

'Ow.' I pinch her back.

'Come on.' She climbs over me to get out of bed.

'What?'

Maya puts a finger to her lips and tiptoes across to the door.

'Where are we going?' I ask.

As we cross the landing, My Henry's laughter floats up the stairs. It makes me giggle. They must be watching something funny.

'Shhh.' Maya pushes open Mrs Glover's bedroom door.

'I don't think we should,' I whisper. The room's dark but my eyes quickly adjust to seeing from the landing light. Maya tiptoes across to the dressing table and picks up a tin of My Henry's tobacco. She opens it, sniffs and screws up her nose as she holds the tin out to me. I shake my head. Maya pushes the lid back on and puts the tin back. Next to it is a china bowl overflowing with copper and silver.

'Pirate treasure,' I whisper.

Maya takes a handful of coins.

I gasp.

She glares at me. 'Your turn,' she hisses.

I glance at the door then grab a fistful too.

As we creep back onto the landing, the TV's playing music. *"Long live Hooky Street…"*

A floorboard creaks. From below we hear Mr Henry say, 'What was that?'

The sitting room door opens and we freeze.

Then we hear Mrs Glover's voice. 'Not a peep.'

'Well, now you're up,' says My Henry,' gonna make a brew?'

We run back to our bedroom. Maya spreads her treasure out on the eiderdown. 'Come on, you too.' She giggles.

I feel sick. 'It's stealing.'

'Nah,' says Maya. 'Not if My Henry doesn't miss it. He empties out his pockets every night and chucks the money into the bowl like he doesn't care.'

I pour my coins on top of Maya's. 'How do you know?'

'I saw him,' says Maya. 'Besides, we need it. Who knows what's going to happen to us now that we're orphans.'

'Orphans?'

'We've got no parents.'

'Shut up,' The knot in my tummy flips. 'Shut up, Maya.'

Maya shrugs. She rummages around in the top drawer of our dresser, pulls out a sock and stashes our coins in the toe before hiding it back under our clothes in the drawer.

'Suppose Mrs Glover finds it?' I say.

'She's got no proof we took it. It could be our money.' Maya climbs back into bed and she's fast asleep within minutes. I lay down too, but when I close my eyes, I still see Khalu falling...

'Not again,' says Mrs Glover as she drags the wet sheets from the bed.

'It wasn't me,' I whisper.

Mrs Glover tuts. She tutted yesterday, too.

I chew my nail. Maya gives me a defiant look.

'It was Maya,' I say.

Mrs Glover raises an eyebrow. 'If that's the case,' she says, 'perhaps Maya should sleep somewhere else?'

'Did you bring a picture of your dog?' I ask.

'I did.' Miss Bishop reaches into her handbag and takes out a small red purse, but it's not really a purse because it has lots of photographs inside plastic covers. 'Here she is.'

Me and Maya sit on the settee either side of Miss Bishop to look at Blondie on the grass with a ball beside her. On another photograph, Blondie's running along the path, her tongue hanging out to one side. 'I like this one.' I point at the one where she's curled up in an armchair.

Maya nudges me. Her favourite is Blondie sitting on a chair with a Christmas hat on her head. Me and Maya giggle.

Miss Bishop takes the photograph purse and puts it back in her bag. She smiles and pats my hand. 'Is there anything worrying you, Ilona?'

'I'm worried about Maya.'

'Why are you worried about Maya?'

'She won't speak to anyone except me.'

'Perhaps it's the shock,' says Miss Bishop. 'Look, dear, I need to have a quick word with Mrs Glover. Are you all right playing here?' Miss Bishop puts a box of animal cards on the coffee table. She gets up and stands in the doorway for a moment watching us. We start pairing up the animals and she goes into the kitchen. When the door closes, Maya and me tiptoe out into the hallway and listen behind the kitchen door.

'So, have they set the date for the hearing?' asks Mrs Glover.

'What are they talking about? Hearing what?' I whisper.

Maya puts a finger to her lips.

'Wednesday,' says Miss Bishop, 'but children don't attend.'

'No, of course not,' says Mrs Glover.

'The case notes make sorry reading,' says Miss Bishop. 'David and Annie Parrish had no extended family.'

I grab Maya's sleeve. 'They're talking about Mummy and Daddy,' I hiss.

Miss Bishop carries on. 'The mother was an only child, orphaned years ago. The paternal grandmother's dead and the paternal grandfather is in a care home up north. There's an uncle in Australia but it sounds like his marriage is on the rocks.'

'Australia? Are they talking about Uncle Clive?' I whisper.

'No friends?' asks Mrs Glover.

'No-one has stepped forward to take on the responsibility.'

'Such a shame. But you've found somewhere?'

'Oh yes, a lovely couple in Wateringbury. Willing to provide a long-term foster home with a view to adoption.'

'I'm not sure Ilona understands what's happened. You know about the bed wetting...'

I nudge Maya. 'She's talking about you wetting the bed.'

Maya thumps my arm.

'Yes, I'm sorry about that. I've arranged bereavement therapy to begin next week. All being well, and I don't foresee any problems, I'll arrange the transfer for Friday.'

As we lie in bed that evening, I whisper to Maya. 'Mrs Glover's washing all our stuff.'

Maya wriggles around to face me. 'That means we're leaving,'

'I hope so. I want to go home. I wonder where they'll take us this time?'

'You do know it's just us now?'

I pinch her arm. 'Shut up, Maya.'

Maya pinches me back. 'Mummy and Daddy aren't coming back.'

I turn away from her and hug Brown Bear tight. I'm not listening to her. I don't want a new home and I don't want a new mummy and daddy.

CHAPTER THREE

A soldier on TV pops up inside a *Punch and Judy* box. He has his arm around a puppet. 'Can't beat Elvis,' says Mrs Glover, swaying as the soldier sings *Wooden Heart.*

I'm doubled up on the settee, clutching my belly.

The soldier starts singing in another language and Mrs Glover shoots me a look. 'Try going to the lavvy again.'

I shake my head. I've been twice already. Maya says she doesn't need to go either. I hope she won't wet the bed in the new place.

The doorbell rings. Mrs Glover goes to answer it. A few seconds later, Miss Bishop pokes her head around the sitting room door. 'Are you ready?'

We go out to the hall. Miss Bishop lifts our coats down from the pegs and we put them on. 'What do you say to Mrs Glover?

'Thank you for having us.' I zip up my coat.

Maya says nothing, she just stares at the carpet.

'You're welcome.' Mrs Glover smiles. 'Good luck in your new home.'

Mrs Bishop drives past shops and houses we don't recognise. It's scary when we go through a tunnel of trees, the sun flashing between the leaves. Something's rolling around in the car. A blue ball. It must be Blondie's.

As we pass a field, Maya points to the lambs. 'Wonder if we're nearly there,' she whispers.

We can see Miss Bishop smiling at us in her driving mirror. 'We're here now.' She stops the car outside a house made of stone with four windows. It has pink flowers hanging from the wall around a purple front door. I read the sign on the gate. *Lavender Cottage*. That's pretty. The roof is crooked like a fairy tale cottage in one of our books. A lady stands on the doorstep, shielding her eyes from the sun.

'That's Mrs Taylor,' says Miss Bishop. 'You'll like her.'

Mrs Taylor has blonde curls. I wonder if she puts rollers in to make them curl like that. Mummy's hair was long and straight but sometimes she made it curly with rollers. Mrs Taylor walks towards the car. We clamber out as a man with a beard and black fuzzy hair follows her down the path.

'It's a pirate.' Maya edges sideways to hide behind me.

'Hello.' Mrs Taylor rests a hand on my shoulder. 'Welcome to your new home.'

I take a deep breath. 'I'm Ilona, and this is Maya.' I nudge Maya to come forward. She's hopping from leg to leg. She needs a wee.

'Hello Ilona and hello Maya,' says Mrs Taylor. 'You can call me Fiona. This is my husband, Jack.'

Miss Bishop lugs our case out of the boot.

'Here let me.' Jack the Pirate smiles. His eyes crinkle up like Daddy's and I bite my lip.

Fiona holds my hand and leads us up the path and into the cottage. 'I'll show you your room.'

The wooden stairs creak as we climb up them. We imagine we're in the crooked house from the fairy story and we try not to tread on the cracks.

Fiona lifts the latch on a wooden door. 'Here we are.'

We love the bedroom. It has a white chest of drawers with a pretty pink box on top. The walls are white too and they have teddy bear pictures. I nudge Maya when I notice the tiny bookcase with books crammed on the shelves. Toys spill from a pink basket in the corner while Pooh Bear and Tigger sit on the bed.

I turn to Fiona. 'But there's only one bed.'

'We thought you and Maya wouldn't mind sharing.' Fiona moves Pooh so he's propped up against the pillow. 'Miss Bishop says you've been sleeping in the same bed at Mrs Glover's?'

I glance at Maya. She nods and smiles.

'Jack will bring up your case in a while.' Fiona fluffs her hair with her fingers. 'Let's go down and have tea. I've made iced buns.'

We follow Fiona downstairs and into the kitchen. It's cosy and warm. I love the big green cooker. It's like the one Mummy always wanted. I think it's called a range. Maya points at the fridge covered in magnets, letter ones like we had at home, but lots of animal magnets too.

'Sit down.' Fiona points at the bench seat.

We can't tear our eyes from the plate of buns on the table. They have pink and yellow icing with butterflies on top and look yummy.

'Tuck in,' says Jack.

We slide onto the bench and I take two of the yellow buns from the plate and pass one to Maya. I leave the pink ones because pink is Khalu's favourite. We nibble at the icing while Fiona makes the tea.

'Would you like a cuppa, Miss Bishop?' Fiona lifts mugs from hooks on the pine dresser.

'Thank you, dear,' says Miss Bishop. 'By the way, I've arranged an appointment with a counsellor. Doctor Lewis, next Friday, ten-thirty.'

Does she mean for us? We're not ill. Perhaps it's to help Maya stop wetting the bed.

'That's fine.' Fiona writes it on her wall calendar.

Maya's staring at the dresser. I turn to see what she's looking at and see a bright orange goldfish swimming round and round a glass bowl.

Fiona flips open a little tub and sprinkles flakes into the water. 'This is Mister Bubbles.'

Maya and me run across to look at him. He's enormous. Little bubbles float to the surface as his mouth opens and closes.

Miss Bishop finishes her tea. She stands up and brushes crumbs from her coat. 'I need to get home and walk Blondie.'

'Blondie's her dog,' I tell Fiona. 'She's a Labrador.'

'Yes,' says Miss Bishop, 'and she'll be missing me. I'll see myself out.'

Fiona claps her hands. 'Right, time for the tour.' She touches Jack lightly on the arm and we leave him washing up.

I like that the cottage is small. It reminds me of our house with a kitchen, sitting room and bathroom downstairs. Our bathroom has a toilet in it too.

We follow Fiona upstairs. 'This is Jack's office. That's your bedroom. Silly me, you've seen that already...' She opens another door. 'And in here is ours.' Fiona's bedroom has a big bed like Mummy and Daddy's.

We go outside to the front garden next. I think it's pretty

because it has lots of flowers. Next, we go back through the house to the back garden. Maya grins when she sees the big area of grass for us to play.

'Down there, through that little gate' – Fiona points – 'is a vegetable garden. It's a bit overgrown. I try to keep up with it but Jack's too busy to help. Perhaps you'll give me a hand? You could have your own little patch.'

As we walk back towards the cottage, a black and white cat comes towards us. 'And this,' Fiona bends to stroke him, 'is Boris. Rather thinks he owns the place, don't you Boris?' Boris purrs, rubbing against Fiona's legs. 'Oh, he's a beautiful boy, yes he is…'

Boris walks over to me, prodding at my legs before rolling onto his back showing off his white tummy. Maya creeps behind me.

'You've made a friend,' says Fiona.

I kneel on the grass next to Boris and stroke his tummy. It's soft and warm. I nuzzle his fur with my nose. Boris purrs loudly. Maya hangs back.

'I'll leave you to get acquainted.' Fiona walks back to Jack who is standing at the door of the cottage. When Fiona reaches him, he wraps his arms around her. She stands on tiptoe to kiss him. His beard must tickle.

I turn back to Boris. He's rolling back and forth, enjoying the attention. I pick a blade of long grass and dangle it in front of him. He crouches, wriggling his bottom, before pouncing on it like it's a mouse. I run down the path, laughing with Boris chasing me. We go through the little gate into the vegetable garden. Maya follows at a distance. I drag the grass along the ground, then flick it in the air, Boris jumps to catch it like he's a circus cat. I can't stop laughing.

Suddenly a small stone whizzes through the air. Boris turns towards Maya and hisses.

'What did you do?' I say.

Maya shrugs.

Boris runs off so I follow Maya back to the cottage.

We have a bath that night and Fiona makes bubbles like Mrs Glover did, but Fiona's bubbles smell of flowers.

Maya puts some on her chin like a beard. 'Like Jack,' she giggles. I copy her.

Fiona laughs. 'Out you get or you'll be wrinkly as a prune.'

We climb out and Fiona wraps us up in her towels They're so soft and fluffy. When we're dry, we put on our pyjamas and clamber into bed.

'Would you like a story?' Fiona goes over to the book-case. 'I think we have all the Roald Dahl's.'

'Daddy used to read us Roald Dahl,' I say.

Fiona reads to us from *James and the Giant Peach.* After she's finished, she tucks us in and kisses us goodnight.

'Leave the door open,' I say.

Fiona smiles. She blows another kiss from the doorway, like Mummy used to do.

When we wake up, Fiona is kneeling on the floor beside our dressing table.

I sit up, rubbing my eyes. 'Is it time to get up?'

'It's Saturday, there's no rush.' Fiona takes a pile of clothes from our suitcase and places them in a drawer.

'What are you doing?' I ask.

'I came to see if you had any dirty washing,' she says.

'You haven't unpacked properly. You know this is your home now?'

Maya tugs at my arm.

'What's this?' Fiona lifts out the sock filled with money.

'That's ours,' I jump out of bed and grab the sock.

'Okay. I'll leave it here then.' Fiona puts the sock on the dressing table before bundling up our clothes from yesterday and heading downstairs. 'Breakfast in ten minutes,' she calls over her shoulder.

I dip toasty soldiers in my dippy egg. Maya does the same.

Jack comes into the kitchen and places a funny toy on the table. It looks like a tiny dustbin, but with yellow feet and hands, and a face with a big red nose. 'He's called Dusty Bin.' Jack's voice is gruff but his eyes twinkle. 'Thought you might like him. It's a money box.'

Fiona smiles. 'Better than a sock?'

When Jack laughs, he sounds like Baloo from the jungle film.

'Here you go, Boris.' Fiona puts Boris's bowl on the floor. He gobbles up his food. When he's finished, he strolls over to sit beside my chair and starts washing his whiskers with his paws.

'He's abandoned me since you arrived,' says Fiona.

'Does he love me?' I ask.

'He does. See how he follows you around?'

'But he still loves you too.'

'I know. I don't mind sharing. Don't worry. Boris and I have special time after you've gone to bed. He curls up on my lap and makes a nuisance of himself when I'm trying to knit.'

After breakfast, I head out to the garden. Boris trots along behind. Suddenly he spins around, his fur on end.

I turn around and see Maya tiptoeing along behind us. 'He knows you're there before I do.'

Maya points her fingers like she's a scary monster. 'Grrr.' She runs at Boris.

Boris jumps, twisting in the air before running towards the cottage.

Fiona's calling so we follow him back.

'We're going to the park,' she says, 'Jack's coming too, aren't you Jack?'

'Will there be swings?' I ask.

'Of course.' Fiona helps us put our shoes on. 'We'll need to get you some wellies for when the weather turns.'

'We had wellies at home, but Miss Bishop didn't bring them.'

Fiona laces up her boots. 'No, I expect you had to leave a lot.'

Jack carries a football, whistling as we walk down the lane. The houses are more spread out here than the ones at home and they all have big gardens.

'Do you know this one?' Fiona holds up a blade of grass. 'Here's a tree in summer.' She runs the grass between her fingers and all the tiny seed bits come off. 'And here's a tree in winter.' Fiona pinches the seed bits together between two fingers. 'Here's a bunch of flowers, and here's the April showers.' She throws the seedy bits up in air and they shower down on us like rain.

Maya and me giggle.

'I'll show you how to do it.' Fiona picks another blade of grass.

Jack raises an eyebrow. 'Is that a good idea?'

'Oh dear.' Fiona brushes tiny grass seeds from our heads. 'I'll have to wash your hair tonight.' She points at the hedge. 'Look, there are going to be loads of blackberries this year, but they're not ready yet. We have to wait for them to plump up and turn black.'

We reach the park and Maya and me run straight to the swings. 'You don't have to push,' I say to Fiona. 'Mummy taught us how to do forwards and backs.'

'I'll help get you started.' Fiona gives us a little push while Jack watches. After we've been swinging for a while, Fiona says, 'Why don't you have a kick around with Jack?'

'Yes. Maya loves football.' We jump off the swings and follow Jack as he runs ahead to a field with nets. He kicks the ball but instead of rolling away, it stays near his foot. 'Come on, I'll teach you to dribble.' He kicks the ball to me. 'That's it, tiny moves forward. Good girl. Stay close to the ball...'

Jack gets the ball and makes it move around his foot, balancing it on top like it's glued.

'It's got to be a trick,' whispers Maya.

'How do you do that?' I ask.

'Takes a bit of practise, but I can show you. Can you do headers?' Jack runs backwards. 'Oof.' The ball sails between the goalposts. 'Score.'

I want to laugh but I feel sad. It reminds me of when we used to play football with Daddy.

'Oh,' Fiona says as we trek back from the park. 'I meant to bring something for the pony.'

'Pony?' I say.

'He's here.' Fiona stops at a big field and whistles.

Maya and me climb onto the wooden gate and a pony comes trotting over. He's only a little bit bigger than us.

'Is he a baby?' I ask.

'No. He's a Shetland,' says Jack. 'They're always that size.'

'What's his name?'

'I don't know his name.' Fiona pats his neck. 'I always call him pony.'

I reach in to stroke his forehead. Maya stares into his big brown eyes.

'Sorry, pony,' says Fiona. 'We'll bring you an apple or a carrot next time.'

'Can we come and see him every day?' I ask.

'I thought this morning we might make cookies.' Fiona lifts a big bowl down from the shelf in the kitchen. 'Do you like baking?'

Maya and me look at each other. 'Yes please.' We loved making cookies with Mummy.

'First of all we need to clear these breakfast things.' Fiona stacks the dishes and takes them over to the sink. Afterwards she opens a big red cookery book. 'Can't beat *Betty Crocker*. I bet you like cookies?'

'Mummy makes them with oats, bananas and honey,' I say.

'The peanut butter cookies were scrummy,' says Maya.

'Well, you haven't lived until you've tried *Betty's Best Ever Chocolate Chip*.' Fiona drags a bench over to the work-top. 'Stand on here and then you'll be able to reach.'

We clamber up.

Fiona ties tea towels around our waists so we don't spill

flour on our clothes, then she fetches a sieve from the dresser. 'Right. I'll get everything out, and you can measure and mix.'

She reads out the ingredients while me and Maya take it in turns to spoon out the right amounts. We stir everything together and when it's a creamy mixture, Fiona sticks her finger in the bowl and licks it. 'Better even than *Delia's*. Okay. Now we get a teaspoon and spoon it out onto the baking sheet like this.' We watch Fiona before having a go ourselves. Maya drops a big dollop of the sticky mixture onto the worktop.

'Don't worry, what the eye doesn't see...' Fiona scoops up the spilled mixture to make one last cookie. 'Now they're ready to pop in the oven. Stay back, it's hot.' Fiona opens the oven door and slides the tray inside.

I can't wait until the cookies are ready. My tummy rumbles.

Fiona smiles. 'Do you want to scrape the bowl?'

Me and Maya use wooden spoons and scrape the bowl clean.

'My, I'm not sure I need to wash this.' Fiona winks as she places the bowl in the sink. 'Now, out you go to play. I'll call you when they're ready.'

Fiona unties the tea towels, and me and Maya run outside. Butterflies flutter around the flowers and bushes. We chase them through the vegetable patch and down to the fence dividing our garden from the neighbours. I climb on the bottom rung of the fence and lean over. In the next garden, a man in a tatty waistcoat is crouching down by the runner beans.

Maya clambers up on the fence beside me. 'Is it a scarecrow?'

As we watch, the man pulls off his straw hat revealing huge sticky out ears. 'Perhaps it's the BFG,' I hiss.

'No,' says Maya, 'not big enough.'

The man's pulling up plants and laying them in a wooden crate. After a while he lays down his fork and hauls himself up to standing. 'Dear, oh dear.' Replacing his hat, he picks up the crate and staggers towards the path.

Maya laughs. 'He's not the BFG, he's a cowboy.'

'Yes,' I whisper. 'Boris could run through his legs without touching. Let's go back inside and see if the cookies are ready.'

We charge through the back door as Jack comes downstairs, sniffing. 'Mmm, what delights can I smell?'

As he sidles up to grab a cookie from the wire tray, Fiona smacks his hand. 'Chef's perks.'

Me and Maya help ourselves to a cookie. I bite into one. It's still warm and lovely and crunchy. And mmm, the chocolate chips are all melty.

'May I have one now please?' Jack sticks out his tongue and begs with his hands like he's a dog.

We laugh. Fiona offers him the tray.

'Now that's what I call a cookie.' Jack rubs his tummy. 'You'll have to make these again.'

'*Betty's Best Ever*.' Fiona puts the cookbook back on the shelf. 'Can't beat them. No more now though, or you'll spoil your lunch.'

'They're good, but I like Mummy's best,' whispers Maya.

I lick chocolate from my fingers. 'We saw a scarecrow man down the garden.'

Jack looks up. 'That'll be Old Mr Simpson. Don't you go pestering him.'

CHAPTER FOUR

Fiona buckles our seatbelts. Her car is dark blue and cleaner than Miss Bishop's.

'Where are we going?' I ask.

'Don't you remember?' Fiona smiles at me in her driving mirror. 'It's Friday and we're going to see Doctor Lewis. We spoke about it last night.'

'The lady with the toys we can play with?'

'That's right.'

Fiona parks in an underground car park and we walk along a street with lots of shops. 'This is Maidstone,' says Fiona. 'Look, Army and Navy Store. We'll come here to kit you out for school.'

Maya nudges me. 'We don't go to school.'

Fiona pulls a piece of paper from her coat pocket and glances at it before pointing to a white building opposite. 'Here we are.' We cross the road and Fiona pushes open a door. She leads the way up a staircase and through another door at the top.

A lady with yellow curly hair is sitting at a desk. She

stops typing, takes off her glasses and smiles. 'Good morning.'

Me and Maya giggle at a splodge of red lipstick on her teeth.

Fiona rests a hand on my shoulder. 'Fiona Taylor. We have an appointment.'

The lady scrolls down a big book. 'Ah yes.' She ticks off the name. 'Please take a seat in the waiting room.' She points to a door behind her desk.

There's a big leather settee in the room and me and Maya sit down while Fiona goes over to a basket in the corner. She picks out some books and brings them over to us, but we don't feel like reading.

A lady with pink spiky hair pokes her head around the door. 'Won't keep you a minute.' After what seems like ages she comes into the room. I like her short skirt and long boots. As she bends down to us, her dangly earrings jangle. 'Hello,' she says, 'my name's Helen. Would you like to see my playroom?'

She doesn't look like a doctor. 'Can Fiona come too?' I ask.

'No,' says Helen. 'If it's all right with you, Fiona will wait here.'

I glance at Fiona. Mummy always said we shouldn't go off with strangers.

'Go on,' says Fiona. 'It'll be fine.'

Maya holds my hand and we follow Helen into her play-room where toys are laying all over the floor. Tatty toys, not nice ones like ours at home. Someone must have left them here.

'You need to tidy your room,' I say. 'It's messy. Mummy tells us off if we leave our room that way.'

'It is,' laughs Helen. 'That's because lots of children play in here.'

'Will they be playing today?' I ask.

She smiles. 'No, today is for you. Would you like to look around?'

I turn to Maya. She shrugs. We wander round looking at the toys. 'You have lots of babies,' I say.

'You can play with them if you like.' Helen sits down. 'You can do anything you want in this room.'

I pick up one of the babies from the floor and jiggle her about, but one of her eyes stays closed. I think about how much I want a Cabbage Patch Doll. Mummy said I'd have to wait until Christmas. But how will Father Christmas find us if we're not home? I bite my lip.

'She wants to sleep.' I make room in the cot and the baby hugs the one already in there. There's another baby on the floor. She looks sad so I pick her up too.

I sit on a chair and look around the room while rocking my baby. In the middle there's a blue table with coloured pencils, and next to it is a sand pit. Maya's looking at the boys' stuff, a garage with cars, and big boxes full of trains and Lego.

I run over to the corner to a Wendy house. 'Let's go into the house, baby. Are you hungry?' I put a pan on the cooker. 'Oh look, Maya, dressing up clothes.' But Maya doesn't want to dress up today. 'Come on, baby, let's go for a walk. I put my baby in the doll's pram and wheel her around the room. Helen's watching me. Maya grabs my arm and tugs me towards the blue table. We sit down on the little chairs. I lift my baby out of the pram and rock her on my lap.

'Would you like to draw a picture?' says Helen. 'I have some paper.' She fetches some from a shelf beside her desk and lays a piece in front of me.

'Don't forget Maya,' I say.

Helen puts down another piece, 'and one for Maya.'

I stare at the blank paper. Maya's waiting. I reach for a red pencil and start drawing.

'That's a lovely house. I like your door and windows.' Helen points to the Wendy house. 'It's a bit like my house.'

'It's not her house,' whispers Maya.

I draw yellow and pink flowers beside the door.

Maya watches me. 'That's not our house.'

'What else would you like to draw?' says Helen.

I chew the end of the pencil. I want to draw Mummy and Daddy and Khalu, but I don't. 'Trees,' I say, adding green trees and a path going up to the front door.

Maya hasn't drawn anything. Helen writes on her pad. I draw Boris rolling around on the path.

Suddenly Maya reaches across me, grabs a black pencil and scribbles all over my picture.

'Hey, don't,' I yell.

Helen looks up. 'What's the matter?'

'Maya spoiled my picture.'

Maya glares at me.

Helen comes over and picks up my picture. 'I can still see your house and… is that a dog?

'No,' I say. 'Miss Bishop's got a dog called Blondie. This is Boris. He's a cat.'

'Oh yes,' says Helen. 'I see that now. Perhaps you'd like to play with something else? We've only got five more minutes.'

I go back into the Wendy house, leaving Maya to sulk at the table. I pick up the baby's bottle from the top of the cooker and sit down to feed my baby. 'Good girl,' I tell her as she drinks her milk.

'It's time to go,' says Helen.

'Can I bring my baby?' I ask.

'No,' says Helen. 'I'm afraid the toys must stay in the playroom, but you can play with her next time. Why don't you take your picture to show Fiona?'

I pick up my picture. Helen opens the door. Maya trails behind as I walk out to find Fiona.

'Did you have a nice time?' says Fiona.

I nod. 'I made you a picture.'

Maya says nothing.

Fiona walks down the garden path towards us with a sheet draped over her arm. 'I thought...' she says as she reaches us, 'we might make a den.'

'Can't we use the shed?' I ask.

'No, it's not safe; full of sharp tools and the floor is rotten.' Fiona throws the sheet over the washing line. She pegs one corner to the fence and another to the branch of a low hanging tree, leaving the other half of the sheet hanging down. 'There.' She stands back, surveying her work.

'It's good,' I say.

'I'll call you when lunch is ready.' Fiona heads back to the cottage.

Maya and me crawl into our den.

I sit down cross legged. 'I like it here.'

Maya shrugs. 'S'okay.'

'You're sulky because Jack wouldn't come to the park today.'

Maya stares out from the open side of our den. Suddenly she jumps up. 'Come on.'

I follow her through the long grass. Maya climbs onto the

bottom rung of the fence and I step up beside her. Smoke from next door's garden makes us cough.

'Mind now.' Old Mr Simpson adds a handful of plants to the fire. 'Won't do you no good breathin' that in.'

'Is it a barbecue?' I ask. 'Jack says when it's a nice day we can have a barbecue and cook sausages outside.'

'No, it's a bonfire.' Old Mr Simpson takes off his straw hat and wipes his brow with a handkerchief. His hair is like tufts of grey wool. 'I heard yer playing out here. Who's that you talkin' to?'

'My sister, Maya,' I say, 'and I'm Ilona.'

Old Mr Simpson stares at us before scratching his head and putting his hat back on.

'Why are you burning the flowers?' I ask.

He turns his attention back to the bonfire. 'Them's not flowers, them's weeds.'

'They look like flowers to me.'

'It's a weed if it's growin' in the wrong place.'

'But they're pretty,' whispers Maya.

'They may look pretty' – Old Mr Simpson stares at Maya – 'but let 'em set down roots and they spoil the other plants. Stop the veggies growing good and strong.'

'Fiona puts her weeds in the garden bin,' I say.

'Better to burn 'em.' Old Mr Simpson throws the last of the weeds onto the bonfire. 'Only way to get rid of 'em once and for all.'

The bonfire flares up. We cover our mouths and noses with our hands until the flames die down.

CHAPTER FIVE

'Mmm.' Fiona's carrot and coriander soup is sweet and creamy. I break my bread into pieces and dunk it.

We mop up the last of our soup with our bread.

Fiona clears the table. 'Why don't you do some colouring while I wash up?'

I fetch paper and colouring pens and sit back up at the table beside Maya. Suddenly there's a terrible commotion from the garden.

'Whatever's going on out there?' Fiona drops the washing up brush in the sink and runs outside, me and Maya at her heels.

A blackbird is on the washing line, flapping her wings and making a horrible 'chink-chink' noise.

'She sounds distressed. Oh no!' Fiona puts her hand over her mouth when she spots Boris crouched low on the grass. As she approaches him, he tries to run but is slowed down by the thing he's carrying in his mouth. Fiona grabs him. Boris twists and wriggles, but Fiona doesn't let go. She holds him by the neck and gently squeezes. With a cough and a splutter, something grey and bedraggled falls to the grass.

'What is it?' I ask.

'A baby bird. You bad boy.' Fiona picks up Boris, scolding him as she carries him indoors. 'You wicked bad boy.'

Maya and me creep closer. The little bird stares up at us. It looks frightened.

'What's up with his wing?' asks Maya.

One of the bird's wings is bent, sticking out at the side.

'Poor thing,' I say.

Fiona comes back with a dustpan. 'Don't touch him. His mum and dad will abandon him if he smells of people.' She gently slides the baby bird into the dustpan. A smear of blood glistens in the sunlight. Fiona winces.

'What shall we do?' I clasp my hands together like I'm praying.

'We'll put him over here' – Fiona moves towards the hedge – 'and hope his mum comes back for him.'

We can't see the blackbird on the washing line anymore, but she must be close because we can still hear those throaty 'chink-chinks'.

Fiona lays the dustpan down. 'Come away, we must leave things to Mother Nature.' Fiona heads back inside, muttering under her breath. 'What a bad cat…'

'You see?' says Maya. 'That cat's evil. You wait. He'll get what he deserves.'

'What do you mean?' I ask.

'Fiona's cross. She doesn't love him anymore.'

'She doesn't love him? How will he bear it?' My heart beats fast as I run into the cottage where Boris is prowling up and down.

Fiona holds him back with her foot as we squeeze past. 'Don't let him out.'

Boris is like a tiger in a cage. 'Fiona,' I say, 'don't you love Boris anymore?'

Fiona crouches down to me. 'Of course I still love him, beastly cat, but I don't like him much right now.' She hugs me. 'I'll always love Boris, no matter what he does.'

I grin.

Fiona smiles. 'Okay, want to help me lay the table?'

I set four places. I never have to remind Fiona about a place for Maya, not like at Mrs Glover's.

Boris meows all night. I bet he's cross because he has to stay indoors.

Early next morning we follow Fiona out to the hedge, hoping to find the dustpan empty.

Fiona puts a hand to her mouth. 'Oh dear.'

The baby bird is lying on his side. His eyes are wide open and his feet stick out like twigs.

'What can we do?' I ask.

Fiona sighs. 'I hoped his mum or dad would come back for him.' She squats down and puts her arms around me. 'Nature is cruel sometimes, but we did what we could.'

'We could call a doctor?'

'I'm afraid even an animal doctor won't do anything for little fledglings. I'm sorry. I'd hoped he was just shaken up, but he must have been badly injured.'

'We have to do something.' I start to cry.

'I know,' says Fiona. 'Let's bury him. We'll give him a good send off, okay?' She holds my hand and we go back indoors. Maya follows.

Fiona sits down at the bureau under the stairs and rummages through the drawers. She pulls out a pretty box covered in tiny flowers. 'This will do nicely.' She opens the box, takes out the envelopes and tosses them loose in the drawer. 'Let's go outside and you can find some soft grass to line the box.'

'And Maya?'

'Yes, Maya can help. We'll put the baby bird in here and bury him under the rose bush.'

Fiona goes into the shed and comes back out with a shovel. She digs a hole under the rose bush, while Maya and me pull handfuls of grass and moss from the lawn to line the box. Fiona lays the little bird gently on the soft bed we've made.

'Can we put some flowers in with him?'

Fiona smiles. 'I think that would be lovely.'

Maya and me run about gathering daisy and buttercup heads, and tiny blue petals from the edge of the flower bed. We make a blanket of flowers for the little bird.

Fiona places the lid on the box and lays it carefully down in the hole. 'Did you want to say anything?'

'Like what?' I ask.

'Well, something about the little bird…'

'Do you want to say anything?' I whisper to Maya.

Maya shakes her head. I think for a moment, hopping from leg to leg. *Perhaps it should be like a letter?* 'Dear little bird. I'm sorry naughty Boris caught you before you learned to fly. And I'm sorry your mum and dad couldn't make you better. We hope you like your box and we'll think about you when we play in the garden. We love you. Ilona, Maya and Fiona.'

'That's beautiful.' Fiona wipes her eyes. 'Okay. We'll cover him up now.' She scoops soil over the box.

I stare at the bare earth. 'Is this what happens to people when they die?'

Fiona sits down on the grass and pulls me onto her lap. 'Sometimes.'

'Is this what happened to…' – there's a lump in my throat and it's hard to make the words come out – 'to Mummy and Daddy?'

Fiona hugs me. 'Did you go to a funeral for Mummy and Daddy?'

'What's a funeral?'

'Well, a bit like this really. It's a chance to say goodbye. Sometimes people are buried like this, under the soil, but sometimes the box is burned and the ashes are scattered somewhere special.' She puts a finger under my chin and lifts my face to look at her. 'Did you get a chance to say goodbye to Mummy and Daddy?'

I shake my head. 'Are Mummy and Daddy somewhere special?' I stammer.

'I'm sure they are,' says Fiona. 'And they'll always be special in your heart. Like you said about the little bird when you play in the garden.'

Fiona holds me until I can't cry anymore. I lift my head to look for Maya. I turn back to Fiona. 'And in Maya's heart too?'

'Yes.' Fiona's crying now too. 'In Maya's heart too.'

I bury my face in Fiona's shoulder. Maya comes closer and wraps her arms around me.

'Poor little bird,' I say to Maya as we lay in bed that night. 'He didn't even get to fly.'

'I'd love to fly,' says Maya.

'Where do you think Mummy and Daddy are?'

'I don't think they're in the ground. The hole would have to be very big. I think they burned up in a fire.'

I shudder. 'I don't want to be burned up in a fire.'

'It might be a bit like flying,' says Maya.

'Being burned up isn't anything like flying.' I roll over to face her. 'If you could fly, where would you go?'

'Far away,' says Maya. 'I'd have red and yellow feathers, and I'd fly over jungles with elephants and monkeys and tigers and I'd never come back.'

'Take me with you,' I whisper, hugging Brown Bear.

We're pulling out loads of weeds. Maya giggles as a worm wiggles through the soil.

'If we can finish clearing this bit,' – Fiona sits back on her heels – 'you can have your own little garden.'

'Can we grow flowers?' I ask.

'Well, I've got a packet of mixed flower seeds in the shed, but it's probably too late for this year. We might be able to grow some salad stuff. Perhaps we should ask Mr Simpson? Now, this is couch grass. Pull up as much of this as you like, but don't touch those thistles. If you haven't got gloves, they prickle.'

'What about this one?'

'Yes, that can come out,' says Fiona.

Smoke wafts across from Old Mr Simpson's garden.

'He's sending SOS signals,' whispers Maya.

Fiona puts a hand to her back as she struggles to stand. 'Ow, shouldn't have knelt for so long. 'Hello,' – she calls – 'Mr Simpson?'

Old Mr Simpson steps across his vegetables to reach the fence. 'See yer got some help.'

'Mr Simpson,' says Fiona. 'Is it too late to plant things this year?'

'Well now.' Old Mr Simpson takes off his hat and scratches his head. 'There's winter veggies, broccoli and beetroot…'

'Beetroot would be good,' says Fiona. 'Thanks, that's great. Oh, I was going to ask, the mint in my herb box is taking over, pushing everything else out.'

'You need to separate yer mint. A pot or a box will stop the roots spreading. I got mine in an old sink. Does the job.'

'Okay, I'll give that a try.' Fiona picks up the box of weeds we've pulled. 'Right, Jack will be wanting his lunch…'

'Give us that here.' Old Mr Simpson reaches over the fence and takes the box.

'Thank you.' Fiona smiles at us. 'I'll give you a shout when lunch is ready.'

We watch Old Mr Simpson throw the weeds on to the bonfire. He picks up his fork and prods at the flames.

'What's that white stuff?' I ask.

'Ashes,' says Old Mr Simpson. 'You mind now, because 'em ashes stay hot long after flames 'ave gone. Yer don't want to be messing around with 'em.'

'What will you do with them?'

'Rake 'em up and use 'em on the garden.'

'What for?'

'All sorts o' things. Some'll go in the compost, the worms love 'em.'

'Yuk,' I say.

'Ashes should be scattered somewhere special,' whispers Maya.

'Ashes to ashes, dust to dust…' Old Mr Simpson stares at Maya. 'We all ends up back in the earth one way or t'other. I scatters 'em round the gooseberry bushes and roses. Stops the slugs eating 'em. You like raspberries?'

Maya and me nod.

'Hang on a mo.' He hobbles across to a plastic container resting on top of a broken metal chair. Next to the raspberries is a box of matches with a swan on it. Old Mr Simpson picks up the raspberries and staggers back. 'You take these and give 'em to Fiona.' He hands the container to me. 'If yer lucky, she might 'ave some cream to go with 'em for your pudding.'

'Thank you.' I tug at Maya's arm. She's staring at the matches.

'Good morning, Mister Bubbles. Ohh!' Maya gasps.

I spin around. 'Mister Bubbles!' Mister Bubbles is floating on top of the water.

'What's the matter?' Fiona steps closer. 'Oh no.' She glances at Boris, who is innocently munching his biscuits.

'Was it Boris?' I ask.

'I don't think so.' Fiona prods Mister Bubbles with her finger. 'Mister Bubbles wouldn't be in the bowl if Boris had anything to do with it.'

Maya's eyes fill with tears. She loved Mister Bubbles. Every morning she watched him swim round and round, opening and closing her mouth in time with his.

'What about the animal doctor?' I say.

'No darling, I'm sorry. Oh dear.' Fiona throws a towel over Mister Bubbles' bowl. She washes her hands before pouring our cereal.

Maya sobs quietly into her cornflakes.

I sniff, trying not to cry too.

Jack comes in. 'What's up with everyone today?'

'Mister Bubbles,' says Fiona.

Jack lifts the towel. 'Oh no.' He runs a hand through his hair. 'That might be my fault.'

Fiona raises an eyebrow.

'Fly spray,' Jack whispers.

Maya glares at him.

'Oh, Jack,' says Fiona. 'You know I always cover Mister Bubbles whenever I use it.'

'I know, I know.' Jack puts both hands over his face. 'I'm so sorry, I forgot. There was this great beast of a hornet buzzing around the window...' He puts his arms around Fiona. 'Sorry, love.' He buries his head in her shoulder.

'Can we dig a hole for him?' I ask.

Fiona holds her tummy and runs for the toilet. It sounds like she's being sick.

'Jack?' I say.

Jack stares at me.

'Can we bury Mister Bubbles in the garden?'

Jack's gaze travels from me to the door of the toilet and back to me. 'I don't think so... I'll take care of it.'

Maya and me are eating breakfast when Jack comes in. 'Mind out.'

Fiona moves aside so Jack can get to the sink.

Maya scowls.

'What's the matter?' I whisper.

'I hate Jack,' she hisses. 'He wouldn't let us bury Mister Bubbles.'

I'm cross with Jack too. It's his fault Mister Bubbles died. Jack's a grown-up, he should know about fly spray...

Maya plays with her cereal. 'Nobody cared about Mister Bubbles except me.'

Jack's taking ages to wash his hands. They're covered in mud like he's been gardening, but Jack doesn't do gardening, it's always Fiona.

'What have you been doing out there?' asks Fiona

Jack glances in our direction. He lowers his voice. 'Something's been digging again.'

'Badger?' says Fiona

'It's been at your roses.'

Fiona puts a hand to her mouth.

Jack nods. 'It's okay, all sorted. Weetabix? Lovely. Hope you've left some for me.'

We finish our cereal and carry our bowls to the sink.

'Can we go out to play?' I ask.

'Okay.' Fiona squirts washing up liquid in the sink. 'But don't be pestering Mr Simpson.'

We run out of the back door and down to the bottom of the garden. I climb onto the bottom rung of the fence. 'He's not there.'

'He's had another bonfire,' says Maya, as little flakes of ash float gently over the fence. 'Catch them.'

I jump down and we skip about trying to grab them. Tiny black and white butterflies skitter about us. We make starfishes with our fingers, giggling as we capture the flakes between our palms. But when we open our hands, they've disappeared, like melting snowflakes.

'Boris! Boris!' calls Fiona. Closing the back door, she steps back into the kitchen. 'I haven't seen him all morning.'

'He's still sulking about that baby bird you confiscated,' says Jack.

Fiona clears the lunch plates from the table. 'He didn't have any breakfast either.'

Jack gets up, yawns and stretches. 'Better get back to it.' He heads upstairs to his office.

'Is Boris missing?' I ask.

'He's probably out hunting.' Fiona sets up the ironing board and lifts the iron from the shelf. 'Jack's right. He'll come back when he's ready.'

I fetch colouring pens and paper, and slide onto the bench opposite Maya. 'Let's make missing posters.' I draw two circles, one on top of the other, and add eyes, ears, whiskers and a tail. Picking up the black pen, I colour Boris in. I glance across at Maya's poster. She's drawing Boris laying down. When I've finished colouring, I choose a blue pen and write across the top of my paper in big letters: *BORIS IS MISSING.*

'There.' I hold it up for Fiona to see.

'That's super darling, but I'm sure Boris will be back in time for tea.' She picks up the pile of ironing and heads upstairs.

I look at Maya's poster. It's a picture of a black and white cat lying on its back. Its feet are stuck up in the air. Across the top Maya has written *RIP*. She's gone over the letters so hard it's made a hole in the paper.

'That's horrid,' I say.

Maya grins. 'He's a stupid fat cat and I hate him.'

'Boris isn't stupid or fat.'

'Well, I'm glad he's gone.'

'Maya, you haven't done anything to him?'

'Me? What would I do? He's probably shut in somewhere.'

Next morning, Boris still hasn't shown up.

'First the baby bird, then Mister Bubbles and now Boris.' Fiona blows her nose on a tissue. 'They say bad things come in threes.'

'Try not to worry.' Jack passes Fiona a mug of tea. 'He'll come home when he's ready.'

I stare down at my marmite soldiers. I'm not hungry. 'Perhaps he's shut in somewhere?'

'We've checked the loft and the shed.' Jack is using his jolly voice. 'Come on, everyone. You need to keep your strength up.'

'Maybe he's got shut in someone else's shed or garage? I know,' – Fiona picks up a slice of toast – 'why don't we go and knock on some doors later and get the neighbours to check?'

'We can take my poster,' I say, lifting a soldier from my plate and taking a bite.

When we've finished eating, Fiona and me put on our coats. Maya doesn't want to come.

'We've already asked Mr Simpson, let's try the other neighbours.' We walk along the lane and stop at the house next door. Fiona rings the bell.

An old lady answers. 'Hello?'

'Sorry to bother you,' says Fiona, 'but our cat is missing.'

'He looks like this.' I hold out my poster.

The lady looks at it. 'I know the cat you mean. He's a big fellow, isn't he? I'm sorry, I haven't seen him the past few days.'

'I wonder if you might keep an eye out?' Fiona brushes her hair from her face. 'Perhaps he's shut in a shed or garage?'

'We haven't been out in the car for a week, but I'll certainly keep my eyes open.'

The man in the next house checks his garage while we wait. He comes back shaking his head. 'Sorry, no sign.'

We knock at lots of doors and our feet are tired as we trek back home. On the way, we pass Old Mr Simpson walking back from the newsagents, his *Daily Star* tucked under his arm. He tips his cap. 'No sign then?'

Fiona shakes her head sadly. 'It's not like him.'

When we get home, I run upstairs looking for Maya. She's lying on our bed fiddling with something. As I come into the room, she closes her fist. She tries not to smile. 'Not found the cat then?'

I stare at her. 'Do you know where he is?'

'Me? How would I know?'

'You've done something.' I jump on her, trying to open her fingers.

Maya pulls away from me. She smirks as she opens her hand. I spot the yellow and green box with the swan. I lunge at her again. We roll off the bed, falling with a thud to the floor.

'What's going on?' calls Fiona from downstairs.

'Nothing,' I shout back.

'Well, keep it down,' calls Jack.

I glare at Maya. 'If you've done something to Boris…'

'You'll what?' Maya tucks the matches under her pillow, climbs back onto the bed and flicks through a comic.

That night I sleep on the edge of the bed. I don't want to be close to Maya. In my dreams I hear Boris meowing and scratching, like he's stuck somewhere under the floor.

CHAPTER SIX

Maya nibbles up to the edge of her toast and discards the crust.

'Daddy says we should eat the crusts,' I say.

'The edges don't have enough marmite.' At the sound of heavy footsteps above our head, Maya shoots me a quizzical look. 'What's that?'

I stare up at the ceiling. 'I don't know.'

She pushes her plate away. 'Let's go and find out what's going on.'

We race upstairs. Peering into Jack's office, we see it's almost empty. His desk's already been moved to the front bedroom, squeezed in under the window.

'What are you doing, Jack?' I ask.

'Clearing out the little bedroom.' Jack adds another box to the stack next to his desk. It wobbles as if about to topple over.

'I bet Jack's clearing out the little bedroom so we can have a room each.' I whisper to Maya.

'I don't think so,' she says.

'What shall we do today?' I ask.

'Let's go and find Old Mr Simpson. He might give us some more raspberries.'

She runs on ahead and I follow.

Maya leans over the fence to look for him. 'Oh, he's not here.' She fiddles with the padlock on Fiona's shed.

'What are you doing?'

She swings the door open. 'Fiona forgot to lock it.'

I stare at the spider webs. 'We're not supposed to go in there.' But Maya's already inside.

She clambers over the lawn mower. 'We should ask Jack when we can have a barbecue.'

'We have to wait for a nice day.' Specks of dust dance in a ray of light from the window. A fork, two spades and a rake hang from hooks on the side wall. Over on the shelf is Fiona's toolbox – snippers, clippers, a knife.

Maya pulls at the black plastic sacking tucked around the metal barbecue. 'If we're still here.'

'What do you mean?'

'Wait and see.' Maya rips off the sacking and rummages in the wire basket below.

'What are you doing?'

'Just looking.' She lifts out a plastic bottle and holds it up. *BBQ lighting fluid.* 'They shouldn't leave stuff like this lying around. It's dangerous.'

'Bath night,' says Fiona that evening.

'I don't want a bath,' says Maya.

'Do we have to?' I ask.

Fiona's tone is firm. 'Yes. I need to wash your hair.'

'Two little ducks went swimming one day,' I sing. Maya squirts me with water and I shriek with laughter.

'I'm home!' Jack calls up the stairs.

'Won't be long,' calls Fiona. 'Just doing bath time. Right, out you come.'

We get dry, pop into our clean pyjamas and curl up in bed. Fiona is halfway through reading *Matilda* when Jack yells. 'Oh my God, the shed.'

Fiona drops the book onto the bed. 'Stay here.'

We jump out of bed and peer out of the window. Jack's stumbling down the path carrying a bucket in each hand.

'Wouldn't the hose be better?' calls Fiona.

'It won't reach,' Jack shouts back.

Old Mr Simpson and another neighbour who we don't know are there too. They carry bucket after bucket, but it's no good.

The neighbour says something to Jack, but we can't hear what. He pats Jack on the shoulder and leaves. Old Mr Simpson is looking at the smouldering building. He shakes his head and turns for home.

Jack stays out there, staring at the blackened remains. Suddenly he spins around and looks up at our bedroom window.

We duck down and scoot back to bed.

Jack's footsteps race upstairs. He stands covered in soot at our doorway. He looks like a chimney sweep from *Mary Poppins*. 'Fiona says you were playing down the garden this afternoon?'

We hide under the covers.

Jack sits on the bed.

We peek out.

He stares at us. 'Did you go into the shed?'

Maya turns her face towards the wall.

'No,' I whisper.

'You weren't playing with stuff in the shed? Fiona says you've been pestering about a barbecue.'

'We're waiting for a nice day,' I whisper.

Fiona stands in the doorway. 'Leave it, Jack.'

'This is serious, Fi. If the shed had been closer to the house, something bad could have happened. To you and…'

Fiona closes her eyes. She strokes her tummy. *When did her belly get so big?*

'This has got to stop.' Jack's voice isn't loud, but we know he's angry. 'First the cat, now this.'

'Jack,' Fiona says, 'why don't you go and have a shower.'

Jack shakes his head, gets up and strides from the room.

'Try to get some sleep,' Fiona says to us in a sad voice.

'I'm sorry,' I say.

'What for?'

'All the bad things.'

Fiona usually leaves the bedroom door ajar, but tonight she shuts it. Everything in the room is black.

'Pretty soon,' says Maya, 'they won't want us around.'

'They won't want *you* around,' I hiss.

Maya rolls over to face me. 'What do you mean?' Her eyes blaze even in the dark.

'They'll want me, but they won't want you.'

'But we're a team,' says Maya. 'Mummy said no matter what, we always look out for each other.'

'We haven't got Khalu.' I wipe my eyes. 'You spoil everything.'

———

'How are you today, Ilona?' asks Helen

'I'm colouring in my princess.'

'I like her dress. Is pink your favourite colour?'

'No, pink is Khalu's favourite. I like purple.' I finish the princess's skirt.

'Do you miss Khalu?'

I shrug and add a yellow crown.

'How is Maya?'

'She didn't want to come.'

'And are you all right with that, Ilona?'

I put down my crayon and look at Helen. 'Me and Fiona are going shopping.'

'That's nice.' Helen writes in her book. 'If you've finished colouring, we could have a go at this jigsaw?' She carries the box over to the mat and sits down.

I slide from the chair and join her. Opening the box, I tip the pieces onto the mat. Helen joins the edges while I look for pieces to make the jungle tree.

'Maya didn't have anything to say today, then?' Helen asks.

'Maya only speaks to me since Mummy and Daddy went away.' I pick up a piece with a monkey's head and try to fit it to the tree.

'Try the other way.' Helen moves the piece in my hand. 'That's it. You know it would be all right for Maya to speak here? This is a safe place.'

I shrug.

'Does Maya want to speak now?'

I sigh. 'I told you, she's not here.'

'Can you talk to me about the fire, Ilona?'

'I don't want to talk about it.' I pick up another piece of the puzzle and turn around.

'It must have been scary. Did you see what happened?'

'Not really.' I slide my nail under the picture side of the piece. It starts to separate from the cardboard backing. 'We saw Jack and Old Mr Simpson and another man putting out the fire with buckets of water.'

'Do you know how it started?'

I close my eyes.

'You don't want to talk about it?'

I shake my head. After a moment I answer. 'I dream about it.'

'What do you dream, Ilona?'

If I whisper, perhaps Maya won't hear? 'I dream Boris is in the shed and he can't get out.'

'Fiona says you were in the garden earlier that day. If Boris was in the shed, wouldn't you have heard him?'

I open my eyes and stare at Helen. 'Maybe.' I don't tell Helen everything about my dream. How, when I step into the shed, Boris puts his paws up through the floorboards and grabs my feet. I haven't told anyone about that. Not even Maya.

'What are we going to buy?' I ask Fiona as we walk back to the shops.

Fiona smiles. 'You'll see. Ah, here we are.'

We walk into The Army & Navy. 'This is a really big shop,' I say.

'Yes, it is.' Fiona stops at the bottom of a moving staircase and reads the noticeboard. 'This tells us what's on each floor.'

I look at the long list. 'It must sell everything.'

'Yes, it probably does.' Fiona holds my hand. 'These escalators always make me feel a bit giddy. Ready?'

We go up two lots of moving stairs. When we step off, we're in a café.

'Lots of yummy things,' says Fiona. 'You can have anything you like, we're celebrating.'

I stare at the pictures on the wall and point at the banana split.

'Good choice. And a pot of tea please,' Fiona tells the lady behind the counter.

When we sit down, Fiona can't stop smiling. A waitress brings our food over to the table. I pick up a long spoon and dunk it down into the cream.

'I've got some good news.' Fiona stirs her tea. 'Jack and I are going to have a baby.'

'A real baby?' I say. 'Not a doll like at Helen's?'

'Yes, a real baby. That's why Jack's emptying out the little bedroom. He's going to paint it to become the nursery. Do you want to help me choose the first present for the baby's room?'

'A real baby?' I repeat.

'Yes,' says Fiona. 'And you'll be able to play with him or her.'

'And feed him and change his nappy?'

'Yes.' Fiona smiles. 'And read stories and sing nursery rhymes.'

My tummy flips. I always wanted a little brother. I dig into the ice cream and lift a spoonful to my mouth. It's too big and dribbles down my chin. I grin and wipe my mouth with my sleeve. Fiona laughs.

She says we can go back down in the lift and lets me push the buttons. We get out on the first floor and walk around looking at all the prams and cots.

'I like this one.' I stop beside a baby crib with pretty yellow frills.

'It's too early to get the big things.' Fiona moves across to a shelf with lots of baby things in boxes. 'And anyway, Jack's got to paint the nursery first, but we can buy the baby something small. How about a mobile?'

'What's a mobile?' I ask.

'It's something for the baby to look at, fixes to the ceiling over the cot. Look, they've got animals.' Fiona holds up two boxes. 'Butterflies or fishes? Which do you like best?'

I like the butterflies but I know Maya and Fiona miss Mister Bubbles. 'The one with fishes.'

'Excellent choice,' says Fiona.

CHAPTER SEVEN

Next time I go to see Helen, Maya comes too.

'I like her trousers,' whispers Maya. Helen's trousers are baggy, like Aladdin's. She's wearing blue satin shoes that match her hair.

I look around the room. My baby is in her buggy, so I walk her around for a bit. After that I lift her out and carry her into the Wendy house to give her some milk and put her to bed in the cot. I sing to her. 'Rock a bye baby…'

'You're singing to your baby,' says Helen.

'Yes, she needs to go to sleep. It makes my baby happy when I sing.'

'You seem happy today, Ilona?'

'Soon we'll have a real baby. Fiona says me and Maya can sing to him.'

'Is Maya happy today?' asks Helen.

'Maya's still sad about Mister Bubbles.'

'Mmm,' Helen writes something on her pad. 'What's Maya going to play with?'

I glance over at Maya, cross legged in front of the garage. 'She's playing with the cars.'

As I move across to join Maya, Helen comes too and kneels on the mat. 'Are you going to play with the cars now?'

'Yes, just while my baby is asleep.' I put a finger to my lips. Reaching into the box, I pull out a blue car. 'This one's like Daddy's.'

'Daddy had a blue car?' asks Helen.

'Yes. It got broken when it crashed.' I rub my fingers over the wheels, making them turn. Maya's whizzing a red sports car up and down the garage ramp.

'Does it make you sad to talk about the crash?' asks Helen.

I bite my lip. 'Mummy and Daddy and Khalu got broken too.' Suddenly Maya crashes the red car into the blue car. My fingers are squashed between them. Tears run down my face.

'It's all right to cry.' Helen is quiet for a moment. 'Would you like a tissue?'

'Mmm,' I say.

As Helen goes to fetch the tissues from her desk, Maya picks up the blue car and hurls it. The car flies past Helen's head, bashes the wall and lands on the floor.

I gasp.

Helen spins round. 'It's okay to be angry, Ilona, but we don't throw things. The toys could get broken or even worse, we might hurt someone.'

'It wasn't me.'

Helen picks up the car and drops it back in the box.

'I think yellow is sunny and cheerful.' Fiona gives the Bolognese sauce a stir.

Maya and me set the table. I'm doing knives and forks, and Maya's doing the spoons.

'What's the rush?' Jack washes his hands. 'Once we have the scan, we might know if it's a boy or a girl, then it can be blue or pink.'

'Mind out.' Fiona shoos Jack aside so she can drain the spaghetti. 'I'm not sure I want to know what we're having.'

Maya picks up the wooden salad spoon and chucks it across the room.

Jack spins around. 'Ilona!' he yells.

My cheeks go hot. 'It wasn't me.'

Maya smirks.

Fiona stares at me. 'What did you do that for?'

I clench my fists. 'I told you, I didn't.'

Jack dries his hands on the towel. 'You'd better go to your room.'

'But it's not fair.' I stamp my feet. 'It was Maya.'

Fiona dabs her eyes with the edge of her apron.

Jack throws the towel in our direction. 'You'd better both go to your room then.'

Slowly I climb the stairs with Maya behind me. When we get to our bedroom, Maya slams the door so hard it shakes the whole cottage.

Jack bounds up the stairs.

'Leave it, Jack,' calls Fiona.

We hear him go back down.

Maya flops on the bed. 'Told you.'

'What? About the baby? It was me who told you.'

Maya stares at me. 'I didn't need you to tell me about the baby. It was obvious. I told you they won't want us around anymore.'

'Yes, they will. Fiona says we can help.'

'Wait and see.'

I pick up Brown Bear and finger his ear.

'Aren't you getting a bit old for that?' Maya grabs him.

'Hey!' I say.

Maya holds Brown Bear up high. I jump to get him but she climbs on the bed and dangles him out of my reach. I climb up too, but slip and land on the floor.

Maya goes crazy, bouncing up and down on the bed and tugging at Brown Bear's head. His stitches give way and his head falls to the side, dangling by a couple of threads.

I scream. Maya drops him.

Fiona races in. 'What on earth is going on?'

'Maya ripped Brown Bear's head off,' I wail. Maya's standing on the bed, staring defiantly at Fiona.

'For goodness' sake.' Fiona grabs Brown Bear and marches back downstairs.

I lay on the floor and sob. I didn't do anything and now we've had no supper. I want Brown Bear.

In the night, I wake and find myself in bed with Brown Bear in my arms. I pull him out and hold him up to the light from the open door. Fiona has sewn his head back on.

A few days later, Miss Bishop comes to visit. We're told to stay in the kitchen while she talks to Fiona and Jack in the sitting room. After a while, the door opens. Jack comes out and walks past without looking at us.

Fiona comes out too. She sits down at the kitchen table. 'Miss Bishop wants to speak to you.'

Me and Maya go in.

'Sit down.' Miss Bishop nods towards the settee. 'Things are not going as smoothly as we'd hoped.'

'Is it the shed?' I say. 'That wasn't me.'

Maya pinches my arm.

'Ow.'

'Well yes, there was the shed.' Miss Bishop sighs. 'But now the Taylor's are expecting a baby and that does rather change things. Also, your therapy needs to continue for longer than we'd thought.' Miss Bishop clasps her hands in her lap. 'We think it might be best to move you to a children's home. Just for a while. That way we can increase sessions with Doctor Lewis to see if we can get to the bottom of things.'

'Do we both have to go?' I ask.

'Do you want to go on your own, Ilona?'

'No.' I don't look at Maya. 'I want her to go and me to stay here.' I feel Maya glaring at me.

'I'm not sure that's possible.' Miss Bishop puts her note-book and pen in her shoulder bag. 'I'm going back to the office to discuss things.' She brushes hairs from her navy slacks as she stands up. 'I'll let you know what's happening as soon as I can.'

'If we go to the children's home, will we come back?' I ask.

'We'll see, dear.' Miss Bishop picks up her bag and leaves the room.

We go up to our bedroom. 'If you don't behave, Maya,' I say, 'we'll be sent away.'

A smile spreads slowly across Maya's face.

I get a cold feeling inside. 'Please don't do anything.'

Someone's tugging my arm. I open my eyes, but I can't stop coughing. Our bedroom's full of smoke. Maya's standing beside the bed. She's dressed.

'What's happening?' I climb out of bed, hugging Brown Bear.

Maya reaches for my hand. Holding my breath, I follow her down the narrow stairs. The front door is unlocked. When we get outside, I look back. Flames light up the sky. I feel heat on my face and arms as the cottage crackles and groans. Sparks and tiny pieces of ash float around us.

Jack and Fiona are shouting from inside. 'Ilona!'

'Fiona!' I yell.

Maya turns and runs off down the lane.

'Maya!' I scream.

I stare at the doorway until Jack finally comes out with Fiona. He has his arm around her shoulders. I glance along the lane, but Maya's disappeared.

Fiona spots me. She runs across and holds me tight.

One of the neighbours claps his hand on Jack's shoulder. 'Everyone out?'

'Yes, thank God,' says Jack. 'I need to call…'

'Fire and ambulance already on the way,' says the man. 'You can do no more, Jack.'

We watch flames climb the wooden trellis on the front of the house, licking their way towards the windows of the upstairs rooms. Sirens become louder and flashing lights are coming down the street – a fire engine and two ambulances.

I remember someone wrapping me in a scratchy blanket and lifting me into an ambulance. Fiona must have been in the other one. On the way to hospital, I call for Maya. No-one can tell me where she is.

The ambulance stops outside the hospital and they wheel me inside.

A doctor comes to look at me. 'Hello young lady.' He shines a torch in my eyes and puts a flat stick on my tongue.

'Open wide.' Using his stethoscope, he listens to my chest before putting it back round his neck. 'Nurse is going to give you something to help you rest.'

The nurse smiles as she steps forward and takes my arm. 'You'll feel a little scratch.'

———

When I roll over and open my eyes, Miss Bishop is sitting on a blue chair by my bed.

'Maya?' I say.

Miss Bishop shakes her head.

My sister has gone.

CHAPTER EIGHT

The next day, Miss Bishop brings me grapes. I finger the crisp white sheets on the hospital bed.

Miss Bishop smooths my blanket. 'Fiona and Jack are okay, a little smoke inhalation, but their kitchen is a mess.' She sits down on the plastic chair. 'Ilona, what happened?'

I turn my head away.

'You need to tell me the truth.' Miss Bishop moves closer, speaking in a quiet voice. 'Did you have something to do with the fire?'

'No.'

Miss Bishop nods. She leans back, then quickly sits forward. 'And Maya? Did Maya have anything to do with it?'

I shake my head. *I'll never tell.*

'Thank heavens.' Miss Bishop pats my hand. 'Well, it sounds as if the fire started in the kitchen. Must have been a chip pan or a tea towel too close to the range.'

Fiona doesn't have a chip pan and she never leaves anything hanging over the range. I cough. Miss Bishop pours water from the plastic jug and holds the glass to my mouth. I take a sip.

She puts the glass on my bedside table. 'Fiona and Jack are staying with friends while the fire damage is repaired.'

'And me?' My voice is croaky.

Miss Bishop pats my shoulder. 'Get some rest. When you're well enough, I'll take you to the children's home.'

That night, I dream we're being driven away from the cottage. Fiona and Jack stand together on the doorstep and Jack has his arm around Fiona's shoulder like he did when we arrived. Fiona's crying. On the back seat of the car I reach for Maya's hand, but she's not there.

'Hello, Ilona. Feeling better?'

I look up. The man's not wearing a white coat like the other doctors.

When I don't answer, he sits on the chair beside my bed. 'My name's Doctor Chowdhury. I'd like to have a little chat if you're up to it?'

I stare at his eyebrows. They're so thick they almost join in the middle.

'Joan here tells me you've been asking for Maya?'

I glance towards the foot of my bed. Joan, the nurse who's been looking after me, is smiling. I nod.

'Maya's your sister?'

I face Doctor Chowdhury, looking into his dark eyes. 'Do you know where Maya is?' I ask.

He sits forward. 'When did you last see her?'

'She ran away after the fire.'

'And you've not seen her or heard her speak to you since then?'

How could I hear Maya if I didn't see her? 'Will she be coming back?'

'I'm not sure she will, Ilona,' says Doctor Chowdhury. 'But perhaps that's no bad thing, eh?'

No bad thing to never see my sister again? I hate Doctor Chowdhury. I wipe my wet cheeks. 'Will Fiona come and see me soon?'

Doctor Chowdhury gets up. 'You're upset. Try to rest. We'll talk again when you're feeling better.' He winks at me before nodding at Joan and striding off down the ward.

———

Two doctors move from bed to bed. I pretend to be asleep.

'What's wrong with this patient?' says one.

'Smoke inhalation as far as I can tell from the charts,' says the other. 'Oh, no wait. There's a psych referral.'

'Any reason she can't be moved up there now?' says the first as they walk away.

Miss Bishop said Fiona had smoke inhalation and she's already gone home. Why hasn't she come to see me? Why do I have to stay?

———

When I open my eyes, Maya's beside me. I struggle to sit up. 'Maya, the fire. You didn't…'

She puts a finger to her lips. 'Shhh. Go back to sleep.'

I lay back down. 'I thought you'd gone.'

Maya tucks Brown Bear in bed beside me. She puts her arms around me and rubs my back. 'I'll never leave you.'

They move me to a little curtained bit near the door. Through a gap, I peek out at the other people in the ward. They don't seem to have anything wrong with them, either.

Doctor Chowdhury comes to see me. He always asks the same things. 'Tell me about Maya.'

'She's my sister.'

'Your twin?'

'My triplet. There were three of us.'

'When did you last see your sisters?'

'Why can't I talk to Helen?'

Where is Maya? She promised she wouldn't leave me. I miss her. I miss Khalu too, and Mummy and Daddy. Why do all the people I love go away?

'When can I go home?' I ask Miss Bishop when she comes to visit.

'Soon,' she answers.

'When can I see Fiona and Jack?'

Miss Bishop straightens my covers. 'I don't know.'

'Is Fiona all right?'

'Fiona's fine, but she and Jack can't go back to their cottage yet.'

'What about the baby? I'm supposed to help with him.'

'The baby's not here yet,' says Miss Bishop.

Her touch wakes me. I sit up in bed. 'Where were you?' I hiss.

'Hiding,' whispers Maya.

'I thought you'd run away.'

She shrugs. 'Didn't take the treasure, did I? You seen Fiona and Jack?'

'No.'

'They don't want us around.'

'Why don't they? The fire wasn't our fault.'

Maya doesn't answer.

'Are you seeing Doctor Chowdhury too?' I ask.

'Yes.'

I play with Brown Bear's ear. 'He asks about you.'

CHAPTER NINE

Joan sticks her head around the curtain. 'You're still here? What's the holdup?'

'Miss Bishop's gone to get my medicine.'

'Got all your stuff together?' Joan opens the bedside locker to check.

I touch the white plastic bag full of my clothes. 'I don't have a suitcase anymore.'

Miss Bishop comes back. 'Ready, dear?' She smiles at Joan. 'Thank you.'

As we walk through the hospital doors and across the car park, I glance back over my shoulder.

Miss Bishop notices. 'What's the matter?'

'What about Maya?'

'I doubt she'll be far away.' Miss Bishop unlocks the car door and puts my clothes on the back seat. 'Hop in.'

'Where are we going?' I ask, buckling my seatbelt.

'St Agatha's.' Miss Bishop checks her mirror and reverses from her parking spot.

'Is it far?'

'About thirty minutes.' Miss Bishop pulls out onto the road.

We don't drive through the town, instead we travel across country. Soon we're passing a sign to Wateringbury.

I sit forward. 'Do we go past Fiona and Jack's cottage?'

'No.' Miss Bishop's lips become a thin line.

Further on, I spot a signpost for Paddock Wood. 'That's where Mrs Glover and My Henry live.'

We keep going for ages. Eventually Miss Bishop turns into a driveway and stops. 'Here we are.' She opens the back door of the car and takes out the plastic bag.

The house is massive and covered in bumpy paint that looks like porridge. We climb the grey steps and Miss Bishop rings the bell.

It echoes inside before the door is opened by a man in jeans and a black t-shirt. 'Hello. Ilona, is it? I'm Robbie. Glad ta meet you.'

I stare at the sprinkling of white dust on Robbie's shoulders as he holds the door open wide and we step into a big hallway. Yellow paint is peeling off the walls.

'Sorry, we're about ta have lunch.' Robbie turns to a girl sitting on the wooden staircase behind him. 'Jane, will you be taking Ilona upstairs with her stuff? She's bunking in with you and Becky.' He glances at the plastic bag in Miss Bishop's hand. 'This it?' Grabbing the bag, he tosses it to Jane. 'Here. Be quick. We're about ta dish up.'

Jane, taller than me with lanky brown hair, shoves my bag under her bony arm and slopes off upstairs.

Miss Bishop gently nudges me. 'Go on. I'll see you soon.'

I follow Jane up two flights of stairs. At the top, the ceiling slopes. Jane leads me past three doors before stopping outside the fourth. She kicks it open with her foot.

The room's no bigger than our bedroom in the cottage, but there are two sets of bunk beds. Jane chucks my bag on a lower bunk. 'Don't be long or you'll miss lunch.' She runs off, her footsteps clattering along the corridor and down the stairs.

I stare at the grubby green curtains and bird poo on the outside of the window.

'Boo!' Maya pokes her head out from the bunk above mine before climbing down the ladder.

I hug her. 'I thought we'd left you behind.'

'Nope. Told you, I'm always here.' She wanders across to the dresser and rummages through the top drawer.

'Have you been here all the time?'

'Course. Except when I was visiting you.' Maya pulls out a silver locket and stuffs it in her pocket. 'Come on, we'll miss lunch.' She runs from the room.

I try to keep up, but before I'm halfway down, Maya's gone. Holding tight to the handrail, I follow the sound of voices. I push open the double doors in the hallway and walk into a large room full of noisy kids. They all look older than me.

The children are split between two long tables and, at the far end of the room, two ladies wearing hairnets and aprons serve food from big silver tins. Jane stands beside one of the tables. Robbie leans over her, waggling his finger. She stares at the floor. I wait by the door.

Robbie looks up. 'All right, Ilona? Jane here will show you the drill.'

Scowling, Jane leads the way to the serving ladies. She takes a tray from the stack and thrusts it towards me.

'Shepherd's pie,' says the first lady. Scooping up a heap, she plops it onto a plate and places the meal on my tray before waving me along.

'Chocolate pudding,' the second lady says, 'and you'll be wanting sauce.' Her knife squeals as it scrapes against the bottom of the tin. She dishes up a huge slice of pudding and pours lumpy brown custard over it.

My plate and bowl slide about on the tray as I follow Jane to one of the tables and take the empty seat opposite her.

At the end of the table, a big girl is filling beakers from a metal jug. 'Here, pass these down.' When the boy opposite her doesn't respond right away, she kicks him. 'John, did you hear me?'

John puts down his fork and hands out the beakers.

The big girl glances my way. 'Give her some cutlery, too.' This time John springs into action, grabbing a spoon and fork from the basket in front of him. He gives the spoon a quick wipe on his jumper before passing them along.

'Eat as much as you can,' says a yellow-haired girl beside me. 'If they think you're a bad eater, they watch you.'

Gravy has spilled onto my tray. I bite my lip. *Where's Maya?*

The girl next to me slides my plate and pudding bowl onto the table and props the messy tray between our chairs. 'My name's Becky.' She speaks with her mouth full, and her cheeks are fat and pink.

I lift a forkful of shepherd pie and wrinkle up my nose. It smells like Boris's food. Closing my eyes, I pop it in my mouth, rolling it around before taking a swig of water to wash it down.

Halfway through my dinner, I spot Maya. She's on the

other table with her back to me. The other kids are already on
their pudding. I pick up my spoon. When I poke the custard,
the skin wrinkles.

Becky smiles. 'Try it. It's good.'

I lift a small spoonful and sniff. It smells like Mummy's
brownies. Apart from the burned bits, it tastes like chocolate
cake. The chocolate custard is yummy and sweet. I eat it
all up.

John and the big girl gather up the dirty plates and bowls,
stacking them on two trays. Everyone stands up.

'Come on.' Becky holds my hand, tugging me towards
another set of doors to the garden. It's half lawn and half
concrete. High on a wall hangs a basket with a torn net, and
girls are taking turns to throw a ball through it. Maya's
kicking a football around on the grass with a group of boys.

Me and Becky sit on a bench near the swings. 'You're
bunking with me and Jane.' Becky's still holding my hand,
making mine sweaty. 'It's Ilona, right?'

'Yes,' I say.

'This your first time?'

I try to stop myself from crying.

'You'll be fine. Bet you won't be here long. You're so
pretty, someone's bound to give you a new home.'

'We had a new home, but there was a fire.'

'Oh no.' Becky's eyes are wide. 'Did people get burned?'

'No,' I say, 'but I don't want to talk about it.'

'You and me will be best friends. Come on, I'll show you
around.'

———

We go back inside. Becky opens a door fast and the handle
slams into a hole in the wall. 'This is the games room.'

I look at the chairs lined up against the wall. There are two tables – one with a net and abandoned ping pong bats; the other with coloured balls in a wooden triangle. Battered board games are stacked on shelves: Monopoly, Cluedo and my favourite, Buckaroo. A large television stands on a unit in the corner of the room. It's not switched on though.

'Come on,' says Becky. I follow her across the hallway. She pushes open a door. 'This is the quiet room.' I stand at the entrance and look around. Old armchairs and a big saggy settee with a wrinkly red cover. Becky points towards a dark wooden table. 'The kids come in here to read or do home-work.' She jabs her finger at me, 'but no games or rough play. And it's out of bounds if there are visitors.'

Next, she shows me the downstairs toilet and points to a door at the far end of the hall. 'That's the offices. We're not allowed back there. Come on, upstairs next.'

On the first floor, Becky waves her hand dismissively. 'You've already seen our room.' Grabbing my hand, she pulls me past the bedrooms and along another corridor to a narrow staircase. Becky puts a finger to her lips. 'The big kids sleep up there,' she whispers.

We head back the way we've come. 'Is that where the mummies and daddies sleep?' I ask as we pass a door labelled *Staff*.

'There aren't any mummies and daddies. If you mean grown-ups, they don't sleep here. They work in the offices. Sometimes, if the boys are fighting or someone's sick in the night, they come through to our side, but we're not allowed to go through to theirs. Let's go back downstairs.'

We head to the games room. I put my hands over my ears to block out the noise. A couple of girls play ping pong while two big boys roll around on the floor punching each other. Becky chooses a jigsaw puzzle and we take it to the far corner, where the carpet has funny dark patches. I don't really want to sit on it, but at least it's away from the others. Maya sits nearby watching, but she doesn't join in. I finish the jigsaw with Becky. There are two pieces missing.

'Teatime,' calls Robbie from the doorway.

Everyone charges into the canteen. I sit next to Becky as we tuck into jam sandwiches and biscuits with a cup of milk.

Robbie puts a hand on my shoulder, making me jump. 'All right, Ilona?' He turns to Becky. 'It's been a long day. Why don't you take Ilona up and show her the bedtime routine?'

I follow Becky upstairs to a room near our bedroom.

'This is the girls' bathroom.' She pushes open the cubicle doors. 'Two toilets and two showers.'

I wrinkle my nose at the funny smell and I don't like the black stuff between the tiles.

'Your toothbrush goes in here.' Becky points to a row of plastic beakers spaced out along a wooden shelf. Each one has a name by it.

I read *Ilona Parrish.*

'And this is your peg.' Becky points out hooks under the shelf; a greyish towel and flannel hang from each. She moves across to the row of basins and passes me a bar of yellow soap with brown in the cracks. 'Here.'

I copy Becky, taking the flannel from my hook to soak it in the basin. When it's softened, I rub on the soap and wash my face. Becky passes me my towel. It's scratchy, not like Fiona's soft towels. Becky brushes her teeth, so I do mine.

Shivering from the cold, we run into the bedroom to change into our nighties.

Becky pulls open an empty drawer. 'You can put your stuff in here.'

I lay my clothes in the drawer and sit Brown Bear on my pillow.

'He yours?' Becky glances at her own bunk, the lower one opposite mine. On her bed sit two dolls, a baby doll in a pink dress and a little girl doll with blonde hair in plaits.

'I like your babies,' I say.

Becky lifts the baby doll. 'This one's Penny. She has a bottle and wets her nappy.' She lays Penny down on her bed before picking up the little girl doll. 'This one's Christine. You can watch me play with them tomorrow if you like. Do you want to give Christine a goodnight kiss?' She holds Christine up so I can kiss her on the lips.

Becky's asleep before Jane and Maya come up. I close my eyes, pretending to be asleep too, as they creep around getting ready for bed. How come Maya's settled in so well? And why hasn't Jane spoken to me since lunchtime? I bet she doesn't like me because Robbie told her off.

Maya climbs up the ladder making the bed springs above me squeak.

I squeeze Brown Bear tight. 'Night-night Maya,' I whisper to the darkness.

'Night-night,' she murmurs back.

CHAPTER TEN

I thought Maya would be happy now I'm here with her, but instead she's sulky and won't speak to Jane or Becky. She only talks to me when no-one else is about. Most of the time she hangs around with the older kids, but I'm scared of them. They're too loud and run everywhere. Especially the boys. When I hear them coming, I close my eyes and stand sideways, so they don't push me over as they rush past. Jane's older too, but at least she's not horrid. She just ignores me.

When the other kids play *What's the Time Mr Wolf?* and *Simon Says*, I want to join in, but I'm too shy. Becky comes to sit beside me, so I won't be on my own. She says she doesn't mind not playing with the others because I'm her best friend.

Becky lets me look at her dolls. She holds Christine up so I can see how her eyes open and hear her cry 'Mama' in a strange robotic voice. I'm allowed to watch Becky dress Christine, but I'm not allowed to dress her myself in case I mess up her hair. Christine's hair ribbons must stay the way they are. Penny has a special potty to do her wees. I'm not allowed to touch her potty or change her nappy either, because I might do it wrong. Sometimes Becky lets me give Penny her bottle.

I'm watching Becky wheeling Penny around in her buggy when Robbie comes to find me.

'Ilona, Miss Bishop is here ta see you. She's waiting in the quiet room.'

I get up, go across the hallway and peep around the door. 'Hello, Miss Bishop. Shall I find Maya?'

'No,' Miss Bishop says. 'Come on in and let's chat on our own.'

I sink down into one of the tatty armchairs.

'How are you getting on?' Miss Bishop asks.

'Okay.'

'Your throat sounds better. Are you sleeping all right?'

I think about night times. How I hug Brown Bear, trying not to let Jane or Becky hear me crying.

Miss Bishop looks down at her notepad. 'Right, we need to talk about school.'

'Fiona says we're going to the school next to the church.'

'I'm afraid, now you're living in Southborough, that St Mark's is much too far. But don't worry. You can go to the local primary with the other children here.'

'But Fiona bought us cardigans for St Mark's.'

'I can sort that out.' Miss Bishop writes something down in her book. 'Now, have you made friends?'

'Becky in our room is nice.'

Miss Bishop smiles. 'That's a good start.'

Maya and me wear the grey pinafores and white blouses that Fiona bought us, but we're not allowed to go to St Mark's. Instead, we have to put on green jumpers with 'Five Oaks Primary' written on them in horrid gold letters, like the rest of the younger kids at the home.

The school is huge, and me and Maya are in different classes. Because Maya won't speak, the teachers think she can't read and put her in a class with 'special children'. Maya's always been a good reader and it makes her cross, but it's her own fault.

My teacher, Miss Naylor, sits me next to a girl called Yvette with tiny plaits all over her head. When she smiles, it makes me want to smile too.

Miss Naylor pins a picture of Hastings Castle on the board. She explains it's a Motte and Bailey Castle and points out the keep and moat. I know this stuff but I don't say anything. Next, we copy writing from the board and draw a picture. I concentrate on getting the drawbridge right, but Yvette draws the whole castle. It looks like a house with thin windows.

'Okay.' Miss Naylor claps her hands. 'Clear up time, then out to play.'

'Colouring pencils go in here.' Yvette lifts a plastic tub from the shelf. 'And you put your book here in this green tray.'

We run outside holding hands. I look around the playground.

'Who are you looking for?' asks Yvette.

'My sister,' I say.

'Her class probably has a different playtime.' Yvette leans her back against the wall and pulls a satsuma from her pocket. As she peels it, the smell tickles my nose and makes me sneeze.

She pulls it apart and holds out a few segments. 'You want some?'

'Thank you.'

'Numbers next. Know your times-tables?'

'Yes, but I'm better at stories and pictures.'

Yvette grins. 'I can't draw for toffee. Did you see my castle?'

'I could show you how to draw a cat?' I offer.

'Really? Okay, and I'll help you with numbers and science and stuff.'

I'd been scared about starting school but now I've been here a few weeks, it's okay. I like Miss Naylor. She smiles a lot like Fiona and she knows loads of stuff like Daddy. Yvette and me help each other and share things. I don't have to watch her play like I do with Becky.

Every day the kids at St Agatha's walk to and from school together. One morning we stop to pick up conkers. Watching the big boys squabble over them, I remember how Daddy used to make a hole in conkers and put them on string.

When Miss Naylor has done the register, she lifts up a big plastic bag and empties it on her desk. A pile of coloured leaves tumble out – red, purple, yellow and gold.

'Take two each, children,' she says. 'Aren't these colours glorious?'

I lift up a leaf and it crackles. It's the colour of my hair. I raise my hand. 'Miss Naylor. Why aren't the leaves green?'

Miss Naylor smiles. 'That's a very good question, Ilona. In the winter there's less sunlight so the leaves stop producing chlorophyll. Once that happens, the green colour fades and the reds, oranges and yellows become visible. Aren't they beautiful? We're going to use them as inspiration for some lovely autumnal pictures.'

As well as the leaves, we're allowed to use felt tip pens, paints and anything else from the craft box. I spend ages screwing up pieces of tissue into tiny balls before sticking them onto my paper to make flowers and trees. It reminds me of Fiona's garden. I wonder if the leaves on Fiona's trees have turned into magical colours.

'Oh, that's pretty. Show me how to do that,' says Yvette. Soon she has tissue trees and flowers too, but they're not as neat as mine. Along the top of her picture, Yvette writes, *To Mummy love from Yvette.*

I chew the end of a green pen. I know, I'll give my picture to Fiona. I don't know how I'll get it to her but perhaps Miss Bishop will help? I add Boris and a baby beside a tree. I don't know what Fiona's baby looks like, so I draw Becky's baby doll instead.

Yvette leans closer. 'Show me how to draw a cat.'

I draw two circles, one on top of the other. Yvette picks out a blue crayon and copies me. She doesn't have a cat but says her mummy will like it anyway. I don't write on my picture. I'll do that back at St Agatha's. Maya might want to send it from both of us.

When I get home from school, I carry my bag up to our room before going down for tea. Where is Maya? I can't wait to show her the picture I made for Fiona. After tea, I head back upstairs. I open the bedroom door and gasp. The picture has been taken from my bag. Someone has torn it up. Tiny pieces of paper and tissue are scattered over my bed.

Jane and Becky are asleep when Maya hangs her head over the side of the bunk. 'Don't go getting friendly with the other kids.'

'But you've made friends.'

'I don't like that kid at school you hang about with.'

'Yvette?'

'Yeah.'

'My teacher put me next to her. Yvette's nice. It's not my fault you're in a different class.'

Maya flops back on her mattress. 'I'm just saying, it's not worth making friends cos we won't be here long.'

'You think Miss Bishop's going to find us a new home?'

'Maybe. We need to hold out for the right place.'

'Don't spoil things, Maya.'

CHAPTER ELEVEN

Becky turns from the noticeboard, her eyes sparkling. 'A cartoon, my favourite. *The Rescuers*.'

'Shall we bring your babies to movie time?' I ask.

'I'll bring Penny,' says Becky, 'because I'm her mummy. You can be Auntie. Christine can't come because she's got to go to school.'

We bag cushions near the front of the screen.

'Oh,' says Becky, 'I forgot to bring Penny's nappy. Go and get it, Auntie. I'll save your place. It's still the adverts.'

Racing back to our room, I search around for the nappy on Becky's bunk. I hear a sound above me but when I check the top bunk there's no one there. Grabbing the nappy, I run downstairs as the film starts.

After the film's finished, we go back upstairs.

'How's my big girl?' Becky lifts Christine into the air. 'How was school today? Did you miss me? Oh!' She drops Christine onto her bunk.

Jane comes through the door. 'What's the matter?'

Becky falls to the floor, wailing noisily.

Jane picks Christine up. 'Oh no.' She puts a hand over her mouth, stifling a giggle. 'Poor Christine.'

She turns the doll around and I gasp. Someone's drawn on Christine's face, giving her black lips, a down-turned mouth and black teardrops running down both cheeks.

Maya snorts with laughter from the top bunk. 'Perhaps she's sad because you made her miss the film?'

Becky stops crying and glares at me. 'I hate you.'

My heart pounds. 'I didn't do it.'

Becky jumps up. 'Who else would?' she yells.

'Don't look at me.' Jane throws Christine onto Becky's bed and climbs the ladder to her own bunk.

I back away. 'It wasn't me. Cross my heart.'

Becky comes right up close. 'You did it when you came to get Penny's nappy.'

'Why would I do that?'

'You're jealous because I've got two dolls and you've only got that stupid bear.' Becky picks Christine up, but the doll's plaintive 'Mama' is too much for her and she begins to sob again.

'In here?' Helen frowns as she looks around the quiet room.

I laugh.

'Hmm. Well, I suppose it saves you coming all the way to my office.'

She's wearing a sort of thick blanket instead of a coat. I reach out to touch the fringe. 'Is this a blanket?'

'It's called a poncho.' Helen slides it over her head. Opening her shoulder bag, she pulls out paper, colouring pens and her notebook. 'Sorry, I couldn't bring my toys.' She sets everything out on the table.

I climb up onto a dining chair. 'S'okay.' Pulling the lid off a red pen, I start to draw. 'Your pens are good. The ones in the games room don't work.'

Helen sits on the settee and places the notebook on her lap. 'So, Ilona, how are things going?'

I carry on drawing. 'Are you seeing Maya too?' I ask.

'I've been in touch with Doctor Chowdhury. You met him at the hospital, remember? He suggested I meet you without Maya.'

I draw a picture of Fiona and Jack's house. 'I'm making Fiona's flowers look really nice.'

'Miss Bishop tells me you've made a friend?'

I pick up a green pen to colour in the grass.

Helen looks at her notebook. 'Becky, right?'

I chew my lip and add a tree next to the house.

'Ilona, did something happen?'

I put the lid back on the green pen. 'Becky doesn't like me anymore.'

'Why? What happened?'

There's green ink on my hands. 'Something happened to her doll.'

'What happened to her doll?'

I rub my fingers, but it doesn't come off. 'She got drawed on.'

'How did that happen?'

'Don't know. It happened when we were watching a film.'

'It wasn't you?'

'No. I like Becky's dolls.'

'But Becky thinks it was?'

'I suppose.'

'And it wasn't Maya?'

'No.' I push the paper and pens away. 'Maya shouted at me when I asked her about it.'

'Have you tried talking to Becky about it?'

'Robbie made us sit together and we both had to say how we were feeling. Becky said she was cross 'cos I spoiled Christine and I said I didn't do it.'

'Christine is Becky's doll?'

With my fingernails, I work away at a lump of chewing gum stuck under the table. 'Mmm.'

'And Becky's still cross?'

'Yes. Robbie made me say sorry, but I didn't do it.'

'You shouldn't have to say sorry if you didn't do it.' Helen scribbles stuff in her notebook.

I turn my paper over and pick up a blue pen. 'Someone put a note under our bedroom door. It said this.' I hold up the paper and show Helen what I've written. *Becky's a Fat Pig*. 'Becky got upset again, so Robbie's moving me and Maya to a different room.'

'Oh dear.' Helen rummages in her shoulder bag. She passes me a tissue. 'I'm not surprised you're upset, Ilona, but I'm sure things will settle down.'

I didn't know I was crying. I wipe my eyes.

Helen watches me. 'Tell me about school. Have you made friends there?'

'I've got a friend called Yvette. She helps me with numbers and stuff, and I show her how to do drawing.'

'Yvette...' Helen's writing again. 'It sounds like you and Yvette make a good team.'

CHAPTER TWELVE

The picture of Hastings Castle droops in front of my knees. I'm supposed to be holding it up so the other kids can see but my arms ache. The girl on stage stops talking. All the kids clap. Now it's my turn.

I look out at a sea of faces. My cheeks go hot. Miss Naylor selected four of us to show our work in assembly. Maya is sitting cross-legged at the front with the rest of her class. She sticks out her tongue. I search for Yvette. She smiles back at me.

'Ilona Parrish,' says the Headmistress.

I try to speak but my tongue fills my whole mouth.

'Hold your work higher,' hisses the girl who's finished speaking. It's all right for her, her bit's over.

'Erm,' I cough. 'This is Hastings Castle…'

Miss Naylor stands at the side of the stage mouthing something. Her lips go small and then big. 'Nor…man…'

'It's a Norman Castle,' I say in a quiet voice.

'Can't hear.' A boy at the back sniggers. 'Looks more like a cat.'

The other kids laugh.

I turn my drawing towards me. It does look a bit like a cat, two circles, one bigger than the other... 'Sorry.' I turn it back, pointing to the smaller circle, 'This bit is the Motte.'

Daddy's voice pops into my head. *'And what's a Motte?'*

'A Motte is like a hill. The bit where they defend the castle. Sometimes they have a keep on top.'

'And the other bit?' asks Daddy.

I point at the bigger circle. 'That's the Bailey where the people live. It has a fence around it called...' I can't remember what it's called. I blink. My throat is dry. I glance at Miss Naylor. She nods encouragingly. 'Anyway,' I say, 'the fence keeps the people safe. This is the drawbridge and it has a chain or rope to let it down.' I take a deep breath.

Miss Naylor claps and, when the Headmistress joins in, so do the rest of the kids.

I stand to the side and the boy next to me takes over.

The bell goes. As we leave class for morning break someone pushes past. I look up. It's the horrid boy who said my picture looked like a cat.

'Little Miss Smarty Pants,' he sneers. His friends laugh.

When we're outside in the playground, I notice Maxine Stubbs from our class staring at me. She whispers something to her friends. They look my way and giggle.

Yvette takes my arm. 'Ignore them,' she says as we walk across to the other side of the playground. 'You were good.'

'I couldn't remember it all.'

'You did it though. Should be proud of yourself.'

'But the other kids think I was showing off.'

'They're jealous,' says Yvette. 'My daddy always says it

doesn't matter what other people say. Do your best and be proud of who you are.'

In the canteen at teatime, Jane, Becky and a girl called Katie sit at the other end of our table.

'So, you and Becky have the room to yourselves now,' Katie says in a loud voice.

'Yeah.' Jane nudges Becky. 'She's a bit of a baby but least I don't have to worry about my bed being set on fire.'

Becky sticks her tongue out and Jane grins at her like they're best friends.

'What d'you mean?' says Katie.

'Didn't you hear?' Becky nods in our direction. 'Two fires at the foster home.'

'Bit of a coincidence.' Jane looks down the table at me and Maya.

'You saying it was deliberate?' says Katie.

Jane shrugs. 'Just telling you what I heard.'

Katie shakes her head. 'We don't want that sort around here.'

When Maya and me enter the games room, everyone turns to stare. 'Watch out,' someone hisses. 'Where's the fire extinguisher?'

We sit down in front of the TV but there's nothing I want to watch.

One of the boys playing pool calls across to me. 'Hey, Ginger Nut, got a light?' His friend nudges him and sniggers.

'Doesn't it upset you?' I whisper to Maya.

'Not really.' She tosses her hair. 'If they've got nothing better to do, that's their problem.'

In bed that night, I hear the rustle of sweet wrappers. 'What are you eating?' I ask.

Maya emerges from under the covers. 'Topic.'

'But you picked a Mars bar.' After supper on Friday's we get a treat from the tin. 'You chose the same as me.'

'I grabbed a few extra.'

I sit up. 'How?'

'When the canteen ladies were clearing the trays.'

'You'll get caught.'

'Didn't though, did I? You want one?' Maya chucks a Topic over to me.

'Thanks.' I slide it under my pillow.

'You not eating it?'

'No, I'm saving it to have at school.'

At morning break, Yvette and me sit on the playground bench. Yvette always shares her snack – banana, apple, sometimes a KitKat.

Today I pull the battered Topic from my pinafore pocket. I unwrap it and I'm about to break it in half when Yvette puts a hand on my arm. 'Wait. That chocolate bar got nuts?'

I examine the wrapper. 'Yes.'

'I can't have none then.'

'You don't like nuts? I saved it all weekend.'

'You're a good friend,' says Yvette, 'but I can't have nuts. They make me ill.'

I look up when someone sniggers. Maya, playing hopscotch nearby, pauses mid-hop to smirk at me.

We're back in class when Yvette starts making funny noises in her throat. Her eyes are wide.

'What's the matter?' I say.

She has her fingers over her mouth.

I shoot my hand up. 'Miss Naylor, quick. Yvette's feeling poorly.'

Our teacher comes over. Yvette's wheezing. She can't breathe. 'Maxine Stubbs,' says Miss Naylor, 'run and fetch Mrs White from the school office.'

Maxine returns quickly with Mrs White and the Head-mistress. Mrs White puts her fingers around Yvette's wrist.

The Headmistress takes one look at Yvette. 'Phone an ambulance.'

'Should I phone her mother too?' asks Mrs White.

'Yes,' says the Headmistress. 'But 999 first and hurry.' She puts an arm around Yvette and walks her slowly from the classroom. Yvette is bent over like an old lady. Her breathing sounds all wrong.

'Carry on with your work, class.' Miss Naylor sits down at her desk and rubs her forehead.

I try to carry on with my story but I can't concentrate.

Nee nah, nee nah… Leaping out of our seats at the sound of the siren, we run to the window.

Two ambulance men hurry into the building. A few minutes later, Yvette is carried out on a stretcher.

Harry Haytor shakes his head sadly. 'She's a goner.'

'Shhh,' says Miss Naylor. 'Sit back down children and finish your stories.'

Yvette's not at school next day or the day after that. During Friday's assembly, the Headmistress talks about nut allergies. She explains how it's important to be careful and, if someone has an allergy, you must never give them anything with nuts. You shouldn't even eat nuts near them. My cheeks burn. I feel sick. Did I make Yvette ill when I unwrapped the Topic?

All weekend I barely eat, spending most of the time laying on my bed. Have I killed Yvette? Will the police come to get me? I don't speak to anyone about it. Not even Maya.

On Monday, Yvette returns to school.

'Did I make you sick?' I whisper as Miss Naylor hands out textbooks.

'No.' Yvette smiles. 'Unwrapping that Topic wouldn't have done it. I have to actually eat nuts to make me bad.'

'But you didn't eat any of it.'

'I didn't eat any nuts that day.' Yvette's tongue pokes out as she copies questions from the blackboard. 'I only ever eat what's in my lunch box.' She gestures to her rucksack hanging on her named peg inside the classroom door.

CHAPTER THIRTEEN

We've been at St Agatha's for five years now. Sometimes I
wonder what Khalu would have made of it. She wouldn't like
not coming first, that's for sure.

Maya spends all her time around the big girls. They braid
each other's hair and try out new nail polish or lippie. I'm too
shy to join in so, when she's with them, I hide out in our
room. I hate the way she abandons me. All I can do is wait
for her to come back.

The big girls hang around with the boys too. They're all
over Kevin, who's twelve and already in big school. Maya
follows him everywhere, sometimes going up to the room he
shares with two other boys. The boys listen to *Queen* and
Guns N' Roses. Maya pretends to like those bands too.

Some days I creep along the corridor and up to Kevin's
room. Even though the music is turned up loud, I can still
hear Maya laughing. I'm sure Kevin's not interested in her. I
bet he only shows her attention because he's got nothing
better to do.

One afternoon Kevin brings home a friend from school. She's called Sophie and has straight blonde hair. I wish I was that pretty. Sophie sits next to Kevin at teatime, gazing at him through her long fringe. When he says something funny, she snorts with laughter.

Maya watches their every move, while I concentrate on my cheese on toast.

Kevin and Sophie get up and leave the table.

'Where're you going?' calls Maya.

Kevin turns in our direction, a cocky look on his face. 'To the quiet room to do homework. Not that it's any of your business.'

'Yeah right,' Maya whispers to me. 'I know what they'll be up to.'

'What?'

Maya rolls her eyes. 'You're such a baby. You've got no idea what boys like.'

Once we've finished, we get up too. As we're passing the quiet room door, Maya stops to listen.

'Come away,' I hiss.

Outside, Maya stomps around on the concrete terrace before pushing her way through the shrubbery.

'Where are we going?' I whisper, following her through the overgrown bushes.

Maya glances back over her shoulder, a glint in her eye. 'You'll see.'

Crouching low, we make our way past the games room and canteen windows, until we reach the back of the building. From inside the kitchen comes the chatter of canteen ladies, a clatter of plates and chinks of cutlery as the dishwasher is loaded.

Maya puts her finger to her lips. 'Shhh.' She reaches through an open window and snatches something from the sill before ducking down. Grabbing my arm, she drags me back the way we came.

When we reach the cover of the hydrangeas, I stop. 'What did you get?'

Maya opens her fist to reveal a sparkly diamond ring.

I gasp. 'You need to put that back.'

Maya shakes her head. 'It's our running away treasure.'

'But it's stealing.'

Maya shrugs. 'Cook will think it fell out of the window. Serves her right for leaving it there.'

Robbie gives Kevin permission to bring Sophie home several times over the following weeks. They're supposed to be doing a science project together, but spend most of their time in the games room watching *Grange Hill*.

At teatime we join them in the canteen so Maya can keep an eye on them.

Kevin keeps shifting on the bench and glancing at Sophie as if working up to ask her something. 'A few of us are going bowling Saturday afternoon.'

'Yeah?' says Sophie.

Kevin runs his fingers through his hair. 'Yeah, so, if you're free…'

Sophie blushes. 'That'd be cool.'

Maya nudges me and I follow her up to our room.

'Forget him,' I say. 'He's not that special.'

'Like you know,' says Maya. 'You don't even like boys.' She grabs a piece of paper and a pencil and sits at our dressing table.

'What are you doing?'

'Nothing.' But she shields what she's writing with

her arm.

———

Next day, when I walk past Kevin and his mates, they're laughing. Kevin has Maya's note in his hand. She must have slid it under his door.

———

Maya's mooching around in our bedroom. I'd rather she was with her mates than have her sad like this. 'We could play a box game?' I suggest. 'Or do a puzzle?'

Maya frowns. 'We've done them all.'

I sigh. 'What shall we do then? I don't think there's anything on telly…'

Maya grins. 'Let's be each other.'

'What d'you mean?'

'I'll dress up in your clothes and you dress in mine.' She rifles through our drawers, chucking clothes over the floor.

'Hey, that's my nice skirt.' I pick it up and lay it on the bed.

Next, she pulls out a pair of jeans and a tatty t-shirt. 'Here you go. Put these on.' She snatches my skirt from the bed. 'I'll wear this and that top you've got on.'

We wriggle out of our clothes and dress in each other's before standing side by side in front of the dressing table mirror. Maya tilts it so we get a better view. It does feel funny. I look in the glass and Maya stares back at me. I turn to real Maya and she mirrors my moves. We giggle.

Maya pulls her hair back into a ponytail. 'Let's see if we can get away with it downstairs.'

'I'm not sure…'

'Oh, come on. I thought you wanted to cheer me up?'

'Okay.' But I drag my heels.

We're halfway down the stairs when Maya grabs my arm. 'This won't work if you don't act more like me.'

I stop. 'Let's go back then.'

'No,' says Maya. 'You have to do what I say.'

My heart thumps. 'I can't.'

'Yes, you can.' She whispers some words into my ear.

I follow her down to the hallway and she drags me towards the games room. I hang on to the frame, not wanting to go in but Maya pushes me and I almost fall into the room. No-one seems to notice. Three kids straddle across the *Twister* mat, while Kevin and another boy play pool. Two friends of Maya's are in the corner painting each other's nails.

'Go on,' Maya hisses.

I shake my head. Maya gives me another shove. I move towards the girls. As I get closer, I look back at Maya.

'Go on,' she mouths.

Leaning towards the first girl, I whisper, 'Kevin says you snogged fat Jeffrey round the back of the sheds.'

'I never,' shouts the girl, splodging nail polish over her friend's fingers.

'Hey!' says her friend.

I take a step back. 'That's what I told him, but he says Jeffrey told him you was gagging for it.'

'That's a fucking lie,' screams the girl. 'Kevin…'

Maya tugs at my sleeve and we run from the room. Out in the hall, Maya doubles over clutching her belly. 'Kevin's so gonna get it,' she laughs.

'You made it up?'

Maya stares at me. 'You're such a pillock. Course I made it up. But that's not the point.' She grins. 'They really thought you were me.'

CHAPTER FOURTEEN

I tug the sleeves of my school jumper down over my hands while Helen reads through my file. Today her hair is magenta.

She looks up. 'I guess it's a longer journey now?'

'Yep, bus to Tonbridge, then a train.' I pull a thread on my cuff. 'At least I get to miss an afternoon of school when I come to see you.'

'You don't like school?'

'You kidding? I hate it.'

Helen closes the file. 'What is it about school you don't like, Ilona?'

I don't tell her about the days and weeks passing in a blur without me speaking to anyone other than teachers. Instead, I shrug. 'I don't know anybody.'

'Sounds like you've lost a bit of confidence since moving to secondary school.' She smiles kindly. 'Haven't you made any friends?'

'Nope.'

'Yvette didn't transfer with you?'

'No, she went to the girls' grammar. She always was good at science and maths.'

'Are you disappointed you didn't pass the eleven plus exam?'

I shrug. 'I wouldn't have coped at a grammar school. I'm always behind, even at Kingley High.'

'Why do you think that is?'

I've worked a small hole in my cuff and I poke my thumb through it. It doesn't matter how hard I try. Sometimes it seems like I miss whole lessons and yet my attendance record is fine. 'Because I'm thick?'

'That's not true, Ilona, you're a bright girl. Grammar school might have suited you.'

'Kingley High suits Maya,' I mumble.

'Sorry?'

'Maya likes it. She doesn't care how she does as long as she's got her mates around.'

Helen stares at me. 'Do you think, Ilona, that Maya's preference might have influenced your results?'

I wake up sweaty and sit up with a start. *Have I wet myself?*

'What's the matter?' asks Maya.'

'I think,' my voice shakes, 'I'm bleeding.'

Maya inspects my bottom sheet. 'It's your time of the month.'

'What?'

'Don't you remember that talk Mrs Morgan gave? It happens to everyone. Well, all the girls. It's a sign you're growing up. I started mine months ago.'

How could I have forgotten? I remember being horrified at the thought of bleeding every month. Did I blank it out? Perhaps I thought it would never happen to me.

'You'll be all right,' says Maya. 'You'll get used to the

stomach cramps. Shove a wad of loo paper in your knickers and we'll go and ask Mrs Morgan for a hot water bottle and some pads.'

———

The next few days are a struggle. My tummy hurts and my head aches. It's like having a cold but without the snotty nose. I don't want anyone to see me so I hide away in our room.

'I know what'll cheer you up,' says Maya. 'Let's pretend to be each other again.'

I frown.

'Oh, come on. It's fun. I'll be you, worried about everything, and you can be me. It'll be good. Make you feel more confident.'

I shake my head, but Maya won't be put off. Sometimes, when she's bossy, she reminds me of Khalu.

Maya hauls off her t-shirt and chucks it at me. 'It'll be a laugh.'

I stare at her top for a second before tugging it over my head and checking myself out in the mirror. She's right. Maya stares confidently back.

Real Maya peers over my shoulder. 'Not bad, but you need makeup. I'll do your hair too.'

Making me up as Maya takes longer than making Maya up to be me. Normally I wear virtually no make-up. Once ready, we stand side by side, me preening and pouting like Maya, while she lowers her head and peers nervously through her fringe. It's weird, looking at ourselves but seeing each other; like the mirror is playing tricks, showing our reflections in reverse.

We practise each other's mannerisms. Maya finds this easier than me. 'Oh, I'm sorry, it was all my fault.' She looks silly feigning my apologetic body language and has me in fits of giggles.

Maya coaches me how to act boldly, how to sashay across the room and how to give what she calls her *come and get me* look. Finally, she opens the bedroom door. 'Come on. Let's see if we can get away with it again.'

We make our way down to the games room. Maya selects an empty chair set apart from anyone else. She tiptoes nervously across and sits down, chewing at her nails.

I take a deep breath before strolling over to where Robbie and Kevin are playing pool. Robbie's our primary carer now. The one who looks out for us and the closest thing we've got to a parent. Or perhaps more like a big brother? I lean against the wall. Kevin looks up and nods.

Robbie squeezes past me when it's his turn to shoot. 'All right?' He places a hand gently on my shoulder. 'Mind your back.'

I glance over at Maya. She points towards the refreshment table in the corner of the room. I nod. 'Anyone fancy a drink?' My voice cracks but no one seems to notice.

'I'll take one, ta,' says Kevin.

Wiggling my hips, I sashay over to the table. Aware Kevin's watching me, I help myself to two cans, shove a straw in each and swagger back. The straw of my Fanta is between my lips as I gaze at Kevin in a Maya kind of way and offer him a can.

He raises an eyebrow before finishing his shot. The ball thunders down into the pocket. Kevin grabs the Fanta. 'Cheers'. He yanks out the straw and lifts the can to his mouth. As he necks the fizzy drink, his eyes don't leave my face.

My heart races. I don't know what to do. I glance towards Maya.

She's frowning. Suddenly she stands up and walks out of the room. The door bangs closed behind her.

I follow her out to the corridor, my cheeks flushed with success. 'I did it.'

'Yeah.' Maya's face is thunder.

'What?'

'I never said you could try it on.' Her spit sprays my cheek.

'But I…'

'Don't you ever flirt with Kev again.' She turns and runs upstairs.

CHAPTER FIFTEEN

Maya doesn't stay annoyed for long. She needs a confidante. Alone at night, she shares intimate details of encounters with boys, while I listen wide-eyed and eager to learn. I begin to dress more like her, rolling skirts over at the waist and stuffing wads of loo paper into my bra. As my confidence grows, old Ilona fades, while Maya becomes ever more precocious.

Perhaps that's why I'm so excited the night I get back from France? Although the whole of Year 8 will experience a residential trip, not all classes go the same time. Maya's class have to wait another few weeks. For once I have something to share with her.

I sit on Maya's bed recounting all the silly things that happened. How we struggled to buy baguettes in the *pâtisserie* and haggled for cheese at the market in Boulogne. '...and then we realised these French boys were following us...' I glance at Maya for reaction and notice her eyes are watery. 'What's the matter?'

'Robbie had a right go at me while you were away.'

I touch her arm. 'Why?'

'He caught me in Kev's room.'

'Oh my God!'

'Robbie hit the roof.' Maya blows her nose into a tissue. 'And now I'm grounded.' She sniffles.

I gasp. 'What about the match?' Maya has been desperate to be part of St Agatha's pool team. She's due to play next weekend for the first time.

She snorts. 'Robbie'll never let me go.'

'Do you want me to talk to him?' I offer. 'I might be able to get round him.'

'No,' says Maya. 'Leave it.'

'All right, Ilona?' Robbie asks before returning his attention to the noticeboard.

'Yes thanks.' I walk across to Maya, who's practising shots at the pool table. 'Wow,' I whisper, 'talk about an atmosphere!'

Maya makes a rude hand gesture behind Robbie's back. I stifle a giggle.

Robbie looks round again. 'What?'

'Nothing.' I grab two cans from the refreshment table and offer one to Maya, but she shakes her head.

I step towards Robbie. 'Did you want a cola?'

'Nah, I'm good.' He tuts. 'Every flippin time…' Using a black marker pen, he scribbles over *cod* and writes *haddock*.

'Bad day?' I ask.

'You could say.' Robbie runs his finger down to *Wednesday*. 'Not chips again.' He crosses through *chips*, replacing the word with *rice*.

I move back to where Maya's racking up for a new game. She breaks, making a ball in a pocket before shooting again.

I pick up my cue and wait.

Robbie, finished with the menu, tucks the marker pen into his jeans pocket. 'Sorry, Ilona. I didn't ask how your day's been?'

'Okay. I finished that history assignment.' I rest my cue between my fingers and take my shot.

'Nice.' Robbie scratches his chin. 'You know, Ilona, you're not bad. I might have a spot free for the game if you're interested?'

I glance at Maya. 'I'm not sure…'

It's Maya turn and she makes another excellent shot.

Robbie blanks her completely.

Maya glares at him before dropping her cue on the table and heading for the door.

Robbie starts as the door slams, but he continues to watch me until I finish the game.

Afterwards, I head up to our room.

Maya looks up from her bed. 'Did you see how he was with me? It's like I'm not even there.'

I sit down next to her and pat her shoulder. 'It's okay, everything will calm down.'

'It won't. Robbie says I've let him down.'

'Let me talk to him.'

'No.' Maya sits up quickly. 'Promise you won't.' She sighs. 'I just have to let the dust settle and hope he comes round.'

Maya and me are flicking through magazines in the games room when Robbie walks in. He takes the TV remote from the shelf. 'Anything you want ta watch?'

'There's a *Friends* omnibus starting soon,' says Maya.

Robbie continues to look at me as if Maya hasn't spoken.

'See?' Maya whispers. 'It's no better than yesterday.'

'*Friends*?' I say.

'All right.' Robbie switches on the TV and chucks me the remote. 'Back in a mo. Gonna make myself a cuppa.'

After he's gone, Maya throws a cushion at the door. 'Bastard.'

I shake my head. 'That was weird.'

Maya snatches the remote and turns the volume up high.

I take it from her and turn the volume back down. 'Is there something you're not telling me?'

Maya picks bobbles from her jumper.

'Maya?'

She shrugs. 'Tried it on, didn't he?'

'Who?' I gasp. 'Not Robbie?'

She nods.

'When?'

Maya's bottom lip quivers.

I grab her arms and give her a little shake. 'Tell me.'

'The other night. After he caught me in Kev's room.'

'What happened?'

'He kissed me.'

'Robbie? No!'

Maya pushes me away and jumps up. 'I knew you wouldn't believe me.'

'I do, it's just... I didn't think Robbie was like that.'

'They're all like that.' Maya sits back down. 'After he caught me in Kev's room, Robbie marched me to the office, closed the door and started to come on to me.' She shudders. 'He said if I didn't let him, he'd report me for being in Kev's room after hours.'

'But you didn't...'

'Course not. I'm seeing Kev. Anyway, Robbie's way too old. I don't even fancy him.'

'Maya, you've got to tell someone.'

'You think?'

'Yes. Robbie shouldn't get away with this.'

———

'We're supposed to be doing homework.' I look up from my maths books spread across the desk. 'You're no help at all.'

Maya, lounging on the bed, is doodling on her pencil case. 'Dwayne's so dreamy!'

'Oh, the new boy. I suppose that's why you're wearing your shortest skirts and rolling your top over so everyone can see your belly,' I retort.

'Don't you think he looks like Patrick Swayze?' Maya sits up, eyes sparkling. 'You know, the one in *Dirty Dancing*.'

'I do know who Patrick Swayze is.'

'Dwayne's so good looking he could be a film star too.'

'He's not gonna be making films around here.'

'You wait. He just hasn't been spotted yet.'

I put down my pencil. 'You really like him, don't you?'

'What's not to like? He's gorgeous.' Maya lays back, gazing up at the ceiling. 'He's my soul mate.'

I snort. 'Is that why you keep following him around?'

Maya grins.

'What about you and Kevin?' I ask.

'Me and Kev are history. He's such a kid.' Maya rolls about on the bed with her pillow between her legs. 'Oooh, Dwayne…'

I laugh. 'Why don't you marry him then, if you love him so much?'

'Perhaps I will,' says Maya.

I open my eyes. It's dark. 'What time is it?' Maya doesn't answer. I sit up. 'Maya, are you asleep?' As my eyes adjust to the dark, I see her bed is empty. Where is she? She can't have gone downstairs. 'Lights out' was an hour ago.

I get out of bed and pull on my dressing gown. Easing open the door, I tiptoe along the landing and up the narrow stairs to where Dwayne shares a room with another boy. I put my ear to the door. I can hear a TV; the older boys are allowed a portable in their room.

I knock on the door. Dwayne opens it, wearing boxers and nothing else. I step back.

He scratches his spotty chest. *Definitely not Patrick Swayze.* 'What?'

I try to see past him but he grabs my arm. 'What?' he repeats. Suddenly he pulls me forward and I feel his penis hard against my belly. 'Come looking for something have you?' He grabs my hand and tries to push it down his boxers.

'No,' I cry.

His mouth is close to my face. 'You know you want it.'

I try to slap him, but he blocks me. 'Little prick teaser.' His eyes glint. 'Someone needs to give you what you're asking for.'

He releases his grip and I run back to our room, slamming the door behind me.

'Where have you been?' hisses Maya from her bed.

'Looking for you.' I climb into bed, my heart hammering against my chest. *Did Dwayne think I was Maya?*

A few days later, I wake in the early hours and sigh with relief. Maya's laying on her bed, staring up at the ceiling. Several times I've woken to find her bed empty but, since the episode with Dwayne, I've not gone looking for her.

'You okay?' I ask.

Maya turns to me. 'Wanna know what me and Dwayne did last night?'

I shrug. 'I'm not sure.'

'We did it.'

'Did what?'

'You're such a baby. We – did – it. Had sex.'

I stare at her. 'But we're only twelve.'

'I'm mature for my age.' Maya climbs out of bed and pulls on her clothes. She avoids eye contact as she brushes her hair.

'You'll get caught,' I warn her.

Her smile is smug. 'Don't know what you're talking about.'

When Maya slips out of bed, I pretend to be asleep. I sneak a look at the alarm clock – 23:15. I wait a few minutes before tiptoeing after her. Downstairs, a light is on in the canteen. I creep past the empty dining tables and through to the kitchen where the fire door is ajar. I push it open and step out onto a square of concrete littered with fag ends discarded by the canteen ladies.

A scuffling noise. I peer at shadows around the over-flowing bins and shudder. Rats. *Why haven't the security lights come on?* My heart thumps as I step forward.

Suddenly someone grabs me and I'm pushed against the

brick wall. It's Dwayne. He latches his lips onto mine, forcing his tongue into my mouth.

I can't breathe.

He pins my arms above my head, his other hand snatching at the hem of my nightie.

I squirm as he gathers fistfuls of fabric, working his way up towards my knickers. He prods and probes before thrusting a finger deep inside me.

A scream bubbles in my throat but has nowhere to go.

Dwayne bites my lip.

I twist my mouth to the side. My scream escapes.

He clamps a hand over my mouth and leans back.

'What's up?'

I stare at him, wide-eyed.

'Don't go all frigid on me.'

As he loosens his grip on my mouth, I lunge forward and bite his hand.

'You fucking bitch.' Dwayne withdraws his hand fast and examines it.

I'm shaking. *Is he going to hit me?*

He adjusts his crotch and does up his zip. 'You been leading me on for a fortnight.' He spits on the ground before turning and walking back into the kitchen.

My legs give way. I slide down the wall. Crouching, I bury my head in my hands and sob.

After a while I manage to pull myself up. I stumble back to our room and find Maya asleep. I crawl into bed, pulling my knees to my chin. If this is what it's like to be Maya, I want no part.

Maya's already gone down for breakfast when I get up. I pull off my soiled knickers, feeling sick at the smear of blood in the gusset. I'd expected Maya to ask where I was last night but, although she must have seen my bed was empty when she came up, she said nothing. I can't bring myself to tell her what happened. She'll accuse me of trying to get off with Dwayne like she did with Kevin. I screw up my knickers, wrap them in toilet paper and throw them in the bin.

I can't bear the thought of eating, so I skip breakfast. Instead, I make my way down to the staffroom door and loiter outside, trying to pluck up the courage to report Dwayne. My heart is racing. Suppose Mrs Amos thinks I agreed to meet him? I shouldn't have been out of my room. Perhaps it was my fault?

Grabbing my bag and coat, I run to catch the bus to school.

———

All day I can't get it out of my head. There's no-one I can tell.

I'm alone in the canteen at teatime when Mrs Morgan touches my shoulder. 'Ilona, Mrs Amos wants to see you as soon as you've finished.'

I put my cutlery down beside the uneaten beans on toast. 'I'll come now.' Picking up my tray, I carry it across to the clearing racks before following Mrs Morgan through the 'staff only' door. It's the first time I've been this side. The floor has the same black and white tiles as our side but without the scuff marks.

There's a door in front of us. Mrs Morgan gives it a small tap.

'Come in.'

'Wait here.' Mrs Morgan disappears inside.

The name plate on the door reads *House Manager's Office*. I stand at the foot of a staircase but don't dare to sit down. Our side, the stairs are chipped and faded where the caretaker has bleached away graffiti, but this wood is a deep golden brown. I move closer, inhaling lavender furniture polish. Mmm. Caressing the smooth banister, I trace my fingers around the swirls carved into every other spindle.

The door opens.

I leap away, my cheeks flushed.

Mrs Morgan eyes me suspiciously. 'Mrs Amos will see you now.'

I step into the room.

Mrs Amos is seated at her desk. 'Sit down, Ilona.' She pushes a sheet of paper towards me. 'Read this. If it's an accurate account, sign your name at the bottom.'

I reach for the paper and read the typed words.

'I was in the outside courtyard when he grabbed me, pinning me to the wall...'

I scan the rest of the page. *What? How does Mrs Amos know what happened? Surely Dwayne didn't tell her?*

'Would you like some water?' Mrs Amos asks.

I nod. *What's going on? Had I already told Mrs Amos and blanked it out? Perhaps Maya told on Dwayne? But how would she know? Unless she was there...*

'I need you to sign this, Ilona, so I can start the ball rolling.'

Without reading any more, I sign the statement.

'Good girl.' Mrs Amos slides the paper into a red folder. 'Right. I've got to make some calls, but you stay here. I'll see if I can find someone to sit with you.' She picks up the folder and walks from the room.

While I'm waiting the door opens and Maya pokes her

head in. 'How did it go?'

I burst into tears. 'How did you know? Were you there?'

Maya comes into the office. 'I'm always there.' She wraps her arms around me. 'You should know that by now.'

'I wasn't going to say anything...'

'I know.' Maya rubs my back. 'That's why I had to do it.' She lifts a strand of hair from my face. 'Robbie will get what's coming.'

I pull away. 'Robbie?'

'Yes. Robbie attacked you.'

'It wasn't Robbie, it was Dwayne.'

'Don't be ridiculous.' Maya sticks out her chin. 'I was with Dwayne last night.'

I stare at her. 'Maya, what have you done?'

Maya disappears in a huff while I sit alone, my heart pounding. I feel sick.

Mrs Amos comes back. 'Oh dear, I shouldn't have left you. Here, have some more water.'

I shake my head. 'I'm sorry...'

'You have nothing to be sorry for.'

I take a deep breath. 'I made it all up.'

Mrs Amos pats my shoulder. 'You've been very brave, Ilona. You know we'll support you through this.'

When I refuse to change my mind, Mrs Amos gets cross. 'This is serious, Ilona. I've already spoken to the board. They could have informed the police.' She sits down heavily. 'You'd better go to your room. No wandering about and don't speak to anyone about this. Go on, off you go.'

My cheeks burn as I stumble from her office.

'What a mess,' I hear Mrs Amos mutter. 'But no smoke without fire...'

I'm back in Mrs Amos's office with Mrs Morgan sitting beside me, smiling encouragingly.

'Now you've had a chance to sleep on it, Ilona, I will ask you one last time.' Mrs Amos pats the red folder on her desk. 'If an attack took place on these premises, it is your duty to report it.'

I feel sick. I couldn't face any breakfast. 'I'm sorry.'

'I see.' Mrs Amos sighs. 'Well, if you are found wandering around at night again, there will be serious consequences.'

Mrs Morgan reaches out and takes my hand. 'It's important, Ilona, not to *overstep the mark* when it comes to boys…'

I listen, but don't really understand.

'Well, young lady,' finishes Mrs Amos, 'I hope you've learned an important lesson. I suggest you talk the whole unfortunate episode through with your therapist.'

'So, you withdrew the complaint?' says Helen.

'Yes, it wasn't fair that Robbie got in trouble.'

'And although no criminal charges were brought against him, he quit anyway?'

'I'm not sure he had much choice.'

'And how does that make you feel?'

'Robbie had worked at St Agatha's for nine years. He was always nice to me.' *But if he tried it on that time with Maya, perhaps it's good he's gone?* I sigh. 'I don't see why Dwayne should get away with it.'

'You haven't told anyone else it was Dwayne?'

'Only Maya. She says she was with him. She'll get in trouble if I say anything.'

'Why would Maya say she was with him if she wasn't?'

I shrug. 'She likes Dwayne. He's her boyfriend.'

Helen takes a deep breath. 'You're convinced the assault happened the way you've said?'

'I wouldn't make it up.'

Helen stares at me.

My cheeks are hot. 'I didn't make it up.'

'Why do you think it happened, Ilona?'

I shake my head. 'I don't know.'

She taps her lips. 'Could Dwayne have mistaken you for Maya?'

'Dwayne is Maya's boyfriend,' I scoff. 'I think he'd know the difference.'

Helen watches me.

'Perhaps Maya wanted to get Robbie into trouble?' I say.

'Why would Maya want to do that?'

'Because he tried it on with her?'

'Are you saying Maya planned all of this?'

'No.' I pull at my cuffs. 'I don't know. She wouldn't set me up.'

Helen closes her notebook and leans forward. 'Ilona, I think I'd like to speak to Miss Bishop.'

'You won't tell her what happened?'

'What you say here is between us, but I do have to share with Miss Bishop when I'm worried about you. And I am worried, Ilona. I feel you're in a vulnerable position at St Agatha's. I think it's time we explored other options.'

I stand outside the quiet room. *What is Miss Bishop going to say? Why does she want to see me without Maya?* I knock on the door.

'Come in,' Miss Bishop calls.

I walk in slowly.

'Sit down, Ilona.'

I sit on the lumpy sofa opposite her.

Miss Bishop looks up from her notebook. 'How are you feeling now?'

I don't tell her about the nightmares. Instead, I chew my nail. 'Okay I suppose...'

'Well, Doctor Lewis and I discussed your situation, and both agreed you were a priority. I took your file to the weekly case conference and the team decided to escalate. A new care plan has been drawn up and we'll be placing you somewhere else.'

'Somewhere else? Am I going to borstal?' My heart beats fast. One of the big boys got sent to borstal when St Agatha's count handle him anymore.

'No, of course you're not going to borstal.' Miss Bishop smiles. 'It's a foster home.'

A foster home? Like Fiona and Jack's?

'Now, this won't be a forever home, but we all agree you'll benefit from a more stable and secure family environment.' Miss Bishop clasps her hands in her lap. 'What do you think?'

'With Maya?'

'Would you like Maya to come with you?' Miss Bishop asks.

I look down. *Maya will think I've betrayed her.*

'Ilona, what is it *you* want?' says Miss Bishop.

'No.' I raise my head.' I want to go on my own.'

Miss Bishop nods. 'That's good progress, Ilona.'

'Will Maya be okay?'

'Yes.' Miss Bishop scribbles something in her notebook. 'Yes, I believe Maya wants to stay here.'

I smile. Of course. Maya will want to stay with Dwayne.

CHAPTER SIXTEEN

I unzip the holdall, smiling when I spot Blondie's hairs. Miss Bishop has loaned me her holdall. I still don't own a suitcase.

Maya lays sprawled out on her bunk watching me pack. It doesn't take long. I don't have that much stuff and I'm careful only to take my things. I pick up Brown Bear and squash him in the top of the bag.

'You're really going then?' asks Maya.

I zip up the holdall. 'I'm not happy here. You know that.'

'And you think you'll be happier without me?'

'I need a break. From all the drama, you know?'

Maya slips off her bunk and heads for the dresser. She yanks open the bottom drawer, rummages around and lifts out a silver and blue tin with *Kendal Mint Cake* on the lid.

She sits down on the rug and opens it. I join her, watching as she takes out two boxes of Swan matches, a plastic bag full of copper coins, a child's silver locket and cook's diamond ring.

Maya bites her lip. 'Our running away treasure.'

'You keep it,' I say.

'You won't get rid of me.' Maya places a hand on her heart. 'We'll still be together.'

'I know.'

Maya puts everything back in the tin. She closes the lid and returns it to the drawer, hiding it under a jumper.

I grab the holdall. 'Bye then.'

She doesn't look round.

I run downstairs.

Miss Bishop is standing at the bottom. She smiles. 'Ready then?'

I kick the dog's toy bone under the seat. Miss Bishop has a dark blue Vauxhall now, but it's just as messy. 'How's Blondie?' I ask.

'Getting on a bit, poor love.' Miss Bishop screws up her face. 'Still enjoys her walks, but we don't go far.'

I don't know what to say. I can't imagine Miss Bishop without Blondie. I look out of the window. We head north. As we turn off the A25, there are fields and trees either side. Maya would be bored already. If she was here, perhaps we'd play *I Spy*?

A sign on the grass verge reads, *Welcome to Dunton Green.* Miss Bishop turns into a small cul-de-sac. She pulls up in front of a detached chalet bungalow. Its curved window in the roof makes me smile, it looks like an eyebrow.

Here we go again. I get out of the car and reach into the back for my holdall. I follow Miss Bishop across the gravelled drive to the front door and she rings the bell.

A tall lady opens it. 'Ah, hello. Come in, come in.'

I reckon she must be at least fifty, with her grey streaked hair styled in a neat bob.

There's an awkward moment in the porch until we realise we're expected to remove our shoes. I slide off my trainers and set them beside Miss Bishop's loafers, before stepping onto the cream carpet.

'Won't you come into the lounge?' the lady says. 'Please, take a seat. Would you like coffee?'

I perch next to Miss Bishop on the brown velvet settee. The lady disappears to sort out drinks. I gaze around the room. Pictures of woodland scenes decorate the textured walls. I think they're watercolours. A glass coffee table sits in front of us and a wooden display unit runs across the back wall with strange sculptures inside the cabinet and a music sound system on its shelf. No television though. How can she not have a TV?

The lady returns with a cafetière and three pottery mugs on a tray. She must have had it prepared because she's only gone a couple of minutes.

Miss Bishop gestures towards me. 'This is Ilona.'

'Oh, I'm sorry. How remiss of me. I'm Mrs Shaw, but please call me Rowena.' Rowena gives us a nervous smile before sitting down in one of two matching armchairs. Her hand trembles as she pours coffee. 'I have to admit to feeling a bit nervous.'

Miss Bishop helps herself to a mug of hot coffee. I take one too. I like the smell but don't much like the taste. I pretend to take a sip before placing it back on the tray.

Rowena puts a hand to her mouth. 'I didn't ask if you take sugar.' She goes to stand, then sits back down again. 'Oh dear, I do wish Nigel were here. Right, what happens now?'

'Well, you've kindly offered to provide a temporary foster situation for Ilona.' Miss Bishop pulls paperwork from her bag. 'The principle aim is to instil a sense of stability and order…'

A crunch of gravel on the driveway causes Rowena to leap to her feet. 'Oh, there he is. Excuse me one moment.' She rushes to meet him, leaving the lounge door open. 'Nigel, they're here. Yes, hurry up.'

Miss Bishop and me exchange a grin.

Nigel Shaw enters the room and, perhaps it's his stockinged feet, but he seems a little shorter than his wife. With a mop of thick grey hair and leather patches on the elbows of his tweed jacket, he looks like a mad professor. Taking his pipe from his mouth, he reaches to shake Miss Bishop's hand. 'Hello, Nigel Shaw. Pleased to meet you.' He turns to his wife. 'Is that coffee I smell?'

'Coming right up.' Rowena scurries to the kitchen.

Nigel takes charge and in ten minutes the paperwork's completed.

'Right.' Miss Bishop stands up and shakes hands with the Shaws once more. *Is this how it feels to be a used car?*

At the door, Miss Bishop slips on her shoes. 'Bye, Ilona. I'll be in touch soon.'

'Bye.' I wonder about kissing her, but I don't. Instead, I watch her leave from the window. She waves before getting into her car.

I feel Rowena's hand on my shoulder. 'Let me show you your room.'

Leaving Nigel to finish his coffee, we head up the open staircase. The room allocated to me has a pretty cloud design on the double quilt, matching the soft blue of the walls.

Rowena opens a drawer in the dressing table. 'I've emptied these for your clothes. There's a wardrobe too, of course.'

I move across to the window. The lace curtains remind me of Fiona and Jack's cottage. I look out over a small but well-kept back garden.

'This is our room,' Rowena calls from the small landing.

I follow and stick my head around the door of the other bedroom. It's larger than mine, with a dormer window looking out over the driveway.

Our tour continues back downstairs with the kitchen and dining room. 'You can use this bathroom.' Rowena opens the door to show me. 'We have an ensuite.' She moves along the hallway to the furthest door. 'And this is Nigel's study, where he does his marking.'

I peek in at the old-fashioned desk and walls lined with books before we head back to the lounge.

Nigel folds his newspaper. 'Come in. I don't bite.' He looks up at Rowena. 'What's for supper, old girl?'

'I've made a nice quiche and there are new potatoes from the garden.' Rowena goes out to the kitchen again.

'Sit down,' says Nigel. 'You're making the place look untidy.'

I lower myself onto the settee. A loud ticking draws my attention to the clock on the wall.

'No television, you're thinking.' Nigel puffs his pipe. 'That's because television rots the brain. There are plenty of books in my study if you want to borrow one.'

Nigel would have got on well with Dad.

'So,' Nigel checks his rear-view mirror. 'I'll be waiting here when you come out.'

'Okay, thanks.' I give him a wave. As he pulls back into the flowing traffic, I turn and bound up the stairs to Helen's office.

Helen smiles as I enter the room. 'You're nice and punctual.'

'Nigel dropped me off right outside. He's picking me up when we're done.'

'Lucky you. Take a seat.'

I sit in the swivel chair, letting it swing side to side.

'You've been with the Shaws, what, two weeks? How are you settling in?'

'Okay.' I plant my feet on the floor and stop rotating. 'It's a lot different to the Taylors.'

'In what way?'

'Well, they're older for starters, and Rowena's a bit fussy. She has loads of rules.'

'Such as?'

I wrinkle my nose. 'Take off your shoes at the door; don't eat anywhere other than the dining room; no reading at the table. Also, they have no TV. Maya would never cope.'

'You're pleased to have time apart from Maya?'

'I guess so. It's nice having my own bedroom.'

'Tell me more about the Shaws.'

'They're always busy. Rowena looks after the house and when she's not cooking, cleaning or shopping, she's off to meetings and organising fundraisers.'

Helen thumbs through a file. 'Rowena was a nurse, wasn't she?'

I frown. 'That must have been years ago.'

'Yes, that's right,' – Helen pulls out a piece of paper – 'now she's a member of a local committee for *Looked After Children*. That's how Miss Bishop found the Shaws.'

I laugh. 'I don't think they've fostered before.'

'No,' Helen smiles. 'And I understand it's on a trial basis both ways. It's kind of them though?' She stares at me. 'To have you?'

'Yes, suppose so.' It's me who breaks eye contact.

'Rowena does loads of charity stuff. She's forever going to coffee mornings.'

'And Mr Shaw?'

'Nigel's all right. He teaches History and Latin all week at some posh school. Parents pay for their kids to go there.' I grin. 'I bet he's strict.'

'You said he's picking you up?'

'Yep, he drops me off at the bus stop in the mornings too. He's got a really nice car. A Peugeot, I think.'

Nigel has shut himself away in the study to do marking and lesson preparation. I find Rowena in the kitchen, a starched white pinny wrapped around her waist.

'Can I help?' I ask. I'm dying to have a go on that Kenwood Chef.

'Erm…' Rowena casts her eye across the ingredients lined up neatly along the worktop – flour, sugar, cocoa, baking powder, bicarbonate of soda.

'I won't make a mess.'

'It's just…' Rowena sighs. 'I suppose I'm a bit set in my ways. I don't usually have anyone else in my kitchen.'

I give her my best angelic smile.

'Oh, all right, why not?' She opens a drawer and lifts out a yellow apron. 'Put this on.'

I unfold the pinny and tie it behind me. 'What are we making?'

'Tray bakes,' says Rowena. 'Have you baked before?'

'Lots of times. Shall I grease the tins?'

. . .

While the chocolate brownies are in the oven, Rowena puts the kettle on for coffee and we chat while we wait.

I gaze at the wire racks where lemon drizzle cake and Bakewell tart have been set to cool. 'Are all these for us?'

'They're for the hospital fête tomorrow afternoon.' Rowena hesitates for a moment. 'I'm helping in the tea tent. You can come if you like?'

'I'd like that.'

Next morning, after Nigel's finished cleaned the Peugeot, I help Rowena load the boot.

'Nigel will drive us.' Rowena fixes the cake containers so they won't slide about. 'He can wander around the stalls while we serve teas.'

'My wheels are getting muddy,' Nigel complains, as his car bumps across the field. He parks as close as he can and helps us unload before moving the Peugeot to the car park. Rowena and I make our way over to the marquee, where several women are already setting up. One is topping up a stainless-steel urn, while another places white mugs in regimented rows before adding a carefully measured spoonful of Nescafé to each.

'Hello ladies.' Rowena lays claim to a section of plastic-covered trestle table and peels back the lids from her Tupperware.

The woman next to her is spreading jam onto dozens of scone halves. She glances across at the tray bakes. 'They look good.'

'Thank you, Doris.' Rowena smiles at me. 'I had some help this week.' She hands me a packet of paper doilies. 'I'll cut the cakes and you can plate them up.'

I arrange individual slices on three large platters.

Rowena nods approvingly. 'Lovely.' She hands me a small metal bowl. 'You can take the money. It's donations.'

A few stall holders stand about chatting. Suddenly a whisper reaches our ears – 'gates open' – and they scurry away to their positions. At that moment, the urn comes to the boil and two ladies serving beverages offer each other a congratulatory smile. The trickle of visitors turns into a flood and soon the refreshment tent is heaving. Rowena and Doris refill plates with cake and scones while I collect the money.

An elderly man drops a generous donation into the bowl. 'I must commend you on these brownies,' he says. 'They are absolutely delicious.'

I giggle – his moustache is sprinkled with chocolate crumbs.

Rowena hands him a serviette. 'Ilona made the brownies herself.'

My cheeks flush.

'Did she, by George?' The old man winks at Rowena. 'Then her grandmother has taught her well.'

Nigel pulls up with the car and gets out. 'Everything go all right?' he asks, loading up the empty cake containers and rubbish bags. 'You were both busy when I came in for a cuppa and a scone.'

'Everything went splendidly,' says Rowena. 'Ilona was a real asset.'

As we drive home, I lean forward between the front seats. 'That old man thought you were my granny.'

Rowena laughs. 'Yes, I believe he did.'

'Do you have any real grandchildren?'

'No,' says Rowena.

'Do you have any children?' I persist.

Rowena glances at Nigel, but he's concentrating on driving. She stares out of the side window. 'No, we never did have children.'

It sounds like she's talking to someone faraway.

Having no television is strange. Although Mum and Dad only let us watch a few programmes, that was so long ago. At St Agatha's, the TV was on all the time and I developed bad habits.

One evening, I push open the door to Nigel's study.

He's marking essays but takes his pipe from his mouth. 'Hello, Ilona. Come on in.'

'Could I look at your books?'

'Of course. Good idea.'

I stare at the books, not sure where to start.

Nigel opens a drawer and lifts out a sheet of paper. He clears his throat. 'Actually, I was rather hoping you might show some interest, so I've taken the liberty of drawing up a list of books that might be good for you to read. No obligation, of course.'

I take the piece of paper – *Lord of the Flies*, *Catcher in the Rye*, several novels by Dickens and the Brontës...

'I've probably got most of them.' Nigel gets up and selects a book from the shelf. 'Here, *Wuthering Heights*. It's as good a place as any to begin. If there's anything I don't have, we'll get it from the library. Rowena will take you along and get you registered.'

In bed that night, I open *Wuthering Heights* and read the first few lines. *Misanthropist?* I might have to borrow a dictionary from Nigel, too. It's nice having someone care about my education. I miss Mum and Dad. Sometimes I can't remember what they look like. I miss Khalu too, and I suppose I miss Maya, but I don't want to think about her. She'd be laughing at me, mimicking Nigel's list of novels and making fun of Rowena's clean kitchen obsession. She'd say it was a cheek for Rowena to pretend to be my granny, just because she hasn't got grandchildren of her own. No, Maya wouldn't like any of this and I'm glad she's not here to mess things up.

CHAPTER SEVENTEEN

It's my first day at Briarswood School. Nigel drops me at the gates and I walk hesitantly towards to the main entrance. It feels like everyone's staring, as if they can tell from my pristine blazer that I'm new.

As I step into the foyer, two older kids approach me. They're both sporting *Prefect* badges on their jumpers. 'Welcome to Briarswood,' says the girl.

The boy prefect is holding a clipboard. 'What's your name?'

My voice is a whisper. 'Ilona Parrish.'

'Parrish...' He checks off my name before pouncing enthusiastically on the next pupil to come through the door. 'Welcome to Briarswood...'

The girl prefect points along the corridor. 'All the new kids are gathering in the main hall.' She gives me an encouraging smile. 'It's down there on the left.'

I make my way along the corridor to the hall, where the chatter of excited voices greets me. The kids are gathered together in small huddles. I move silently between them, trying not to look out of place. Although I don't know anyone, I'm grateful to be here. It's all down to Nigel. He'd taken me under his wing, coaching me in English, Maths and Science and, a few months later, entering me for the 13+ entrance exam.

A sudden screeching sound causes everyone to stop talking and turn towards the stage where a tall man struggles with a troublesome microphone. He clears his throat. 'My name is Mr Hinkley. Good morning everyone.'

'Good morning, Mr Hinkley,' we chorus in robotic unison.

'Thank you. I'm in charge of Induction and I'd like to welcome you all to Briarswood School. Now, I'm aware that some of you may know each other…'

A gaggle of girls begin to giggle and two boys standing nearby nudge each other.

Mr Hinkley raises his hand, waiting for everyone to settle. *That would never work at Kingley High.*

When the hall is silent, Mr Hinkley continues. 'It's impor-tant you all have the opportunity to make new friends. Here are some conversation openers.' He waves a bundle of paper strips. 'What I'd like you to do is walk around, find someone you don't know and ask each other questions to get to know them.' Mr Hinkley divides the bundle of paper strips in half and hands them to the two girls nearest him. 'Here, pass these out.'

One of the girls works her way towards me. She passes me a paper strip and moves on. I lift the list to read it. *'What's your name? What's your favourite colour? Where do you live?'* I lean against the wall and roll the corner of the paper between my fingers. Mr Hinkley's occupied on the other side of the hall, trying to persuade a group of lads to take part. I close my eyes. *I hate this.*

A voice whispers in my ear. 'Tell me a secret no one else here knows.'

I open my eyes to see a girl with wavy dark brown hair smiling at me. I look down at my list. Her question isn't there.

'All right, I made it up,' she says. 'Me first then. My mother's French and my father's Spanish.'

'O-kay…' I take a deep breath. 'I'm a triplet.'

'Ooh, you win.' Amber flecks sparkle in her coppery eyes. 'What's that like?'

Me and Emmy become inseparable, I've never had a friend to hang around with before, not since Yvette, and I was a little kid back then. I love going to Emmy's house. Her parents' furniture and unusual ornaments remind me of the mementos Mum and Dad collected on their travels. Whenever Emmy and I take a break from our homework, I examine the curios.

'How old is this?' I hold up a vase that's begging to be caressed.

Emmy shrugs.

I lift an elaborately decorated silver box from the shelf to feel the weight in my hands. 'Look at this velvet lining. Where's it from?'

Emmy shrugs. 'You'll have to ask *Maman*.'

When I ask Emmy's mum, Francine, about a beautiful oil painting of three children, she defers to Emmy's dad. 'Ask Jacint. He knows the provenance.' Francine stares at the portrait and smiles. *'Je sais seulement que j'aime ça.'*

Jacint preens with pleasure, patiently giving me chapter and verse about where each object comes from and how old it is.

The stories behind the items fascinate me and, over time, I build my knowledge. Before long, Jacint is lending me books and magazines and quizzing me on my developing expertise. Perhaps boring to some, it reminds me of the way Dad used to challenge us when we were little, always coming back with another question we hadn't anticipated.

Jacint turns it into a game. Like a magician, he produces a small silver jug from behind his back. '*Entonces?*'

I take it and turn it over, searching for a hallmark.

Jacint smiles.

I frown. 'Late nineteenth century?'

'*Bien,*' says Jacint

'A little tarnished…'

'And does this matter?'

'Better to be in its original state than clogged up with silver polish.'

'*Exacto!* And the design?'

'Could be Victorian… no, Edwardian.'

'*Excelente.*' Jacint claps his hands. 'We make a trader of you, *si*?'

On another occasion, I spot a small tray on top of the cocktail cabinet. 'Is this new?'

'*Si,*' says Jacint.

I pick it up. 'Art deco?'

'Yes.'

'Nice. I like the wooden handles. Valuable?'

'*No mucho*, but what do I say?'

'It depends on whether I like it or not. If I like it, it will probably do well.'

'*Exacto!*' says Jacint.

Since transferring to Briarswood, my sessions with Helen have become more like mentoring.

'So, thirteen.' Helen smiles. 'Did you have a nice birthday?'

'Yes thanks. Rowena and Nigel took me out for a meal at the Steakhouse.'

'That's nice.' Helen turns her attention to the first term report booklet I've brought to show her. She flicks to the summary sheet at the back. 'It says here you're in the top ten percent. That's amazing, Ilona. Well done.'

My cheeks flush. 'Thanks. Emmy and me study together.'

'Emmy?'

'Emmeline Perez. She's my best friend. We hang around together all the time.'

'It sounds like Emmy's a good influence.' Helen scribbles in her notepad.

'She is. Whenever Rowena has a committee meeting or Nigel stays late at school, Emmy and I do homework together round at her house.'

'And Rowena and Nigel approve?'

'Yeah, sure. And Nigel likes Emmy's dad. Jacint is an antiques dealer.'

Helen puts down her pen. She thumbs through the rest of my report. 'French and Spanish... wow, these results are tremendous.'

'Emmy's mum speaks French and her dad speaks Spanish, so I get loads of practise.'

'And how are things more generally?'

'Good. Rowena and Nigel came to my Parent/Teacher evening. There were other kids with old parents, so it was okay.'

'Do the other kids know about your family situation?'

'Only Emmy. The others know I'm an orphan and don't ask much after that.'

Helen nods. 'The Shaws must be proud of you.'

I grin. 'Rowena even gave me money to buy a cheese-burger and chips on the way home, and she can't stand junk food.'

'And have you heard or seen anything of Maya?'

'No.' I wonder if Helen still meets with Maya.

'You don't miss her?'

I squirm in my seat, feeling disloyal. 'I've got Emmy now.'

'Well done, Ilona.' Helen hands me my report booklet back and writes something in her notepad. 'It sounds as if you've really turned a corner.'

Me and Emmy are sitting halfway back in the Odeon watching *Four Weddings and a Funeral*. I've chosen a pink shrimp from the bag of pic 'n' mix between us when a shower of popcorn comes flying down on us. I turn around to see who chucked it, but it's too dark to see the culprits.

Someone lets out a massive belch. A girl yells, 'For fuck's sake, you've tipped it all down my jacket.'

'Shhh.' A man in the row behind us hisses.

'All right, keep your hair on,' another girl retorts.

The gang sitting with her screech with laughter.

The first girl complains. 'Does cola stain?'

'Ignore them,' whispers Emmy. 'The film's starting.'

The troublemakers settle down as the title comes up on the screen. Although they still roar with over-the-top laughter at the really funny moments.

Finally, the credits roll and the auditorium lights come on low.

'That was so good.' Emmy wipes tears from her eyes. 'I love Hugh Grant.'

'I liked the actor who played David. I don't think I've seen him in anything before.'

Emmy gets up but, when the other people in our row don't move, she sits back down. The girl gang have pushed ahead of everyone else and are already at the fire exit. They shove and jostle, waiting for the usherette to open the doors.

Emmy points in their direction. 'That girl has the same hair as yours.'

As the lights come up brighter, I see the likeness, although mine's a little shorter. 'Oh yes,' I say as our row begins to move.

'Wait.' Emmy rummages down the back of her seat. 'I can't find my purse.' She bends forward, feeling along the floor.

I'm still staring at the girl's red hair when she turns around. Her eyes narrow with surprise and recognition.

Feeling a little giddy, I topple back into my seat. I haven't seen Maya for over a year, but she hasn't changed a bit.

We hold each other's gaze. She smiles and I smile back. Then Maya runs a finger across her throat in a gesture meaning, 'You're dead'.

I gasp.

Maya grins, tosses her hair and follows her friends through the exit.

'Oh, it was in my pocket.' Emmy takes my arm. 'Sorry.'

CHAPTER EIGHTEEN

I can hardly believe Emmy and I are almost sixteen. Tonight, we're sitting in Briarswood school hall listening to deputy headteacher, Mr Morris, extolling the advantages of sixth form life.

Emmy nudges me. 'I'm not staying on,' she says.

I turn towards her. 'Really?'

She shakes her head. 'No. I'm going to stay with Mémé and Grand-père.'

'You're going to live in Paris?'

'Shhh.' Our form tutor glares at us from the end of the row.

'I'm going to study for the *International Baccalaureate*.' Emmy's eyes sparkle. 'Mummy and Daddy never did rate the English education system.'

'I'm not sure A-levels are for me, either. I'd much rather leave and get a job.'

Emmy sniggers. 'Rowena and Nigel might have something to say about that.'

I shrug. 'I'll be moving out before I'm eighteen, anyway.'

'So where will you live?' asks Emmy.

'Tom says the Leaving Care Team will help me sort it.'

'Oh well, if Tom says…' Emmy grins. We've both got a bit of a crush on Tom Gilbert, my new social worker. 'I can't believe Miss Bishop's getting married.'

'I know. I always thought she was way too old.'

Mr Morris holds up a Sixth Form Prospectus. 'And now it's time for you to visit the various subject displays. As well as your teachers, we have representatives from Oxbridge, Leeds and Bath this evening. Please, make good use of them.'

Emmy and I leave the hall as soon as the introductory session is over. With little interest in the subject displays, we wander the school corridors. As we pass the RE department, Mr Gilkes gazes hopefully through the doorway. I smile apologetically.

Emmy checks her watch. 'What time's your Careers appointment?'

'In five minutes.'

'Okay, I'll meet you in the foyer. *Papa*'s giving us both a lift home.'

I head back into the main hall and sit in the waiting area, while the student in front of me finishes her interview. When it's my turn, I move across to the chair in front of the Careers Advisor's desk.

While she makes notes on the previous interview, I study her clothes. The navy jacket and skirt is more business-like than the outfits worn by most of the female staff. She finishes writing and turns to her register before looking up with a smile. 'Ilona Parish?'

'Yes.'

'Cindy McCarthy.' She shakes my hand as if this is a job interview. 'Now, remind me, what are your top three subjects?'

'Literature, History and Art.'

She looks at my report card. 'Your grades for those subjects are certainly healthy. Any hobbies or interests?'

I smile sweetly. 'Antiques.'

She raises an eyebrow in surprise. 'That's unusual. Well, I think the best thing would be for you to stay on and take A-levels.'

I nod, knowing I have no intention of following her advice.

Nigel pushes his supper plate away and folds his arms. 'So, how did you get on at the Sixth Form Evening?'

'Complete waste of time. I'm not staying on, whatever that Careers woman says.'

Nigel nods. 'Jacint and I had quite a chat after he dropped you off last night.'

'Really?' I place my knife and fork down on my plate.

'He tells me he's really impressed by your knowledge of antiques. He says you have flair, a natural talent.'

I grin. 'I love talking to Jacint about old things. It's so interesting, thinking about where they've been and how they managed to survive all these years.'

Rowena stacks the dishes. 'We know, Ilona, that you're not enamoured by the prospect of staying on at school.' She looks at Nigel. 'Tell her what else Jacint said.'

Nigel clears his throat. 'Jacint has offered you a job. Well, more of an apprenticeship. He'll train you and even arrange day release for a business management course. How would that suit?'

'Yes!' I jump up and throw my arms around Nigel. I think it's the first time I've hugged him.

Rowena pulls a tissue from her housecoat pocket and

blows her nose. 'Are you sure you don't want to stay on at school for another couple of years?'

I sigh, knowing this is Rowena's way of keeping me here. 'I want to stand on my own two feet.'

Rowena sniffs. 'Well,' – she struggles to smile – 'we'll support whatever you decide.'

CHAPTER NINETEEN

Tom rests a hand on my arm. 'She's waving.'

I look back. Rowena is standing at the lounge window. The last few weeks have been tough. It's not Rowena's fault, but she can be such a mother hen. Sometimes I literally can't breathe.

When I told Nigel and Rowena I wanted to move out, it caused quite a commotion. We'd been watching Princess Diana's funeral together on the TV.

'It's so sad.' Rowena dabbed her eyes with a hanky, as the two princes followed their mother's coffin. 'Those poor boys, losing their mother so young… Oh,' – she covered her mouth with her hand – 'I'm so sorry, Ilona. What am I saying?'

'Don't worry. It was a long time ago and anyway, young people can be very resilient. Speaking of which' – I take a deep breath – 'I've been talking to Tom about the possibility of getting a place of my own.'

Rowena bursts into tears. 'But why, Ilona? I thought you were happy here?'

'I am... I have been. But now I have a job and it's time for me to have my own space.'

'Nothing wrong with wanting a bit of independence.' Nigel puts an arm around Rowena. 'Come on, old girl. She works in Brasted. It's not like she's moving to the other end of the country.'

I raise my hand before hitching my holdall onto my shoulder and following Tom along the road. Tom usually cycles everywhere, but today we're catching the bus. Rowena had wanted Nigel to drive me, but Tom explained it was better to say our goodbyes at home.

We reach the bus stop and Tom peruses the timetable. 'Buses run from Dunton Green to Sevenoaks every thirty minutes. It's easy enough to get back. But it might be wise to limit your visits if you're keen to establish independence and resilience.'

Independence and resilience. During the bus ride, I turn these words over in my mind. Tom had explained it wasn't the norm to leave your foster home before the age of eighteen, but since starting work I couldn't think of anything else. Luckily he was on my side and, when a place came up at Sycamore House, Tom went out of his way to persuade the local authority that a move would be in the best interests of my mental wellbeing.

After a twenty minute ride, we get off the bus.

'Sycamore House is basically a small block of flats,' says Tom, as we walk the rest of the way. 'Ten self-contained bedsits and a reception area. You'll always find a member of staff if there's a crisis or if you need someone to talk to.'

When we arrive, he leads the way upstairs and unlocks a door. Flat ten is compact with magnolia walls and the smell of fresh paint. I take it all in – sofa bed, wardrobe, chest of drawers, television and a kitchenette area with microwave, toaster, small fridge and sink.

Tom opens a door to reveal a small shower room and toilet. 'There's a separate laundry room in the basement for residents' use.'

Rowena had offered to get me groceries, but Tom said there'd be a welcome pack to start me off. Opening the fridge, I find milk, butter and a sliced loaf.

'All right?' Tom asks. 'I think there'll be teabags and biscuits, too.' He opens the cupboard above the sink. 'Yep, in here. I'll leave you to get settled in. Ask at reception if you've any questions.' He lays my key on the draining board before heading back downstairs.

I close the door. From the window, I watch Tom leave the building. I gaze around my bedsit and can't help smiling.

After unpacking, I make toast. Rowena sneaked a small jar of marmite and a Pot Noodle into my holdall, so I add them to the provisions in the kitchenette cupboard.

I turn on the TV for company, but after I've eaten I'm not sure what to do. I don't have any laundry as Rowena washed and ironed all my clothes. Maybe I should check out the facilities? I pick up my key and head down to the ground floor.

A lady at the reception desk smiles. 'Hi, I'm Sue. You're the new girl. Ilona, right? Settling in okay?'

I nod.

'If you need anything, there's a store five minutes along the road. Open all hours and it sells just about everything.'

'Thanks.' I gaze about. 'And the laundry room?'

'Take the stairs through that door to the basement. You can't miss it.'

I make my way down the stairs. It's dark at first, but security lights come on when they detect movement. At the bottom, I follow the sound of a tumble dryer, easily locating the laundry room. It's a mini laundrette with three washing machines and two dryers.

A teenage girl with her back against one of the dryers looks up as I come in. 'Hey.'

'Hi,' I say, taking in her jeans and strappy vest top. Two sections of her hair are braided to form an Alice band.

'You new?' she asks, putting her magazine on the bench.

'Yeah, just arrived. I'm having a look round.'

'Thought I hadn't seen you before. I've only been here a couple of months myself.'

I sit down beside her. 'Where were you before?'

'At home, looking after my mum.' The girl looks down at her bare feet. 'She has multiple sclerosis.'

'I'm sorry.'

The girl shrugs. 'When she got really ill, we had to let the house go. Social moved me here. How about you?'

'Foster home for four years. Before that, St Agatha's.'

'Long time in care. Bummer.'

The dryer finishes its spin. The girl opens the door, yanks out her clothes and shoves them into a black bin liner. She slides her feet into the flip flops discarded under the bench. 'What's your room number?'

'Ten.'

She smiles. 'Hello ten. We're neighbours. I'm nine, but you can call me Courtney.'

'Would you like tea or coffee?'

It's the first time Helen's offered me anything other than water or squash. I touch the back of my hair to check my chignon is still secure. 'Coffee, please.'

'I've only got instant?'

'That's okay.'

Helen switches on the kettle and spoons Nescafé into two mugs. 'You've come straight from work?'

'I took the afternoon off.'

She passes me a mug of steaming hot coffee. 'I must say, you look every bit the part.'

'Thanks.' My cheeks flush. I feel grown-up in my pencil skirt and blouse. 'Jacint likes me to look smart. I'm working four days a week now.'

Helen sits behind her desk and flicks through my file. It's bulging with notes and paperwork from Social Services and the Pathway Team.

I take a sip of coffee and grimace. Jacint and I drink the proper stuff at work.

She peruses a letter on headed paper. 'So, you're all moved in?'

I cradle the mug in my hands. 'Yes, thank you so much. Tom says without your support, I'd never have been allocated a bedsit.'

'You're still under the care of the Local Authority?'

'Yes, but with more freedom and independence. We have our own space, but there are staff on site in case we get into trouble.'

She puts the letter back in the file. 'And you're still friendly with Emmy?'

Although I've barely touched my coffee, I place the mug down on the desk. 'She left for Paris a couple of weeks ago.'

'That's bad timing.'

'Not really. It was always her plan.'

Helen stares at me. 'I expect you miss her?'

'A bit, but it's not like I didn't know she was going.' I sigh. 'Anyway, I've made a new friend. My neighbour.'

Helen leans back in the chair. 'What's she like?'

'Courtney? She's nice.'

'What's her story?' Helen prompts.

I smooth my skirt before looking up at Helen. 'She's in the bedsit next to mine. Her mum has multiple sclerosis. Courtney looked after her until she went into a nursing home.'

'Her father's not on the scene?'

'No. He buggered off when her mum first got ill.'

'So, you and Courtney have become friends?'

'Yeah, we're mates.' I smile. 'We shop, do our laundry together, that sort of thing.'

'And you're eating properly?'

I giggle. 'You sound like Rowena. She bought me a cook-book. *Cooking for One*. It's for students really, but there are loads of easy dinner recipes. Sometimes I cook for Courtney too.'

'Have Rowena and Nigel accepted you've moved out for good?'

'Sort of.' I wrinkle my nose. 'They miss me, but I go back for dinner once a month.'

'It's good to have adults looking out for you. Tell me more about your job.'

'It's going well.' I adjust the clips on my hair. 'Jacint took me to a house clearance this week.'

'Remind me, where's his shop?'

'Brasted, but it's not a shop. It's an Emporium.'

Helen raises an eyebrow. 'Ooh, very prestigious.'

I laugh. 'It is a bit posh but doesn't get that busy. When I'm not shadowing Jacint, I sit out back and read through old antique trade magazines. I'm thinking I might specialise in dolls and teddy bears.'

'And studies for the Business Diploma?'

'I'm in the top three in my class, hoping for a distinction.' I feel myself blush as I rush on. 'Jacint's giving me more and more responsibility. He's taking me to an Antique Fair next month. At the end of the year, we're going to Paris to collect things he's bid on. I'm so excited and you never know, we might even meet up with Emmy.'

'So, you'll get to travel?'

'Yeah.' I grin. 'I love my job.'

Back home, I slump down on the sofa. I didn't tell Helen everything about Sycamore House, or the weird feelings I've been having lately. Am I lonely? Missing Emmy? Or is Maya messing with my head again? Work is fine, but when I get home her presence haunts me.

I scan the room. Thankfully, nothing's been moved. I lean back and close my eyes. I'm dropping off to sleep when I smell something sweet and sickly. Opening my eyes, I sit forward and look around. My heart beats faster. I don't wear perfume but I recognise that fragrance, popular with Maya and her friends at St Agatha's. *Anais, Anais.*

CHAPTER TWENTY

'Slip it into drive, then ease your foot slowly off the brake. That's it. You're doing great.'

I check over my shoulder, indicate and pull slowly away from the kerb.

'That's it, mirror, signal, manoeuvre.' Nigel cranes his head to check nothing's coming. 'You've got it.'

'So, when do you think I'll be ready for my test?'

Nigel chuckles. 'It's only your third lesson. Today we'll try a three-point turn.'

'I'm a fast learner.'

'You do know, Ilona, that taking your test in my car limits you to driving automatics?'

'I know, you told me, but it's not like I'm getting my own car any time soon.' I turn my head towards him. 'And you and Jacint both have automatics I can borrow.'

Nigel drops me outside the shopping precinct, and I head through to *Debenhams*. I spot Rowena as soon as I step off the escalator on the restaurant floor. Sitting on her own, clutching and unclutching her gloves, she looks a little lost.

I make my way over to her and slide into the seat opposite. 'Hi.'

'Hello.' Rowena's face lights up. 'How are you, dear? You're looking a bit pale. Are you eating enough vegetables?'

'Yes, I'm fine.' I pick up the menu. 'Filter coffee?'

I go up to the counter to place our order. While I'm queuing, I glance back at Rowena. *Is it my imagination, or has she gotten older since I left?*

I return with our coffees and set them down on the table.

'Thank you.' Rowena lays her gloves carefully across the top of her handbag. 'How did the driving lesson go?'

'All right, I think. But you should really ask Nigel.'

Rowena takes a packet of sweeteners from her bag and adds a tablet to her black coffee. 'He'll say everything's going splendidly.'

'He's very patient,' I say. 'Perhaps he should consider doing it for a retirement job?'

'Retirement? Nigel?' She laughs. 'I'm not sure he ever will. He always said teaching was a job for life. He's sixty next year, you know?'

'And you?' I help myself to milk. 'Keeping busy with all your committees?'

'I have to find something to do with my time, especially now you don't need me.' She sips her coffee.

I reach across and take her hand. 'I still need you. It's good to know you've got my back.'

She gazes out through the café window. 'We never had children of our own. I don't know why it never happened.' She turns her attention back to me, squeezing my fingers. 'When you came into our home it gave us both a new lease of life. We'll always be here for you, Ilona dear. As long as we're able.'

'I know, and I'm grateful for all you do.'

Rowena lets go of my hand and rummages around in her handbag for a tissue. 'Now,' – she dabs her nose – 'I must stop being so maudlin.' She points at the blackboard behind the till. 'I think we both deserve a nice slice of cake.'

Courtney and I eat together a couple of times a week, although there's no set pattern. Sometimes I make a lasagne and it turns out too big so I'll give her a knock, or she orders takeaway and asks if I want to share.

One evening, I'm unlocking my door as Courtney comes out of hers.

'Hi.' I push open my door.

'Oh, speaking to me now, are you?' She glares at me.

'What?'

'Right stuck-up cow yesterday. Cut me dead.'

'Where?'

'Right outside. I'd just come home from work and asked if you wanted to share a pizza. You looked at me as if you'd never seen me before. Like I was something crawled out from under a bloody stone. Well, I thought, if you're gonna be like that, bugger you.'

I bit my lip. 'I don't even remember. Are you sure it was me?'

'Calling me stupid now, are you?'

'No, I'm sorry. Courtney, wait…'

But she's disappeared down the stairs. Once inside my bedsit, I go to hang up my coat, but the coat hanger from the back of the door is lying on the sofa bed. I'm sure I didn't leave it there. I move to the kitchenette to make dinner. In the sink, there's a baked bean can and a dirty mug. I lift the mug to my nose. Coffee. I bought a take-away coffee this morning at the Italian restaurant near *The Emporium*. I didn't have a drink before I left and I definitely didn't have beans. I frown. There's no way I'd leave an empty can and cup in the sink overnight.

I put a ready meal in the microwave. When it's done, I take it out, stick it on a tray and carry it across to the sofa to watch TV while I eat. I must have dozed off because the bongs of *News at Ten* wake me. I yawn. Making up the sofa bed, I lay out my dark trousers for work tomorrow, but where's my new green jumper? I check both drawers of the dresser before rummaging through the washing basket, although I know I haven't worn it.

CHAPTER TWENTY-ONE

The receptionist at Messrs. Owen and Quinn smiles as I enter. 'Can I help you?'

'I've an appointment with Mr Owen?'

She checks the diary. 'Miss Parrish?'

'Yes.'

After marking a tick by my name, she puts down her pen. 'Mr Owen's on a call, but he won't keep you long. Can I get you some refreshment?'

'No, I'm all right, thanks.'

'Take a seat.'

I ease myself into the low couch. As the receptionist returns to her typing, I pull the letter from my handbag and read through it again.

Dear Miss Parrish,
The trust fund set up for you and your sister on behalf
of Mr Clive Parrish, executor of your parents' estate,
is to be made available on your eighteenth birthday.
Please make an appointment with my secretary at

your earliest convenience, so that the necessary docu-
mentation may be prepared.
Yours sincerely,
Arthur T. Owen. Esq.

A phone buzzes on the receptionist's desk. 'Yes? Very good, Mr Owen. I'll show her in.' Replacing the receiver, she smiles at me. 'Mr Owen will see you now.'

'Thank you.' My pencil skirt has ridden up. I tug it down as I walk into his office.

Arthur Owen, a small man with a bald head, makes a half-hearted attempt to stand. 'Miss Parrish? Sorry to have kept you, but I'm sure Janice has looked after you. Please, take a seat.'

I sit in the leather chair opposite the Georgian reproduction desk.

'Coffee? Tea?'

'No, thank you.' Noticing my hands are shaking, I clasp them together in my lap.

Mr Owen thumbs through a file and pulls out a sheet of paper. 'Now,' – he clears his throat – 'as you are aware, your parents made provision for you and your sibling. We were instructed in this matter by the executor of your parents' estate, a Mr Clive Parrish?'

I swallow. 'Uncle Clive, yes.'

Mr Owen adjusts his glasses. 'I understand your uncle is now sadly departed?'

'Yes, he had a heart attack. My aunt wrote me from Australia to let me know.'

'I'm sorry for your loss.' He turns his attention back to the file. 'The monies from your parents' estate were invested to be held in trust for you and your sister. They will be paid out on your eighteenth birthdays.'

I cross and uncross my legs. 'How much will I get?'

He consults another sheet. 'The investment, although initially modest, has made a healthy profit over the years. The figure is, of course, to be spilt. Now, let me see... yes, the amount paid to each of you will be in excess of twenty thousand pounds.'

I stifle a gasp. Our parents' house was not large. I'd assumed there wouldn't be much equity after the mortgage was paid back. I grin. Twenty thousand pounds is enough for me to move out of Sycamore House and put down a deposit on a flat of my own.

Mr Owen peruses the paperwork. 'Now, your sister...'

'She'll receive the same amount?'

'Yes, yes of course. As I said, monies are to be divided equally.'

'I don't have contact with her. I assume you can sort things out directly?'

'Yes, yes of course. I have her details here.' Mr Owen picks up his phone. 'Janice? Could you come in to witness a signature please?' He slides the papers across the desk. 'Now, read this through and sign when you're ready?'

Janice enters the room and hovers behind me.

Mr Owen hands me his pen. 'That's right, and again here.'

Once I've signed and Janice has witnessed, Mr Owen gathers up the papers. 'There is one other small matter. I notice we have a box of your parents' personal effects in store.'

'Personal effects?'

'Photographs, small personal items, nothing of significant value, but I assume you'd like to have them released into your safe keeping?'

'Yes please.'

Mr Owen nods. 'We've got your address. I'll have them sent over. Before you leave, make sure my secretary has your bank details and the monies will be transferred directly into your account.'

'Thank you.'

'How did it go?' Rowena asks when I ring that evening.

'You won't believe this.' My words tumble out. 'Mr Owen says I'll get twenty thousand pounds.'

'That's wonderful, Ilona. Really wonderful. You see? Your parents made good provision for you and your sister. What do you think you'll do with it? I suppose you might like to get a car, now that you've passed your test.'

'I don't really need a car. Jacint is happy for me borrow the Citroën. I've been thinking about what Nigel said about investing in property. I think I'd like to buy a flat, but I could do with some advice.'

'That sounds eminently sensible, Ilona dear. Come to supper this Friday and Nigel will guide you through the process. Property buying can be a bit of a minefield.'

After a delicious meal of beef bourguignon accompanied by a glass of bubbly to celebrate my good fortune, we retire to the lounge for coffee.

'Do you know what you're looking for?' asks Nigel.

'A one-bedroom flat or even a bedsit, I suppose. I'd like an easy commute to *The Emporium*.'

'Mmm.' Nigel puffs on his pipe. 'Two bedrooms might be a sounder investment. More potential.'

'I'll never get a mortgage on a two-bedroom place.'

'You might with the right broker. Jacint will write you a good reference.'

Rowena refills our coffee cups. 'But would Ilona be able to afford the repayments?'

'She could always rent one room out,' says Nigel.

'Oh, that's an excellent idea,' says Rowena. 'I don't like to think of you being on your own.'

My pulse quickens. 'I'm not sure I can handle living with someone.'

Rowena picks up the framed photo of me, Emmy and Jacint standing in front of the Eiffel Tower. 'Such a shame Emmy decided to stay in Paris for another year. The two of you get on so well.'

'Yes, living with Emmy would be okay.' I sip my coffee. 'Or Courtney I suppose, but she's moving in with her dad.'

'I thought Courtney didn't see her father?' Rowena takes a seat in an armchair.

I shrug. 'She didn't until he got back in touch a few months ago. He's living in Deal now and has asked her to give it a go.'

'We'll advertise.' Rowena reaches down for a magazine from the rack beside her chair. 'What about *The Lady*? I can help you pen something. We'll find you someone nice and reliable.'

Between them, Nigel and Jacint smooth the way with a mortgage broker. Rowena, excited to have a new project, makes a shortlist of flats in Sevenoaks for us to view, although I'll make the final decision. After a few viewings, we find a two-bedroomed flat with an easy bus ride to work. It's spacious and Nigel says being in the commuter belt is a good investment.

I'm reluctant to share, but I must be pragmatic. Rowena helps me word an advert and I'm surprised by the amount of interest. Rowena and I narrow it down to two applicants and invite them for a viewing.

———

I pace the room. 'I'm feeling a bit nervous.'

'No need,' says Rowena.

'Well, I'm grateful to have you to support me.'

Rowena blushes. I can tell she's pleased.

The doorbell rings and I hurry to answer it. 'Hello.'

The girl on the doorstep responds with a small smile.

'Come in,' calls Rowena.

The girl moves hesitantly into the room.

'It's Sophie, isn't it? Sit down, dear.' Rowena gestures to the sofa.

'Would you like some tea?' I ask.

'No, thank you.' Sophie's voice is a whisper.

Rowena sits on a dining room chair while I hover behind, feeling redundant. Rowena smiles encouragingly. 'Why don't you tell us a little bit about yourself?'

Sophie fiddles with her hair. 'I'm eighteen and I live at home.'

'And where is home?'

'Ashford.'

Rowena scribbles on her pad. 'You've got a job?'

'I'm studying. In Maidstone. For an MA in Computer Science.'

Rowena frowns. 'If you're studying, how will you manage the rent?'

'My dad will be paying.'

'She seemed quite studious,' says Rowena, after Sophie has left.

I frown. 'She was a bit quiet.'

Rowena puts a cross against Sophie's name. 'I don't think she'll be much company. Seems the type to shut herself away in her room. I don't want you getting lonely.'

Mel, the second applicant, is pleasant enough, but her clothes reek of cigarettes. She accepts my offer of tea and plonks herself down on the sofa as if she owns it. 'Never say no to a cuppa,' she says, helping herself to two digestive biscuits.

Rowena purses her lips. 'You do know this is a no-smoking flat?'

'Yeah, that's fine' – crumbs spray from her mouth – 'I'm giving up anyway.'

When Mel's gone, I glance at Rowena.

'Early days,' she mutters, thumbing through the folder of applicants. 'I'm sure we'll find the perfect person.'

Back at Sycamore House, I tell Courtney about the interviewees over a bottle of wine and pizza.

'The first one was a complete geek.' I laugh.

'I wish I'd been a fly on the wall,' giggles Courtney. 'I'm surprised Rowena didn't show the second one the door.' She leans across to top up my wine glass. 'So, you haven't found the right person yet?'

'No.' I sigh. 'And I can't manage the mortgage payments on my own.'

'What about me?'

I stare at her in astonishment. 'But you're going to live with your dad?'

She grimaces. 'I'm not sure that's gonna work. And anyway, there's my job. The travel agency in Sevenoaks have offered to make my position permanent and if I stay here, I'm closer to Mum. I can still go down and visit Dad a couple of times a month.'

'Really?' I whoop with glee. 'That would be terrific.'

Next day Courtney views the flat. 'I love it,' she says. 'The bedroom's perfect and the sitting room's big enough that we won't crowd each other.'

I throw my arms around her. 'That's settled then.'

CHAPTER TWENTY-TWO

'What are we doing for Millennium?'

'I don't know.' I pretend to be engrossed in my book. I've been dreading this conversation.

'You don't know?' Courtney plonks herself down opposite me. 'Are you serious?'

I close my book and put it on the coffee table. 'I'm not really a big party person.'

'Hello?' She waves her hands in the air. 'It's Millennium. We've got to celebrate.'

'But Emmy's away.' I sigh. 'I thought I'd watch it on TV.'

'No, no, no.' Courtney slams her hands down on the arms of the chair. 'This is non-negotiable. We're eighteen! We have to do something spectacular.' Her eyes sparkle. 'Leave it to me.'

When Courtney tells me she's wangled us invites to a party at a friend's country house, I have reservations, but Rowena's surprisingly encouraging. 'A Country House Party? How exciting. I must admit I'm relieved you're not going to that Dome thing.'

'Courtney says the Dome's sold out. Do you think Nigel might drive us? We're staying over, so we won't need a lift back.'

'Near Ashford did you say? I'm sure he wouldn't mind.'

'Great,' I say, although I have butterflies in my tummy. I don't know if it's excitement or because I've run out of excuses not to go.

Nigel pulls up on the turning circle and we clamber out of the car.

'Have a nice time.' He checks his mirror and gives us a quick wave. The wheels of his Peugeot crunch on the gravel as he drives off, making way for the limousine following us up the drive.

I turn to look at the house, feeling like Jo in *Little Women*, out of my depth and ill-prepared for the ball.

'Come on.' Courtney grabs my arm and we run up the stone steps before the next guests alight from their vehicle.

The country house looks very grand from the outside but, as we step through the heavy front door, I notice everything's a little shabby. The carpets are worn and the wallpaper's scuffed. Portable hanging rails completely fill one side of the entrance hall. Courtney and I shed our coats and stow our overnight bags before heading for the Ladies to check our appearance.

I stare at my reflection in the mirror. The long turquoise gown and strappy shoes I'd been delighted with on my shopping trip with Courtney now seem over-the-top. Beside other girls dressed in jeans and t-shirts, jostling for space at the basins, I feel overdressed. 'I look like I'm attending a school prom,' I wail.

'You look lovely.' Courtney, unperturbed in her long silver evening dress, reapplies her lipstick and teases her hair. 'Come on. I'm starving.'

Gliding back across the hall, we enter the ballroom. The DJ has set up in the corner of the room, engulfed by two enormous speakers. Strobes and lasers cut through fog from a smoke machine. He's playing Vengaboys – *We Like To Party.* No-one's dancing.

As we head through an archway to the annex, it becomes suddenly noisy. Crowds of people are gathered around buffet tables, making heavy inroads into bowls of crisps and nibbles as they raise their voices to be heard.

A plump girl with a pretty smile runs towards us, her arms open wide. 'Courtney!'

'Julianna!' Courtney and the girl squeal, rocking from side to side as they hug each other.

Julianna's over-tight fuchsia gown looks like a bridesmaid's dress. Suddenly I don't feel overdressed.

Courtney pulls away and turns to me. 'Julianna, this is Ilona, my flatmate.'

Julianna hugs me as if we're old friends. 'I love your dress.'

I smooth my skirt. 'Thank you.'

'Still okay for us to stay?' asks Courtney.

Julianna waves her arms. 'Of course. Daddy said the more the merrier.' Someone behind us catches her eye. 'Melody!' she shrieks, before abandoning us for the new arrival.

Courtney grins. 'Don't mind Julianna. Her family are filthy rich, and she's spoilt rotten. She'll have no idea how many she's invited to stay.'

'Shouldn't we find out where we're sleeping?'

'This place is so big, and anyway,' – she winks – 'there's no guarantee, even if we find a bedroom now, that it'll be free later. Our bags are fine where they are. Don't worry.'

There's a cheer as caterers emerge from the kitchen to fill tables with a bountiful buffet of pizza slices, chicken wings, samosas, rice dishes and salads. Courtney and I load our plates. Every few minutes, another of Courtney's friends arrives, evoking shrieks, squeals, air kisses and hugs. Soon we're a group of a dozen or more. Someone gets a round from the free bar. Someone else has a tray of shots. The noise level rises as the annex fills to bursting.

Julianna climbs up on a chair, her cheeks scarlet, her voice high pitched as she struggles to be heard. 'Come on, you miserable fuckers. Is no-one gonna dance?'

Moving as one, we flow through the archway and onto the dance floor. The DJ plays *Don't Call Me Baby,* following up with *Music Sounds Better With You.*

We're dancing to garage – DJ Luck & MC Neat – when someone yells, 'Fireworks.'

'Nearly midnight,' says the guy next to me. 'Come on.'

We pile out onto the lawn and I put my hands over my ears as I gaze up at the display.

Bang, bang, whizz, whoosh. Rockets light up the night sky, spinning, spiralling and whirling, before splattering into ever increasing puddles of shimmering stars.

'Make a wish,' someone whispers. I close my eyes and smile. *Great job, good friend, flat of my own. What more could I want?*

CHAPTER TWENTY-THREE

'Happy New Millennium,' I yell, bouncing into Helen's office.

Helen laughs. 'You're in a good mood. Take a seat.'

I plonk into the swivel chair and spin around to face her. 'It's great having my own place. The bedsit never really felt like mine.'

'Your friend has moved in too?'

'Yes, and it's working out fine.'

Helen nods encouragingly.

I elaborate. 'Courtney's not fussy like me, but we keep our personal stuff in the bedrooms and the sitting room stays clutter free.'

'Sounds like you've established some ground rules.'

I shrug. 'I s'pose. Courtney's got loads of friends, but she never invites people to stay without checking first and she lets me know when she's going to her dad's. It's good to know there's someone to look after the flat if I have to travel for work.'

'And how do you get on socially?'

'Well, we celebrated the Millennium together. We have

girls' nights in, too – video, bottle of wine, chocolate. Have you seen *You've Got Mail?* You've got to watch it.'

She smiles. 'I'm so proud of you, Ilona. I know your parents would be, too.'

'Thanks.'

Helen rolls the corner of her notebook between her fingers. Her turquoise streaked fringe flops over her eyes.

'What?'

'Perhaps this is as good a time as any…' She sighs. 'You know, Ilona, that my work is with children and juveniles?'

There's a sinking feeling in my belly.

'Ilona,' she continues. 'Do you understand what I'm saying?'

'You're deserting me.'

'Not deserting you but, going forward, you need adult therapy. Anyway, it doesn't have to happen as quickly as all that, but yes, we need to transition you.'

I scowl. 'I don't need a therapist.'

'You might feel you don't need one now, but there may come a time…'

'No.'

'Ilona, it's important for us to talk about this. To prepare you.'

I get up. 'I don't need therapy anymore. I don't need anyone.'

———

I unlock *The Emporium*. Jacint comes in later these days, leaving me to set things up. I switch on the electric till and fill the coffee machine. I'm sorting through the post when I come across a letter addressed to me. No postmark, so it must have been hand delivered. The writing on the envelope is curiously similar to my own. I feel queasy. Ripping the envelope open, I take out the contents and read:

Dear Ilona,

I'm contacting you at work because I thought if I turned up at your flat or rang you, it might freak you out. I've been travelling for a while, but now I'm back. I know you'll have done something sensible with your share of the inheritance, but you know me – must have some of Mum and Dad's wanderlust in my genes.

Anyway, let's meet. I can come to yours. Thursday evening? Around eight?

If you don't want to see me, just be out and I'll get the message. But I hope you'll be in.

So much to catch up.

Love you babes,

Maya. X

Jacint's arrival startles me. 'I swear that traffic gets worse every morning. Everything all right?'

I shove the letter into my pocket. 'Yes, coffee's just brewed.'

Focusing on work is impossible. Several times Jacint reprimands me for silly mistakes. I'm consumed by Maya's voice in my head, my mood fluctuating between excitement and dread. I'm curious to know where she's been all this time. I'd heard on the grapevine that she started an Art Foundation course after finishing school. What else has she been doing?

At lunchtime I have no appetite. Instead, I sit in the back room, sipping water and re-reading the letter. I always thought Maya and I shared a kind of telepathy, but any special connection we had disappeared long ago. Why is she coming back into my life? And why now?

Thursday night is Courtney's Salsa class. She usually goes for a drink afterwards. The question is, should I be in?

'Why don't you knock off early?' Jacint's voice is full of concern. 'You've been out of sorts all day.'

Gratefully I grab my coat and hurry home. Back in my flat, I rush to my bedroom, open the wardrobe and reach up to retrieve the old hat box. I lift out the old photographs returned with our parents' personal effects and rifle through the post-cards beneath. Maya had sent several from her travels around Europe – Paris, Barcelona, Milan.

One card depicts a white village in Andalucía. *Hey, if you ever get to Spain, visit this place. It's beautiful. Hope you're well and living life to the full, but don't worry if you're not, 'cause I'm doing enough living for the both of us. Maya. X*

Once Maya received her inheritance she ventured further afield. A more recent card portrays a Peruvian woman carrying triplets in a carrier on her belly. *Remind you of anyone? Miss you babes. Maya. X*

Has Maya blown her inheritance? Is she back looking for a handout?

I open the oven door and sigh. The Marks & Spencer lasagne has dried out. I'm halfway through my second glass of wine when the doorbell rings. When I open the door, it's like staring into a mirror, except – my heart sinks – how come Maya always looks better than me? Her skin glows with a healthy tan while she pulls off retro style in mini skirt, black tights and Doc Martens. A faux fur stole is draped over her shoulder. Or is it real?

Maya holds out a bottle of Merlot like an olive branch and

when she smiles, I can't help smiling back. We hug and suddenly I don't want to let her go.

I pull away, holding the door wide. 'Come in.'

We sit either side of the small table.

'I can't believe it.' She laughs as she appraises me. 'We haven't changed a bit.'

'Speak for yourself.' I pour her a glass of wine.

'I suppose I thought we'd look different to each other as we got older.' She reaches across to touch a stray tendril of my hair. 'Our hair's still the same, too.'

I scoff. Maya's hair, wild and free, suits her personality. Mine's straightened and clipped back in a French pleat. And yet, if I wore it loose, would it be like hers?

'There's lasagne,' – I get up to retrieve the dish from the oven – 'but it's a bit overdone.'

I bring the lasagne to the table and place it down on a mat. Without waiting for me to dish up, Maya grabs her fork and digs in. I study her as she eats. We may look the same, but we don't dress the same. I try to look smart – it's important for work – but I never quite pull it off. Maya wears charity shop clothes and looks like she stepped off a catwalk.

'So, where have you been?' I top up our glasses.

'Cheers.' She dabs her mouth with the serviette. 'Oh, all over – Italy, Turkey, Canada. Even traced some of the Inca Trail. Remember Mum and Dad went there before they had us? What an experience. How about you? Even been out of the country?'

'France and Spain.'

Maya sips her wine.

'For work,' I add.

'Ah, the antique salon. Classy place. I had a nose through the window when I dropped my letter off. I hope you didn't mind me writing to you there? I didn't want to give you a heart attack turning up unannounced. So, how was life with the Shorts?'

'The Shaws,' I correct. 'Fine, nice, normal.'

'You were well out of St Agatha's. Everything went downhill after you left. Some of the guys got into drugs and there was loads of shop lifting going on. Not your kind of thing at all.'

'Was it yours?' I ask.

'Ouch.' Maya gets up to explore, pausing in front of a silver Art Nouveau picture frame. 'I didn't know we had this?'

'It was with Mum and Dad's personal effects. Uncle Clive asked that a few items from the house be saved. There were loads of old photos, but that's the only one of their wedding. I can get you a copy if you want?'

'Nah, it's okay, I haven't got anywhere to put it anyway.' Maya lifts the photo from the shelf. 'Dad's moustache.' She snorts. 'He looks like he's posing for *Sgt. Peppers* album cover.'

I giggle. 'Mum's dress is more Woodstock than bridal.'

Maya replaces the frame before moving across to the display unit. 'You've got yourself well set up here, haven't you?'

I feel my cheeks flush. 'I've picked up a few nice pieces along the way, but there's nothing of great value.'

Maya picks up a Murano vase. 'This Venetian?'

My pulse quickens. 'How do you know that?'

'Saw something similar in Venice. Oops.' She pretends to drop it.

'Be careful.'

'Still such a worrier.' She laughs. 'You haven't changed. So, no man on the scene?'

'Not at the moment.'

Maya strolls around the flat, pushing open doors. 'Two bedrooms? Someone's living here, you sly cow. Who are you shacked up with?'

'My flatmate, Courtney. She'll be home soon.'

'Courtney.' Maya peers through the doorway into Courtney's room. 'Bit messy, isn't she?' Wandering in, she heads for the dressing table and begins to poke through Courtney's jewellery.

'Leave that.' My nostrils flare. 'Courtney and I respect each other's privacy.'

'Sorry.' Maya drops a silver necklace on the floor.

I stoop to pick it up and return it to the dresser. 'Come out, now.'

'Thing is...' she says, once we're back in the sitting room, 'I'm not in a good place right now.'

Here it comes.

'Had a bit of a break-up with my latest guy and I don't have anywhere to stay tonight.' She pulls that face, the one that always could get round me. 'I was hoping I might kip here?'

I check my watch. Almost midnight and I have work tomorrow. 'Okay, just one night. Take my room, I'll sleep on the sofa.'

'Or we could curl up together like we used to?' Maya grins, scrunching her eyes like she did when we were small.

'No, I'll be fine on here.'

'Hope I didn't wake you?' Courtney touches my arm.

I stretch and yawn. 'No, I need to get up anyway.'

'Why are you sleeping on the couch?'

'My sister stayed over last night.'

'Oh, I'd love to meet her, but I've really got to dash…'

'It's fine.' I sit up. 'Maya hasn't surfaced yet and anyway, I'm gonna have to get going myself. Another time.'

'Kettle's boiled.' Courtney manoeuvres out of the door, the handle of her wheelie case in one hand, a slice of toast in the other. 'Don't forget, I'm straight to Deal after work.'

I creep around so as not to wake Maya. Before leaving, I write her a quick note. *Hi. Sorry, I had to leave early for work. Give me a call when you wake. Love Ilona x*

I add my mobile number.

As I unlock the front door, I call out. 'Maya?' There's no answer. I make my way into the bedroom. Wet towels are strewn across the floor. My toiletries are empty and it's clear she's been rifling through my drawers.

I pick up the note I'd left for Maya from my dressing table. She's scribbled on the bottom. *Thanks for last night. Hope you don't mind, but I borrowed a change of clothes. Speak soon. Luv ya. Maya. X*

Great. How many months before I hear from her again?

Jacint sways a little as he comes through the door.

I giggle. 'Liquid lunch then?'

'Purely business.' He sits down heavily in the chair behind reception. 'Everything all right?'

'Yes, pretty quiet. Apart from that guy who makes lamps from vintage objects. He called by again,' – I signal to a desk light – 'and wondered if we'd be interested in selling them?'

Jacint lifts the upcycled wooden cobblers last from the

table and examines its vintage-style filament lightbulb. 'How much?'

'They retail for fifty quid. He's offering twenty-five per cent commission.'

Ringing comes from Jacint's office. 'That's my phone. I'll get it.' Hauling himself up, he disappears into his office. He's back moments later. 'It's for you. Take it in there. I'll keep an eye on the shop.' He picks up the lamp again.

'Thanks.' I hurry into the office and lift the receiver. 'Hello?'

'Hi, Ilona?'

'Yeah?'

'It's Helen,' she says, as if I wouldn't recognise her voice. 'How are you?'

'I'm good.'

'Listen, I know you said you didn't want to speak to anyone and that's your prerogative of course, but I wanted to tell you about this great guy…'

'A man? I don't think so.'

'Give him a chance. Of course, due to client confidentiality, I can't pass anything on to Lucas without your permission. Perhaps you could come in and chat about it?'

'I'm not sure…'

'Ilona, it's fine. You have every right to find a new counsellor for yourself, but I'd love you to meet Lucas. Look, can you make some time next week? I'm free Tuesday or Wednesday.'

'I'm busy next week.'

'Well, perhaps I can give you Lucas's number?'

'Okay.' I grab a pencil and pad from Jacint's desk. 'Go ahead.' I scribble down the number as she reads it out.

'It feels odd, doesn't it? Finishing like this…'

I go to speak, but there's a lump in my throat.

'Well, good luck, Ilona. I hope everything goes well for you.'

'Thanks.' I put the phone down. Tearing the page from Jacint's pad, I ball it up and chuck it away. I'm heading through the doorway when I have second thoughts. Retrieving the note from the bin, I tuck it in my jeans pocket.

CHAPTER TWENTY-FOUR

I'm settled in front of the TV when Courtney throws my jacket at me. 'Come on.'

'I was about to watch *Casualty.*' I groan. 'Come where?'

'Out. Meeting up with my mates. You can't spend another night in front of the box. You're eighteen, not eighty.'

I haul myself up from the sofa. 'Well, I need to get changed…'

Courtney steps behind me and unclips my hair. 'There, you look gorgeous.' She chucks my hair clip on the side table. 'You can borrow my lippie in the cab.'

Since its refurb, *The Tickled Trout* attracts a trendier clientele. Tonight, it's full of noisy commuters delaying the last leg of their journey home.

'There they are.' Courtney waves at a crowd of people around a large rustic table. She signals to her mates that we're heading for the bar, but they raise a wine bottle and beckon us over.

After lots of air kissing and seat shuffling, I find myself squeezed between two of her friends. Courtney makes introductions, but I only catch the names Dee and Nate – the two people either side of me.

'It's Happy Hour,' explains Dee, as I stare at the row of bottles on the table. 'Two for One.' She turns back to chat with Courtney.

'I guess we'd better crack on with these,' says Nate. 'Red or white?'

'Red, please.'

Nate grins. 'To match that stunning hair.' He fills my glass to the brim. His smile is genuine, but he's not really my type with razor cut hair and slim fit shirt showing off his biceps. 'Cheers.' He raises his glass and clinks it against mine.

'Cheers.' I respond with a shy smile.

'So, how do you know our Courtney?'

'We're flatmates.'

'You're Ilona?' Nate leans back, appraising me. 'We've heard all about you.'

I feel myself blush. 'Oh no, what's she said?'

'Only that she has this beautiful, illusive and intelligent flatmate who never comes out, shuts herself away every night…'

'That makes me sound incredibly dull.'

'Or mysterious. So, are you a vampire?' he teases. 'Or a workaholic?'

'Well, I'm out and it is night-time…' I grin. 'Actually, I work with antiques. That makes me sound even more boring, right?'

'Not at all. I'm intrigued.'

Nate's a great listener. After I've told him about my job at

The Emporium, he tells me he's a teacher. 'Only recently qualified, but I've secured my first position at Briarswood.'

'That's my old school. So, what do you teach?' I ask.

'PE and sport.'

I sip my wine. 'Ah, I should have guessed.'

Nate affects a frown. 'You may think PE is not proper teaching, but let me tell you, it's every bit as stressful. We have to do all the regular assessments and reports.'

I giggle. 'I bet you only know the names of the sporty kids.'

'Well, some kids could try harder…' Nate downs his wine and tops up our glasses again.

For someone sporty, he certainly puts the booze away. But, despite initial reluctance, by the end of the evening I give him my number.

Nate's waiting at the entrance to Knole Park. I'd been surprised to hear from him on Sunday morning. Casting aside plans for a lazy day, I'd donned my trainers and agreed to meet him for a walk and lunch.

He kisses my cheek. 'I expect you've been here loads of times.'

I shake my head. 'To tell you the truth, I'm a little wary of the deer.'

'I'll protect you,' he says, linking arms with me.

As we stroll along, a breeze rustles the leaves of the tall oaks and sun peeks through the branches, making dappled patterns on the dewy grass. We come to a clearing and I look to the sky, enjoying spring's first warming rays.

A twig snaps and I jump.

'What was that?' I say, as a huge stag with impressive

antlers emerges from the trees. He stands wide-eyed, surveying us, the intruders.

Nate backs away. 'Run,' he yells.

We charge through the undergrowth at breakneck speed, not stopping until we've put a couple of hundred metres between us and the beast. Panting, I lean forward, hands on my knees. Once I've got my breath back, I glance up and see Nate clutching his heart. I catch his eye and we burst out laughing.

'My hero.' I gasp through giggles.

'Please,' Nate puts a finger to his lips. 'Don't tell a soul.'

I smile. 'It's our secret.'

Nate takes my hand. We make our way back to the gates and, after leaving the park, stroll up the street towards *The Oak Tree*. It's busy, but Nate schmoozes the young waitress into giving us a table by the window.

'So, you live locally?' I ask once the waitress has gone.

'Digs at the school.'

'Very posh.'

'Not really. I share with one of the other teachers. My family live in Desford.'

'Where's that?'

'Near Leicester. I did my teacher training there.'

'You're a long way from home.'

The waitress returns with two bottles of *Beck's*. She smiles at Nate and sets the beers on the table. 'Are you ready to order?'

Nate looks at me. 'You first.'

'Veggie lasagne please.'

'I'll have the Sunday Roast. Lamb please, with all the trimmings.' He winks at the waitress. She blushes before hurrying away to fetch our order.

Nate turns back to me. 'What were you saying? Oh yes, a long way from home. How about you? Kent born and bred?'

'I'm afraid I am. Told you I was boring.'

'And family?'

'Just me and my sister.' I swallow. 'We don't see much of each other.'

Nate reaches across for my hand. 'I'm sorry.'

The meal is delicious and, despite the huge portions, Nate clears his plate. He sticks to one beer. 'School tomorrow,' he says.

On the way back to the flat, we stroll past *The Majestic Cinema.*

Nate stops to read the upcoming features. '*Fight Club.* Supposed to be good. It's on next weekend if you fancy it?'

I stare at the poster. 'Bit of a bloke's film, isn't it?'

Nate kicks his trainer against the wall. 'Suppose it is…'

I nudge him. 'Well, Brad Pitt's always worth a watch.'

'How was the film?' Courtney passes me the Domino's Pizza box. '*Fight Club,* wasn't it?'

I slide a slice of Margherita onto my plate. 'Mostly men punching each other's lights out.' I help myself to a generous helping of salad and pass Courtney the bowl. 'Okay, I suppose. The twist at the end made up for it.'

Courtney loads up her plate. 'So, how are things with you and Nate?'

'Good.'

'It's been two weeks, hasn't it?'

'Yeah. He's taking me to a football match on Saturday. Leicester City v. Wimbledon.'

Courtney frowns. 'Didn't know you were into football?'

'I'm not really, but our next date's my choice.'

We watch TV while we eat. When the adverts come on, I notice Courtney glance at me.

'What?' I ask.

'Be careful.'

I laugh. 'You introduced us.'

'I know.' Courtney picks up her serviette and wipes her mouth. 'Is Nate your first boyfriend?'

'I wouldn't call him my boyfriend. We've not been seeing each other that long.'

'It's all going a bit quick.' She looks at me. 'I'm just saying…'

'I'm not stupid.' I get up and squash the empty pizza box into the bin before squirting way too much liquid into the sink and tackling the washing up.

———

'It's an away match, Premier League,' Nate tells me on the train journey to Croydon. 'Selhurst Park is the Wimbledon home stadium.'

'Doesn't that make it harder for Leicester?' I ask.

'They'll cope,' – he tugs his blue and white scarf – 'long as we're there.'

'Shall we grab lunch first?' I ask as we join the masses making their way from the station to the stadium. 'If the kick off's at three, we have plenty of time.'

Nate shakes his head. 'Nah, we'll get something in there.'

After queuing to go through the turnstiles, we buy drinks before taking our seats. I nurse my polystyrene cup of tea. Nate swigs his beer while holding a heated debate about line-up and positions with the guy sitting next to him. It's so noisy I can scarcely believe they hear what each other say. As kick off approaches, a tangible sense of anticipation builds. The crowd raise their arms as one, creating a wave and singing what appears to be a rather pointless song. *'We're the left side over here...'*

Nate squeezes my knee. 'You okay?'

'Yes.' I shiver.

The two teams emerge onto the pitch.

'Robbie,' the man next to Nate yells at the top of his voice.

I notice a bit of a huddle with two captains and the referee before the ref blows a whistle. As the match begins, I try to follow what's going on. The mood of the Leicester City fans changes during the first half of the game. Several times they yell out, targeting first the manager then the ref, while swearing with frustration.

When the whistle blows for half time, Wimbledon are one goal up. Nate takes my arm. 'Come on. Let's grab something to eat.'

We head down into the covered area and queue at the food stand for burgers and fries. Nate orders two beers, necking one down while we're waiting. Taking our food, we climb back up the steps to our seats for the second half. I have another tea – pretty disgusting but steaming hot – at least I can warm my fingers. Ten minutes into the second half, Leicester score. The fans roar, chanting *'Leicester, Leicester...'* and singing, *'Oh, when the blues...'* accompanied by much stamping of feet.

Nate rubs his hands together. 'Gerry Taggart, you legend. That's more like it.'

I wonder how his mood will be if the game ends on a draw? I don't get to find out. Three minutes before the end, Wimbledon score again and it's all over.

As we make our way slowly out of the stadium, the Leicester City fans are subdued and everyone's an expert on what went wrong.

CHAPTER TWENTY-FIVE

The doorbell rings. *Has Courtney mislaid her keys again?*

'Hi babe.' Maya smiles, holding out a bottle of wine.

I glare at her. 'You took my clothes.'

'Oh, come on.' She steps past me. 'We were taught to share. Glasses?'

I close the door. Taking two wine glasses from the kitchen cabinet, I set them down on the table.

Maya uncorks and pours the wine. She hands me a glass. 'Friends again?'

I frown, but I sip my drink. 'So, what you been doing for the past couple of months?'

'Travelling.' She plonks herself down on the sofa. 'Did I tell you I spent last summer working in a taverna in Greece? Well, the guy I met out there called me. He was on a road trip through Europe on his Harley and asked if I wanted to ride pillion…'

I study her as she regales me with her exciting adventures. 'You're back for a while?'

'Yeah.' She looks around as the doorbell rings. 'Expecting someone?'

'I ordered Chinese.' I hurry to the door to pay for the delivery. 'Thank you.' Coming back into the kitchen, I set the brown bag on the worktop. 'There's enough for two.'

As I dish up, Maya raises the subject of boyfriends. 'So, how serious is this thing with you and Nate?'

I didn't tell her about Nate.

'I rang to speak to you Saturday,' Maya explains 'and your flatmate told me you'd gone to a football match. Didn't she tell you I rang?'

'No.' Courtney and I hadn't spoken much since our difference of opinion about Nate.

'So,' – Maya handles the chopsticks like a pro – 'what's he like? Must be pretty amazing if he persuaded you to go to a football match.'

I bite into a spring roll. 'These are delicious.' I place the half-eaten roll on the side of my plate. 'It's going well. Nate's fun and we really get on.'

'But…' prompts Maya.

I sigh. 'Courtney told me to be careful, so I guess it's only a matter of time before he gets tired of me.'

'He sounds a bit of a player. You should get in first.'

'What, dump him? Why would I do that?'

'Oh, come off it, Ilona. If you think Nate's working up to letting you go, you're probably right. Do you want to be *poor little Ilona* all your life? Don't be such a victim.'

'But I like him.'

'Like him? Sure, you like him now, but wait until he starts spreading nasty rumours about you all around town. See how much you like him then.'

I stare at her. 'Sounds like you're speaking from experience.'

Maya shrugs. She pushes her plate away.

I've finished too. 'I don't know,' I say.

'Trust me. I know what I'm talking about.'

Is she right? Should I act first? I clear away the plastic containers. 'I'll sleep on it.'

'Ilona, you know I'm the only one who will tell you the truth.'

My mobile phone rings. 'Hello?'

'Hi, it's me.' Nate pauses. 'Sorry, can I get a rain check on Saturday night?'

'Why?' Tears prick my eyes. I'd thought the football had gone pretty well. I'd smiled a lot; feigned interest while he attempted to explain the off-side rule.

'I've got this residential thing. Someone's dropped out last minute.'

'Why do you have to go?'

'Well, Greg just sort of roped me in. It won't be so bad. They'll pay expenses.'

'Is that all it is?'

'What are you getting at?'

'Nothing.'

'You sound funny. Has someone upset you?'

'No.'

'Has Courtney said something?'

'Why do you ask that?'

'I don't know. Christ, I can't say anything, can I? Look, I might be able to meet up Friday afternoon before we leave. If not, I'll call you over the weekend.'

He rings off abruptly. It's the first time we've argued and I'm not even sure what it was about.

I leave *The Emporium* early on Friday afternoon, but Nate doesn't call. Next morning I put in an extra shift. 'May as well,' I tell Jacint. 'Courtney's on her monthly trek to Deal and all I've got to look forward to at home is chores.'

When a call comes through, I expect it to be Nate.

'Hi,' says Maya. 'Want to meet for a drink tonight? My treat.'

'Okay. What about *La Hacienda*?' Emmy introduced me to this Spanish restaurant. It's close to work and has discrete booths. I often sit there with a good book, pretending to be waiting for someone. Sometimes I tell Courtney I'm meeting a friend. I have no friends other than her and Emmy, but my ego doesn't allow me to stay home every night. From the booths I can easily spot if someone I know comes in. It's only happened once, and I'd feigned an incoming phone call. Jumping up, I'd pulled a face as if there'd been a change of venue and rushed out, leaving my glass of wine abandoned.

When I arrive, I scan the bar for Maya. There's no sign of her, so I order a bottle of house red and two glasses, and retreat to my favourite booth.

Maya arrives minutes later. She chucks her tasselled suede handbag on the seat opposite and slides in. 'I was going to get the first one.'

I shrug as I pour the wine. *That was probably unlikely.*

Maya raises her glass. 'I'm surprised you were free. I thought you'd be out having fun with Nate?'

'He's away on a residential. He's supposed to ring me, but I've heard nothing yet. I suppose he's busy looking after the kids.'

'Either that or busy with one of those fit lady PE teachers.' Maya shrugs. 'Sounds like Nate's reached his sell-by date.'

We drink far too much on Saturday night, so it makes sense for Maya to stay. Awaking hungover, we spent Sunday under the duvet watching TV and eating beans on toast and leftovers from the fridge. I let her sleep in my bed – it doesn't seem fair to offer her Courtney's.

When I get home from work on Monday she's gone. I wander into my bedroom and survey the carnage. Maya's helped herself to the *REM* CD we'd been listening to the night before, along with a couple of my favourite tops and a pair of hardly worn ankle boots. Why am I not surprised? Ironically, I'm touched she's attempted to make the bed and hung her wet towel over the back of a chair.

My phone pings. I pick it up. A text from Nate. *Sorry about the weekend. You free to meet for a drink tomorrow?*

I'm a bit busy this week, I reply.

The phone rings immediately. 'I'm so sorry about the weekend,' says Nate. 'Let me make it up to you.'

'No, I don't think so.'

'Why?'

'I don't think we have much in common.'

'Look, I couldn't help that I had to work. I'm the new boy. They say jump and I say how high.'

'I know and I get it. It's just…'

'What?'

'I don't think we're very compatible.'

'Right.'

'I'm sorry,' I add, but he's already hung up.

'You dumped him?' Courtney's tone is incredulous, but at least she's speaking to me again.

'You were the one who warned me to be careful,' I say.

'I didn't tell you to dump him.'

'Well, it's over, and anyway, I'm off to Paris on Saturday.' I slide my paperback into the case. 'Have you seen my new red cords?'

'No.'

I rifle through my wardrobe shelves. 'Never mind. Maya must have taken them.'

'Maya?' says Courtney.

'Yes. She turned up again at the weekend. You didn't tell me she rang here last week?'

'I didn't know she had.'

Jacint and I board the train at *Ashford International*. My heart is racing as we step into the carriage. It's my first time on *Eurostar*. We find our reserved seats, and the steward serves us with coffee and croissants. Afterwards, Jacint disappears behind the *Daily Telegraph* while I thumb through my guidebook. It's my first time in Paris, too.

At *Gare du Nord*, we take a taxi to the *Chambre d'Hote*. After depositing our bags, we head straight out to visit *Les Puces*. According to the guidebook, the flea market at *Porte de Clignancourt* is the most famous in the world. I trail behind Jacint, watching and listening as he negotiates on commissioned items.

In the taxi on the way back, I close my eyes. The flea market was heaving and my feet are killing me.

Jacint clears his throat and I sit up. 'Sorry.'

'You did well today,' he says.

'Oh, I'm not sure I was much help.'

He smiles. 'Nonsense. It was you who spotted the 1920s chandelier by *Müller Frères.*' He pats my arm. 'You have made one of our punters extremely happy. I'm dining with Francine's sister tonight. You're welcome to join us?'

I shake my head. 'Thank you, but no. I think I'll have an early supper. I want to be up early to visit the *Musée d'Orsay* before we leave tomorrow.'

'Very sensible. *Va a ser una larga noche.*'

At the *Chambre d'Hote,* we part company in the foyer and go up to our rooms. Although my bed beckons, I freshen up before heading straight out.

In a café near *Montmartre,* I linger over the *Plat du Jour.* Streetlights reflect in the rain-strewn pavement and sitting at my small table, I pretend I'm a figure in a *Van Gogh* painting.

CHAPTER TWENTY-SIX

Pausing outside, I glance up at the building. *Do I want to do this?* I pull the note from my pocket and check the hastily scribbled directions – *second floor, first door on the right.* I head up a stairwell reeking of fresh paint. The name plate on the door is coated with protective film – Lucas Trent.

He opens the door on the first knock. 'Ilona Parrish? Come in.'

I take the seat in front of the desk. I'm eye level with one of those posh executive toys: five silver balls suspended from a wire frame.

Lucas unbuttons his jacket as he sits down. 'I'm pleased you agreed to meet with me, Ilona.'

'I didn't have much choice, seeing as Helen's dumped me.'

He adjusts his tie. 'You do have a choice. You're the client.'

I stare past him. Outside, the sky is clear blue.

Lucas clears his throat. 'Dr Lewis tells me you'd rather I don't have access to her notes?'

THREE FACED DOLL 201

I focus on him again. 'I thought it best to have a fresh start.'

He steeples his fingers.

I shift on my seat. 'Orpington's quite a distance.'

'We only need meet when you deem it necessary.'

I exhale. 'I don't really know where to start…'

'Wherever you like.'

I gaze out of the window again, watching a fluffy cloud scud slowly by.

After a few moments, Lucas sits forward. 'Would you like me to begin?'

'Yes.'

'All right. Well, as you know, I only recently joined the practice. My experience is with adult clients, which is why Dr Lewis…'

'Helen,' I interrupt.

'Sorry.' His eyes are the darkest brown. 'Helen thought we might be a good fit. Of course, you must make your own decision about that.'

'I haven't decided yet.'

'The first step is to see if we can establish a relationship as therapist and client. It won't be the same relationship you had with Helen. This will be a new one. Some people like to share notes from previous sessions, so they don't have to repeat everything. Others, like you, choose to begin anew.'

'It's nothing personal…'

He waves his hand dismissively. 'You may decide I'm not the best fit. Or I may feel I can't offer you anything. We both need to be happy with the relationship if it's to be beneficial. Would you like to say anything at this point?'

I glance around the office, remembering sessions in Helen's playroom. 'This room is so bare.'

'Yes. These sessions will be different to the ones you had with Helen.'

I tap my fingers on the arm of the chair.

'Would you like to know more about me?' he asks. 'My professional background?'

'Yes please.'

He straightens his tie again. 'Well, I trained in Bristol; did most of my clinical experience there before moving to London. I've been fully qualified for four years. Recently I moved to Kent and I'm building my client base. Because you've chosen not to share your history with me, we'll start with a blank canvas.' He smiles again. 'It may be that you don't want to speak today. Perhaps you've just come to have a look at me? Get a feel for whether we could work together?'

I inspect my hands.

'If that's the case, that's fine. I won't charge for a full hour if you'd like more time to consider…'

I look up. 'I have a sister. Actually, I had two sisters. We were triplets.'

He cocks his head to one side. 'You said "had", past tense?'

I maintain eye contact. 'When we were five, Khalu and my parents were in a bad accident.'

'I'm sorry to hear that.'

'It's okay. It was a long time ago.'

'You have another sister…' he prompts.

'Yes, Maya.'

'And you get on with Maya?'

'I do now. When we were growing up, we fell out quite a bit. We were orphans and spent time in care. At one time we were separated for several years.'

'That must have been tough.'

'In a way, but it also allowed me to form my own identity. I'd always felt a little overshadowed by Maya.'

Lucas sits forward. 'Why do you think that is?'

I study my hands. 'Maya's a very social person. People like her.'

'You think that people don't like you?'

'They like me well enough I suppose, when they get to know me.' I squirm. 'Maya's prettier than me.'

He frowns. 'Sorry, you said you were triplets? You, Khalu and Maya were non-identical?'

'Oh no, we were identical.'

'Right.' Lucas's thumbs have a mock battle.

I glance at the clock.

'Perhaps we've done enough for today?' Lucas gets up from his chair. 'I think we could work together very productively, Ilona.'

CHAPTER TWENTY-SEVEN

Jacint has come in early to conduct my formal appraisal. I've never had one before. I didn't think I'd feel nervous but, sitting in his office watching him pore over paperwork, I catch myself chewing my nails. I slide my hands under my thighs.

He looks up. 'So, it's three years since you started here. How do you think things are going, Ilona?'

'Pretty good. I may have shifted that *Louis XVI* Mantle Clock.'

Jacint guffaws. 'That dreadful thing? I thought we were stuck with it.'

I grin. It is pretty hideous. Circa 1880 and housed in an Ormolu case, the clock was decorated with a creepy gold cherub and mounted on a heavy marble base.

Jacint shakes his head. 'I should never have taken that house clearance. What did you get for it?'

'It was marked up as two grand and the guy offered one and a half. I told him I'd have to check with you first.'

Jacint slaps his thigh. 'We will bite his hand off. *Mejor*

que Bueno. Taking you on was a good decision. Your knowledge and expertise has really grown.'

'I've always enjoyed learning about antiques.'

He clasps his hands together. 'Have you thought about developing a specialist area?'

'Well, I like glassware and jewellery... and toys and teddy bears, of course. Although we don't get them in often.'

'It's a bit early to narrow your field too much, but I believe it's time you started to build your own small collection.'

'I already have a few pieces in my flat.'

'*Bien.*' Jacint drums his fingers on his desk. 'I've decided to invest in you, Ilona. I'll advance you the sum of one thousand pounds to use as a starting capital. Start small, selecting only pieces you like. I'll set you up with a separate account and you'll keep any profit you make.'

My heart races. 'Thank you.'

'I also believe the time has come to delegate more responsibility. You've organised the networking event here at *The Emporium* tonight. Why not take the lead? I'll be here, but I'll take a back seat. Apart from the welcome speech, of course.'

My cheeks burn. 'Are you sure I can do it?'

'*Si*, Ilona. *Estas listo.*'

I'm on a high in my new black dress and kitten heels. Jacint's right, I did do all the organising, hiring caterers for the nibbles and getting the wine on sale or return. After welcoming everyone and handing over to Jacint, I'm feeling pretty pleased with myself.

As I circulate, there's a pleasant buzz in the air and I

approach a small group of local businessmen with confidence. 'Everyone all right here?'

A tall fair-haired guy spins round. I gasp. Nate. I hadn't recognised him in a suit.

'Yes, thank you.' He smiles and I feel myself blush.

'Excuse us,' he says to the men he's with, before taking my arm and leading me a few steps away.

'What are you doing here?' I hiss.

'Finding something in common?' He winks. 'I must say, I'm pleasantly surprised.'

'Oh?'

'I'd always believed,' he whispers, 'that the antiques world consisted solely of middle aged, rather camp men.'

'Seriously, it's been months. What are you doing here?'

'Officially I'm on school business. I've been given new responsibilities this year.' A waitress approaches with a tray of canapés, but Nate waves her away. 'Unofficially, I'm hoping you'll give me another chance. Shall we start again? Hello, my name's Nathan and I'm representing Briarswood School, researching work experience opportunities for our students. And you?'

I giggle. 'I'm Ilona.'

***

There's a cool breeze as we step out of the cab at Tower Pier and I'm glad I'm wearing Courtney's jacket. 'I still don't know where we're going,' I say, gripping Nate's arm so I don't trip on the cobbles.

'We're here.' Nate's smile is smug.

I stare ahead. The boat on the jetty is festooned in fairy lights. 'Wow, I've always wanted to do a *Sundowner Evening Cruise*.'

He squeezes my hand. 'Had to do something to impress you.'

A waiter in a tuxedo and white tie greets us. 'Good evening sir, madam.'

Nate takes two glasses of champagne from the waiter's tray.

'It's all a bit posh,' I whisper as we cross the gang plank.

'Let's grab a good spot.' Nate leads the way up a flight of steps to the viewing deck. He passes me my glass. 'Cheers.'

I lean against the rail. Nate rests an arm over my shoulder.

'What's that building with the flashing light?' I ask as we sail past Canary Wharf.

'*One Canada Square*, tallest building in Canary Wharf. The flashing light warns aircrafts that it's there.'

We glide on towards Greenwich and, despite the borrowed Hobbs jacket, I shiver.

'Are you cold?'

'A bit.'

'Let's go inside and get warm.'

We move down to the saloon. A waiter shows us to our table. Nate orders two more glasses of bubbly. I slip off my coat.

Nate whistles as he appraises my chiffon evening top and black velvet trousers. 'You look lovely, but I'm not surprised you were chilly.'

'Thanks.' I sit down opposite. 'You did tell me to dress up.'

The waiter returns with our drinks and young waitresses circulate with trays of canapés.

We sip champagne while listening to the jazz quartet. As their rendition of *Ain't No Sunshine* draws to a close, I wipe my eyes with the back of my hand.

Nate passes me a napkin. 'Are you okay?'

'Thanks.' The napkin is linen; I try not to soil it with mascara. 'That song always gets to me.'

'Were you thinking of someone special?'

I sniff. 'I haven't seen my sister in ages.'

'Did you have a falling out?'

'No, Maya disappears. She'll turn up when she's ready.'

There's a round of applause as the jazz musicians leave the stage. Another musician seats himself at the piano and begins to play a medley of tunes more conducive to over-dinner chat. Waitresses circulate with the first course.

'Sorry.' Nate unfolds his napkin. 'It's a set meal. I hope you like it.'

I lift my spoon to taste the tomato soup. 'It's lovely.'

'So,' says Nate, 'you were saying? About your sister?'

I tear a piece off my bread roll. 'Maya.'

'Maya. She's older or younger than you?'

'We're the same.'

'What? Wait, I knew you had a sister, but twins? Wow. I've never dated a twin before.'

The waitress clears the soup bowls and brings the main course – chicken stroganoff.

I help myself to rice and pass the dish to Nate. 'Here, you have the rest.'

'Sure you've got enough?' Nate tips the rest of the rice onto his plate. 'These portions are a bit small.'

We concentrate on our food for a few moments.

'The stroganoff is delicious,' I say.

'Should I have ordered red wine?'

I raise my champagne flute. 'No, I'm fine with this.'

'I might get a beer in a minute.' Nate glances around for a waiter. 'You sure you don't want anything else?'

'Nate, you don't have to try so hard.'

. . .

'Well,' I say, placing my knife and fork together on my empty plate. 'The food was great.'

There's a tangible buzz as the jazz quartet step back onto the stage. One of the guys picks up a trumpet. 'Oh…' Nate spins around as the musician begins to play. 'Miles Davis. I love this one.'

We turn our chairs so we can enjoy the music, tapping our feet as the quartet throw themselves into their second set.

A waitress wheels a dessert trolley between the tables. Nate selects sticky toffee pudding, I choose pavlova.

Nate smiles as he takes an envelope from his pocket and slides it across the table.

I put down my spoon. 'What's this?'

'Open it.'

Lifting the flap, I slide out a leaflet about a cottage in the Cotswolds. I shake my head. 'Nate, I'm not sure…'

'Relax, it's just a weekend. This place belongs to one of the masters at school. He's giving me a good rate.'

'But it's too much.' I gesture around the room. 'All of this…'

'I'm upping my game.' Reaching across the table, he takes my hand. 'What's wrong with me wanting to spoil you?' He gazes into my eyes. 'You don't need to worry. I promise I won't go faster than you're comfortable with. Okay?'

I swallow. 'Okay.'

CHAPTER TWENTY-EIGHT

As we stop outside my flat, I put my hand over my mouth, stifling a yawn. 'I'd invite you in for coffee, but Jacint expects me to work for a couple of hours tomorrow.'

'Okay. I'll be off.' Nate pulls me into a bear hug. 'I'd better go.' He kisses the top of my head before releasing me. 'I'll call you.'

I unlock the door and let myself in. Pulling off Courtney's coat, I drop my handbag on the sofa. My mind's buzzing. Shouldn't have had that last cup of coffee as we waited for the late train. Perhaps an Ovaltine would help? I switch on my CD player and sing along to Ronan's *The Way You Make Me Feel* while the kettle comes to the boil.

A few moments later the doorbell rings. *What excuse will he have for coming back?* I'm laughing as I tug open the door. 'What did you…' My smile freezes.

'Surprise!' Maya makes jazz hands.

'What are you doing here?'

'Charming.' She brushes past me and heads for the fridge. 'I'm starving. Anything to eat?' She lifts out a plate of left-over cheesecake and pulls back the clingfilm. She pokes in a finger and brings it to her lips. 'Baileys, yum.'

I glare at her. 'That's Courtney's.'

'It'll go off if it doesn't get eaten.' Maya pulls open the kitchen drawer, helps herself to a spoon and begins to demolish the dessert in huge mouthfuls.

I stare at her.

Maya pauses, her spoon mid-air. 'What?'

'It's been weeks.'

'Yeah, sorry.' She sighs. 'You know what I'm like.'

'No phone calls, no emails, no texts.'

'Well, you didn't contact me, either.'

'I tried. You never answered.'

'Fair point.' Maya continues her impromptu supper. 'This is good.' She smirks. 'In fact, both dishes are pretty good.'

'What?'

'Lover boy. That was Nate, I assume? Saw you smooching on the doorstep. Don't worry, he didn't see me.'

'Are you stalking me or something?'

Maya bursts out laughing. 'What are you on?'

'You always seem to know what's going on in my life, even when we've been out of touch.'

'Don't be ridiculous. I saw you were busy' – she makes air quotes – 'so I waited until he left.'

'How did you know Nate wouldn't stay?'

She taps her nose. 'I know everything.' She tilts her head. 'You haven't slept with him yet, have you?'

My cheeks flush. 'It's really late. What do you want, Maya?'

'Bed for the night?'

I sigh. 'Okay, and then what? Disappear from my life again?'

'Actually, I might stick around. I've got business over the next few days.'

'Just one night?'

'Two tops. Courtney won't mind, will she?'

'She's away until Monday.'

'Great, I can sleep in her room.'

'No, use mine. I'll take the sofa.' I march into my bedroom, pull underwear and a t-shirt from the drawer and throw it on my bed. 'Change of clothes.'

Maya runs the cold water tap and fills a pint glass. 'You haven't introduced me to Courtney yet.'

'You never hang around long enough.'

Maya blows me a kiss and closes the door to my room.

I'm making toast when Nate rings the next day. 'Good morning, beautiful.'

'Thank you for last night. I had such a lovely evening.'

'You're welcome. Look, I know you're working today, but I wondered if you were free for lunch tomorrow?'

'Sorry, Maya's in town.'

'You didn't say?'

'No, it was last minute.'

'So, are you busy with your sister all day? Perhaps we could still do brunch?'

Maya never rises before midday. 'That's fine.'

We meet at the *Black Cat* café, a few streets from my flat. Nate orders a full English, I have coffee and pain au chocolat. I'm distracted. I shouldn't have left Maya on her own.

By eleven-thirty we're walking back. When we stop at the bottom of the steps, Nate wraps his arms around me. 'Can't I come in?'

'You know Maya's here.'

'I'm sure she won't mind. Anyway, I'd like to meet her.'

I loosen his arms. 'She's probably still in bed.'

Nate pulls me closer. 'I wish we were.'

I hold myself rigid. 'Nate, don't.'

'Sorry.' He leans back, gazing into my eyes. 'You've been quiet this morning.'

I turn my face away.

'Have I done something wrong?'

'No, it's just, my sister…'

'Okay, okay.' Nate kisses my forehead. 'I'll call you tomorrow?'

***

'Hiya.' Courtney manhandles her weekend bag through the door. 'Something smells good.'

I glance up from the chopping board. 'Maya's coming for dinner.'

'Great, I can't wait to meet her.' Courtney dumps her bag in her bedroom. 'That's assuming I'm invited?'

'Of course.' I gesture towards the open bottle of Pinot Grigio. 'Help yourself.'

Courtney pours herself a glass and takes a sip. 'Ah, I needed that. I must admit I'm intrigued to meet your sister. You and Maya are identical?'

I continue slicing mushrooms. 'I doubt you'll tell the difference. Mum and Dad could, but even Khalu had problems at times.'

'Wasn't Khalu identical, too?'

'Yes, although sometimes I wonder if we'd have grown more different as we got older.'

'It must be strange, being the same as someone else.'

I frown. 'Me and Maya are not the same.'

'Sorry, that came out wrong. I meant both looking the same.' She finishes her glass. 'Shall I pop out to the offie and grab another bottle?'

At nine o'clock, I give the risotto a prod with a wooden spoon. 'It's gloopy, but I might be able to salvage it.'

'Perhaps she's delayed at work or something?' says Courtney.

'Maya? Work? Sorry, I'm not sure those words go together in the same sentence.' I sigh. 'We can't keep waiting. Let's eat.'

When we've finished, Courtney pushes her bowl away. 'Have you texted her?'

'Yep.' I see pity in Courtney's eyes. Every time Maya comes back in my life, people start feeling sorry for me.

'I'll clear up,' says Courtney.

I don't argue, but slope off into my room and collapse on the bed.

The next day, Courtney comes in from work looking like she's about to burst.

'What?' I ask.

Her eyes are wide. 'I met Maya.'

'Maya was here?'

'No, that organic café where you sometimes go.' Courtney unbuttons her coat. 'I was on my way to meet a client when I saw *you* standing in the queue, so I ducked in to grab a takeaway – you're always telling me how good their cappuccino is. I tapped you on the shoulder and said, "Hey, you skiving?"'

The hairs on the back of my neck bristle. 'But it wasn't me.'

'No.' Courtney hangs her coat on the peg behind the door. 'You turned around and looked at me blankly and that's when I realised. I said, "Oh my God, sorry, it's Maya isn't it?" and she said, "Yes, and you're Courtney, right?" She must have thought I was such a dork, standing there staring.'

Courtney goes to the fridge and takes out a bottle of wine. 'You're so bloody alike, Ilona. I swear if you were sat next to each other, I couldn't tell the difference. Well, except for her clothes. Very Bohemian in her flared jeans and velvet jacket...'

'What did Maya say?'

Courtney pours herself a glass of wine. 'She smiled and said, "Why don't you stop saying sorry and join me."'

I gasp. 'You had coffee together?'

'Yes. Sorry, do you want a glass?' She waves the bottle.

I shake my head. 'What happened?'

'We got our drinks and sat down, and I realised I was still staring. I said, "Sorry, oh crap," and Maya laughed.' Courtney sips her wine. 'I asked what happened to her last night.'

'What did she say?'

'She said she got held up. She'll call you.'

'So, did you chat?'

'No, I had a meeting to get to, but I told her we must reschedule.'

'She hasn't rung.'

'I guess not. God, Ilona. I looked back and there she was, sitting in the window drinking hot chocolate. She's the dead spit of you.'

CHAPTER TWENTY-NINE

It's quiet at *The Emporium* and I'm poring through Jacint's old antique magazines when I come across an article. *Carl Bergner of Sonneberg, Germany, began his doll business in 1890, using factory heads made by Gebrüder Heubach and Simon & Halbig. Bergner produced both two- and three-faced dolls.*

'Ooh, this might be relevant,' I say.

Jacint looks up from his ledger. 'What is it?'

'It's the history of dolls. Carl Bergner made a bisque doll with smiling, crying and sleeping faces in the 1890s. He registered his design for doll bodies with changeable faces in both Germany and Britain.'

'That could be it.' Jacint removes his glasses and cleans them with his handkerchief. 'Does it say whether there's a maker's mark?'

I read on. '*Bergner's multi-faced dolls came in two-faced and three-faced versions. By 1908, Bergner's successor, Alma Maaser, was using the name "Metamorphose" for these dolls.* Metamorphose,' I repeat, exaggerating the vowel sounds. '*The dolls had cloth bodies with composition lower arms and legs.* That's just like mine. *Their three faces revolved by simply turning the brass loop atop their head.* Wait. *The back of the doll's pressed cardboard shoulder-plate is stamped C.B. in a circle.'*

I lay the magazine down. 'I have to check.' I run down to the basement and retrieve the doll from the leather trunk. Bounding back up, I emerge panting on the shop floor. I lay the doll on the desk and slide her tattered pink gown away to reveal her shoulder. 'Yes, there it is.'

Jacint gets up from his desk and comes to inspect the mark. 'C.B. Well done, Ilona. You've doubled if not tripled the value by establishing the doll is authentic.'

Glowing with pleasure, I continue reading. *'The renowned Gebrüder Heubach firm in Germany made many dolls using a ring and rod device. Pull-strings often operated a mama/papa voice mechanism.'* I lift the doll and lean her forward. I expect a pitiful *Mama,* like that of poor Christine, but the doll emits no sound. I repeat the action several times and sigh. 'If she had a voice box, it's not working.'

'You might be able to have it repaired.' Jacint sits down and flips through his business card holder. 'This place has been helpful in the past.' He hands me a card.

'*The Doll Infirmary*,' I read. 'I wonder how much it would cost?'

Jacint returns his attention to his paperwork. 'You need to consider it as an investment.'

I scan down to the last section of the article. *'The realism of the expressions depicted on the dolls' faces is remarkable. The best German doll makers commissioned well-known sculptors to model the heads of actual children with varying expressions.'* I turn the knob under the bonnet, carefully considering each face. *Actual children? That's just creepy.*

Restoring the doll's sleeping face, I return her to the basement.

As I unlock the door to my flat, I hear sounds coming from the kitchen. *Courtney should be out...* I creep forward and spot Maya unpacking food onto the worktop. 'How did you get in?'

'Key under the flower-pot,' she answers.

I stare at the mess – plastic packaging, breadcrumbs and something greasy spilt.

'I'm fixing dinner,' Maya explains. 'My treat to say thank you for giving me a bed for a couple of nights.'

I sit down at the table. 'You left me with a pile of dirty laundry and a sink full of washing up.'

'Sorry.'

'And you're three days late. You were supposed to come Monday. Courtney was looking forward to it.'

'Well, I'll see her tonight.'

'You won't, she's at Salsa class. Anyway, I hear you two already met?'

'Yeah, she seems cool.' Maya tears a French stick into chunks and throws them into a basket. 'We'll get together soon, I promise. The three of us. Now, go and get washed up. It's nearly ready.'

When I come out of the bathroom, Maya's arranging plates of pâté and cheese on the coffee table. She's also bought tomatoes and olives.

I pour us both a glass of wine.

'Cheers.' Maya chinks her glass against mine.

I help myself to brie and bread. 'So, where are you staying?'

'Kipping on a mate's couch. I'll be around another week or so.' Maya bites into a slice of warm quiche. 'Mmm, this is good.' She swallows. 'Nate called round earlier.'

'What?' A crumb goes the wrong way and I choke.

Maya slaps me on the back. 'You all right?'

I nod, my eyes watering, and take a sip of wine.

'He popped in before you got home. I like him.'

My heart's racing. 'What did he say?'

'Not much. I told him we were having a girlie night and he said he wouldn't butt in. He said he'd ring you over the weekend.'

'Okay.'

When Nate calls Saturday, I try to keep my tone casual. 'You met Maya, then?'

He chuckles. 'Well, sort of…'

'She said she met you?'

'She opened the door in a bathrobe with a towel wrapped around her hair.'

'Typical.' My heart starts to pound. 'You didn't mistake her for me?'

'No, she called through the letterbox before opening the door to tell me you weren't home. Don't worry, I averted my eyes.'

'The perfect gentleman.'

'She sounds like you,' he continues.

'I know.' I feel myself relax. 'Once, at college, we recorded role-play exercises on video. When the tutor played it back, it was like watching Maya on screen.'

'Weird.'

'Yeah, and it wasn't just the voice…'

'Anyway,' Nate interrupts, 'I called around to check if you're free next weekend?'

'For our mini break?'

'Yep. I'll pick you up Friday night around seven. Pack light and use a soft bag.'

'You take that end, that's it,' says Jacint to Paul, the guy from the Hardware store. 'Careful now, we don't want to catch the veneer.'

Paul strokes the surface of the *George II* kneehole desk. 'What wood is this?'

'Burr walnut with herringbone inlay.' Jacint tugs open a drawer. 'Lined with ash.'

'Nice.'

The two men huff and puff, loading the desk into the van.

'Coffee?' I say, as they come back into the shop.

'Don't mind if I do.' Paul takes a coffee mug from the tray and helps himself to a gingernut. He nods towards the van. 'How much does a desk like that go for, then?'

Jacint grins. 'Two and a half.'

'Two and a half grand?' Paul's eyes widen. 'I'm in the wrong business.'

Jacint laughs.

Paul dunks his biscuit. 'Is the van yours?'

'No.' Jacint takes a sip of his coffee. 'I hire one when I need it.'

I offer more biscuits. 'Nate's hiring us a Morgan for the weekend.'

Jacint widens his eyes. 'For the Cotswolds? *Estoy celosa.*'

Paul laughs. 'Ever since we went on that tour of the Morgan factory in Malvern, Jacint's dreamed of owning one.

Take plenty of pictures,' – he winks at me – 'then you can really rub his nose in it.'

Courtney pauses, holding the door jamb. 'See you Monday.' She grins. 'Don't do anything I wouldn't do.'

'That leaves me plenty of scope.'

She pokes out her tongue before heading off for the train to Deal.

I return to my packing – a cashmere jumper in case it's cold, plus my little black dress and heels for dinner. I've also treated myself to new lacy underwear and black stockings. Just in case.

At ten to seven, I'm on the sofa with my jacket and bag beside me, waiting. At half past seven Nate still hasn't turned up. I get up, open the door and go outside. I gaze up and down the street. *Where is he?*

At eight o'clock, I'm telling myself he's broken down. By nine, I've convinced myself he's had an accident. Nate's not used to driving a sports car. Suppose he's lying dead in a ditch?

Why don't I ring him? It would be easy enough. It's what anyone else would do. I pick up my mobile phone and put it down a dozen times. He's had second thoughts. He's gone off me. He doesn't think I'm worth waiting for…

At eleven I pick up the landline. I've heard if you dial 141 first, it withholds your number. I dial 141, followed by Nate's mobile number.

He answers right away. 'Hello?'

In the background I hear laughter and glasses clinking. It sounds like he's in a bar. I put down the phone. Not dead then. Not in a ditch. I've been stood up.

CHAPTER THIRTY

Courtney's key turns in the lock. 'Hi,' she says, closing the door and smiling at me. 'So, how did your weekend go?'

I put down my book. 'It didn't.'

'What?'

Hauling myself up from the sofa, I take my dirty cup and plate over to the sink. 'Nate stood me up.'

'Bastard. Wait until I get my hands on him.' Courtney drops her weekend bag and strides across to hug me. 'I'm sorry, Ilona. You were really looking forward to it.' She hesitates. 'Are you free tomorrow night?'

I turn on the tap to wash up. 'I'm always free. Why?'

'I'll order takeaway. We need to have a chat.'

Courtney and I spend the following evening slagging off men in general and Nate in particular. After finishing our curry, I stack the plates and place them on the draining board.

'Come and sit down a minute.' Courtney tops up my glass and moves across to the sofa.

I pick up my glass and join her. 'Sorry to go on. I was really getting to like Nate, especially the past couple of weeks. I don't understand what I did wrong.'

'You didn't do anything wrong.' Courtney grimaces. 'Oh dear, this is really bad timing…' She takes a deep breath. 'I'm sorry Ilona, but I'm moving out.'

My heart beats fast. 'Why?'

'I've got a transfer to a branch in Dover.'

'Is it my fault? I know I'm not much fun to be around but…'

'It's not you.'

Why's she avoiding eye contact? 'I thought you were happy here?'

'I am. I was. But I've been at the travel agency a year. This is a promotion. I'm moving in with Dad, so I'll save loads on rent.'

'If it's the rent, perhaps we can come to an arrangement?'

'It's not the rent.' Courtney turns to look at me. 'Look, this was never going to be forever, was it?'

The bell on the shop door chimes. I look up, expecting a customer.

'Hi.' Maya strolls in.

'Hi,' I say. 'Thought we were meeting at *La Hacienda*?'

'I finished early so I thought I'd come and check out where you work.' She browses *The Emporium*, her eyes taking in everything. 'I've only peered in through the window before. Jacint not here?'

'No, I told you. He's at an Antiques Fair in Bristol. That's why I'm finishing up a bit earlier.'

'Oh yeah.' Maya picks up a crystal decanter. 'I forgot.

Shame, I was hoping to meet him. Well, you carry on with whatever you're doing. Don't mind me, I'll have a poke around.'

There's no way I can concentrate with Maya poking around. She's such a fiddler. I carry on filling in the paperwork to go with the package I'm sending to Henrick, while attempting to keep half an eye on Maya.

She runs her fingers along the top of a walnut cabinet before opening a writing desk and pulling out all the little drawers. Moving on, her attention is drawn to a cocktail cabinet. She lifts out an expensive Fostoria glass and raises it to her lips. 'Mine's a Martini,' – she pouts into the mirror – 'shaken, not stirred.'

Despite interruptions, I finish the paperwork and check it through, aware that Maya's over by the jewellery cabinet, tugging at the glass door.

'Got the key for this?' she asks.

'No.' I don't want her finger marks over everything. 'Jacint has it.'

Maya slopes back to my desk and picks up the long box I'm about to bubble wrap. 'What's in here?' She rattles it like it's a Christmas cracker.

'Don't. It's valuable.' I reach to take the box from her, but she's already undoing the clasp.

'Nice.' She prises the Art Deco platinum bracelet away from the tiny pins securing it to the velvet and lays it over her wrist. 'Are these emeralds? They match my eyes. Wow, look at the diamonds.'

'Put it back. I have to post it tonight.'

'Why don't you let me borrow it?' she pleads. 'Just for tonight? We'll package it up afterwards and post it in the morning. Jacint will be none the wiser.'

'Because I have to send it recorded delivery and, yes, he

will know.' I take the bracelet from her wrist. After carefully securing it in the box, I wrap it in bubble wrap and slide it into the envelope. 'Right. We'll drop this at the post office on the way.'

La Hacienda is unusually busy and the waiter seems a little flustered. 'Are you ready to order?' he asks.

'Paella and a glass of house red, please.'

'*Si, señorita.*'

Maya glances up at him. 'I'll have the same.'

He picks up the menus before going to fetch our drinks.

'Courtney's leaving,' I tell Maya.

'Why?'

I fiddle with the tablecloth. 'She's moving down to Deal to live with her dad.'

The waiter returns with our wine.

Maya raises her glass. 'Well, I call that good timing.'

'Why?'

'I can have her room for a bit.' She clinks my glass. 'Cheers.'

The waiter places the paella on the table. '*Que aproveche!*'

Maya tucks her serviette under her chin and digs in.

Our booth is in the corner, an ideal spot for romantic couples. I become aware of glances from the waiter and eat as quickly as possible, guessing they want the table.

After I've finished, I push my bowl away. 'Look Maya. I don't mind you staying a few days, but you can't freeload.'

'Don't worry.' She pats my hand. 'There's money coming.'

I raise an eyebrow. 'Have you even got a job?'

'Course I have.'

'Because I'll struggle to pay the mortgage without Courtney's contribution. If you don't pay your way, I could lose the flat.' I put my head in my hands. 'God, I can't believe Courtney's left me in the lurch like this.'

I sense Rowena studying me closely as she passes me the vegetable tureen. 'Is there something wrong, dear?' she asks.

'Courtney's moved out.' I help myself to broccoli and carrots, and hand the tureen back.

'Oh no. Why?' Rowena offers the vegetables to Nigel.

I shrug. 'Promotion. It's in Dover and closer to her dad.'

Nigel loads his plate with roast potatoes. 'She'll have fewer prospects down there.'

Rowena picks up her knife and fork. 'Family ties are important.'

Like I'd know. I slice into my pie.

'How will you manage the mortgage payments?' asks Nigel, ever the pragmatist.

'I'm okay at the moment,' I lie. 'Courtney paid up until the end of the month.' I take care not to mention Maya. She'd only been with me for two weeks, but during that time she'd drained my stock of wine and put a big dent in my credit card. I'd arrived home from work one night to find a note propped against a bottle of Merlot. *Babe. Sorry to take off like this, but I've been offered a fantastic opportunity in Milan. I hope you don't mind but I've borrowed a few bits. I'll recompense you big time when I get back.*

'Well, we can help.' Rowena turns to Nigel. 'Can't we?'

'No, really,' I say. 'I'm not looking for a handout.'

'Then I suppose,' – Nigel scoops another spoonful of potatoes onto his plate – 'you need to find another flatmate.'

'Eat up, dear.' Rowena looks at me with that concerned face. 'You're looking far too thin.'

I push vegetables around my plate. 'I'd rather not have someone I don't know living in the flat, but I can't meet the mortgage payments on my salary and it's not like I have any savings.'

'Did you know Emmy's coming back for a while?' asks Rowena. 'Perhaps she'll need somewhere to stay?'

'No. Jacint didn't tell me.'

Nigel looks pointedly at Rowena. 'It was supposed to be a surprise.'

'Oh.' Rowena covers her mouth with her hand. 'Silly me. I hope I haven't ruined it.'

'No, it's excellent news.' I suddenly feel hungry and tuck into my dinner. 'I can't wait to see her.'

———

I poke my head around Jacint's office door. 'You didn't tell me Emmy was coming home.'

Jacint looks up from his paperwork. 'Who told you? She wanted it to be a surprise.'

'Rowena let it slip.' I give a small laugh. 'But don't worry, I'll pretend I don't know. Is she staying with you?'

'I assume so. Why?'

'My spare room is free.'

Jacint smiles. 'She'd love that.'

With the worry lifted, I feel myself standing taller. 'When's she coming?'

'Soon,' – Jacint taps his nose – 'and that's all I'm saying…'

. . .

I arrive back from lunch break to find Emmy waiting. 'Surprise!' she cries.

'Emmy!'

'Bonjour ma chérie. Ça va?'

We throw our arms around each other and skip around like kids in the playground.

'Off you go, you two, before you break something,' says Jacint. 'No more work today. You will want to catch up.'

We both peck him on the cheek before heading out the door, arm in arm. Laughing and giggling, we visit our old favourite – Marks and Spencer – for afternoon tea and scones.

'How come you're back?' I ask as I pour Earl Grey into china cups.

'Checking out Unis. I'm hoping to do a post grad in textiles.'

'So, you're back for a while?'

Emmy slices her fruit scone in half, liberally applying butter. 'Initially a couple of weeks, but depends on what I find. *Papa* says you can put me up?'

'I'd love to.'

Two days later, we take a trip to London.

Emmy stops outside a small boutique in Oxford Street. 'Wait, that skirt is *très chic*. Looks a bit Stella McCartney.'

I stare at the flimsy lace mini skirt. It doesn't even have a price tag. 'Like you need more clothes with all those fabulous Paris outfits. Come on.' I tug her arm. 'Let's try Gap.'

She treats me to a pair of black bootcut trousers from Morgan and we finish the day with cocktails in All Bar One.

It's a little after nine when I arrive at *The Emporium*. The door's unlocked. I push it open and spot Jacint at the reception desk, poring through the books. He looks up. 'You've been having a nice time, the two of you?'

I blush. Emmy's attending an Open Day today, but I haven't done a full day's work since she moved in. 'Yes, it's been great spending time together.'

Jacint seems distracted.

'Jacint, is everything okay?'

'Ilona,' – he runs his hands over his face – 'I have to raise something a bit sensitive.'

'Oh God. I'm sorry. I've taken the mick spending so much time with Emmy…'

'It's not that.' His voice is solemn. 'You remember the Art Deco bracelet we had valued for Lady Smythe?'

'Of course.' I take off my coat and hang it on the coat rack. 'Cabochon emeralds bezel set with fine milgrain edging. Fancy openwork links and bars with French-cut and baguette diamonds.'

'You sent it to Henrick for a clean and valuation,' he continues.

'Yes, the paperwork should be in the file.'

'And it came back?'

'Not yet. Not that I've seen.'

'This is what is so strange.' He scratches his chin. 'I'm afraid I'd forgotten about it until Lady Smythe's assistant rang to ask about the delay. I called Henrick. He said it's a fine example of Art Deco period jewellery and values it at twenty grand.'

'Wow.'

'The thing is, Henrick says he returned it two weeks ago.'

My heart thumps. 'Has it got lost in the post?'

'It was sent recorded delivery and had to be signed for. I've checked with the delivery service. They say it was delivered and they have a signature. Could you have put it somewhere safe?'

My mouth feels dry. 'Last time I saw it was the day I packaged it up.' *When Maya was here…*

Jacint holds out a sheet of paper. 'I asked them to fax the receipt.'

I stare down at my signature. 'I didn't sign for it. Someone must have forged this.'

Jacint watches me. 'Have a think, Ilona. It's been hectic with Emmy here. Perhaps you've forgotten?'

'No, I'd remember.' *Is he going to fire me?*

Jacint sighs. 'It's not just the money, although I'm not sure we can claim on insurance… The thing is, I can't replace it. It's of sentimental value to Lady Smythe and you know what a good customer she is.'

'Honestly, Jacint, I didn't sign for it.'

'Mmm, well, as I say, have a good think.' Jacint goes into his office and closes the door.

I gaze around Lucas's office, taking in the grey designer couch and button back armchair. 'You've got new furniture.'

He takes my jacket and hangs it on the coat stand. 'Hope you approve?'

'I do.' I rub my palms across the soft velour as I sink into the couch. 'Do you mind if I ask a question?'

Lucas makes himself comfortable in the armchair. 'Fire away.'

'Is fear of dolls a thing?'

He raises a quizzical eyebrow. 'What makes you ask that?'

'When my sisters and I were small, we were terrified of an old doll we inherited. She had three faces.'

'Three faces? That does sound creepy.'

'So, is it a thing?'

'Yes. Fear of dolls is a phobia called pediophobia. It's similar to pupaphobia, the phobia of puppets, but most people don't suffer from a phobia. They just find dolls creep them out.'

'Dolls don't creep me out, per se, but this one did.'

'For many, dolls are friendly and human-like, but not real. Some scientists liken fear of dolls to fear of robots. They suggest the phobia stems from the fear that robots might replace them. It's referred to as "uncanny valley". Dolls or robots may be fashioned to be animated and life-like. For some, this seems a threat.'

'A threat?'

'Our brains are trained to recognise faces. We readily identify faces in clouds, trees, a piece of fruit. You must have read that story the other week about someone finding the face of Christ on a banana skin?'

I snort with laughter. 'Yes.'

'Our brains seek faces and search them for clues about emotions and intentions. When we see something in a lifelike doll that makes us feel uneasy, we register it as a threat.'

'Right.'

Lucas studies me. 'How are things going, Ilona?'

'Not great.' I frown. 'My flatmate moved out.'

'I'm sorry to hear that. Will you replace her?'

'I have to.' I sigh. 'I can't afford the mortgage payments on my own. I've got a friend staying with me for now.'

Lucas strums his fingers on the arm of the chair. 'And have you known this friend long?'

'Since school. Emmy's my boss's daughter.'

'That sounds a good fit. Any chance you can make things permanent?'

I examine my fingernails. 'Unlikely. She's off to Uni soon.'

'Well, I'm sure you'll find someone.' Lucas consults his notes. 'We said we'd focus on relationships today, didn't we?'

'May as well.' I squirm in my seat. 'I've got an ex-boyfriend to add to the list.'

Lucas leans back, steepling his fingers. 'Do you want to talk about that?'

'I guess he wasn't that into me.' I shrug. 'I don't care.'

'Yet from your tone it sounds like you do?'

I get up and slope across to the window. The car park across the street is busy. Two cars wait for the same space and, when a parked car moves, they both go for the gap. The drivers wave and gesticulate, but I can't hear what they're saying. 'I don't understand what happened.'

'Tell me about it,' says Lucas.

I return to the couch. 'Things were pretty casual to start – walks, cinema, a football match. Everything was his choice. We didn't seem to have much in common, so when he started messing me around, I finished it.'

'So, you ended things with him?'

'Yes, and I thought that was that. But then Nate came

back and he seemed to want to make things right. He took me up to London. Really pushed the boat out.'

'What happened?'

'He was supposed to be taking me away for the weekend. He even hired a Morgan.'

'Nice.'

'Well, it might have been if he'd bothered to show up.'

'He stood you up?'

Tears trickle down my cheek.

Lucas passes me a tissue. 'What did Nate say when you tackled him about it?'

I blink.

'You didn't call to find out what happened?'

'I couldn't.'

'Nate shouldn't have treated you like that, Ilona. You deserve a reason for why he didn't show.'

I shred the tissue.

'Did something happen between you?'

I shake my head.

Lucas leans forward. 'Nate didn't hurt you?'

I look up. 'No. We never even...' My breath shudders. 'I don't seem to be good at relationships.'

'From what you've told me, it sounds as if things were going well between you and Nate.' Lucas scratches his chin. 'There was nothing to indicate waning interest?'

'No.'

'Perhaps Nate not turning up had nothing to do with you? Maybe the two of you got your wires crossed?'

I stare at Lucas. 'I don't think that's likely.'

'If you rang him, you might be able to sort things out.'

'I can't,' I whisper. 'I just can't.'

I sit for a while without speaking, but sense Lucas watching me.

'Is there something else you'd like to talk about today?'

'Something happened at work. An expensive bracelet has gone missing. My boss blames me.'

'I'm sorry to hear that. What makes you think your boss blames you?'

'I was the one responsible for sending it off to be valued.' I'm careful not to mention Maya or the forged signature.

'These things happen. I'm sure your boss believes you. How has he reacted?'

'Jacint's been really nice, but I can tell he's disappointed. It's so unfair. I didn't take it and now he'll never trust me again.'

'Let things settle down. I'm sure Jacint knows how loyal you are. He's probably as bewildered as you about what's happened. You never know, the bracelet may turn up. These delivery services aren't always reliable.'

CHAPTER THIRTY-ONE

I've been nursing the same drink for the past twenty minutes. At least this two-night stay at the Leeds Castle Hotel has got me out of the flat. Having acquired work experience with a prestigious Fashion House while waiting for her University course to begin, Emmy has stayed longer than anticipated. Her persistent need for entertainment is wearing me down.

'Come on, Ilona,' she wheedled the other night. '*Papa* says you've been working six days a week.'

'That's the way I like it.'

'It's not good. You're twenty. You should be out on the razzle every night.'

'I like my own company. Anyway, I get out and about. I travel, don't I?'

'A whistle-stop trip to Bruges doesn't count. And I bet you stayed in the hotel room the whole time apart from when meeting with dealers.'

. . .

Well, I'm living it up now. Tomorrow I visit an Antiques Fair at Leeds Castle. That's if I survive tonight's charity auction.

I'd spent the Gala Dinner avoiding the advances of the sweaty bald man sitting beside me. After coffee was served, I congratulated myself on staying polite but aloof. My admirer, however, had other ideas. Leaning close, he treated me to a waft of garlicky breath. 'Some of us are hitting a nightclub.' His hand touched my knee. 'I'd love your company.'

'Excuse me,' I said, scurrying away from the table and heading for the Ladies. I stayed there for ten minutes, only creeping out once the coast was clear.

Since then, I've concealed myself here, the smallest table at the back of the ballroom, torn between obligation to attend the auction on Jacint's behalf and a desire to flee.

The waiter works his way in my direction. Abandoning half a glass of wine, I pick up my clutch bag and walk briskly towards the lift.

Exiting on the third floor, I let myself into my room, kick off my shoes and lay down on the bed. Picking up the TV remote, I channel hop, but there's nothing worth watching. I pad across to the minibar and peruse the menu. Five quid for that tiny bottle of gin! I slam the door. This is ridiculous. It's only ten o'clock. Emmy's right, I should live a little.

Sliding my high heels back on, I head downstairs, giving the ballroom a wide berth. Instead, I make for the jazz bar where I perch on a bar stool and order a gin and tonic.

As I sip my drink, I notice the guy playing the piano. Mmm, he's fit. The other guests are chatting so loudly they don't seem to have noticed the music is live. I watch him for a while, noting the way his hair flops forward, a bit like Hugh Grant's. Finishing the tune, he looks up. I love his smile.

I clap and it encourages others to join in.

Piano Guy laughs, plays one more song and pulls his mic

towards him. 'Thank you, ladies and gentlemen. I'm taking a short break now, but don't go away. I'll be back to play more of your favourites.' He gets up from the piano stool, walks towards me and slides onto the bar stool next to mine. 'Hi. Can I buy you a drink?'

Did I just pick him up? 'I should buy you one. You're doing all the work.'

Piano Guy shakes his head. 'No, I need to treat my number one fan.' He winks. 'You can get the next round.'

God, that's smooth.

The bartender waits for our order.

Piano Guy points at my empty glass. 'Another one of these?'

It wouldn't hurt. 'Yes, please.'

'Make that two.' Piano Guy is watching me and I feel my cheeks flush.

The bartender mixes our drinks and places them in front of us before going back to polishing glasses with a bar towel.

Piano Guy chinks his glass against mine. 'Cheers.'

I sip my gin.

He holds out his hand. 'My name's Jamie.'

I smile. 'Ilona.'

'Ilona, that's a beautiful name. So, Ilona, what's a nice girl like you doing in a place like this?'

What a cliché! I fiddle with my hair. 'Well, I'm not in the habit of picking people up at the bar.'

'Neither am I.'

'Yeah? I bet you pull every night.' *OMG, I'm flirting.*

'I wish.' Jamie grins. 'No, seriously, this is not a regular occurrence. I'm standing in for a mate. He was asked to play a wedding at short notice but already had this gig. I owed him a favour.'

'So, what's your day job?'

'I teach at Canterbury Christchurch University. I'm doing a PhD – history and literature.'

'Wow, impressive.'

'Not really. So, what do you do?'

I twizzle my drink. 'I'm in antiques.'

'Classy.' He clicks his fingers. 'Of course, you're here for the conference.'

'Yes.'

'You didn't fancy the night club then? I spotted a gaggle of antiquarians climbing into a minibus as I arrived.'

'Then you probably clocked the average age of said antiquarians was around seventy?'

Jamie winks. 'Perky lot, these antique dealers.'

'You wouldn't believe it.' I sip my drink 'I keep to myself on these things.'

'So, here for the weekend?'

'I'm heading home tomorrow afternoon, after the Antiques Fair at Leeds Castle.'

'I'm staying over too. One of the perks of the gig.'

I bite my lip. *What's he suggesting?*

He downs the rest of his drink. 'Actually, I was thinking of visiting Leeds Castle tomorrow. I don't suppose you fancy sharing a cab?'

'I'm not sure what time I'm going.'

Jamie gestures towards the piano. 'Well, better get back.'

The audience are lively during the second half of the set. While they call out requests, I study Jamie. He's so sexy.

I catch the bartender's eye. 'Excuse me?'

'What'll it be?' he asks.

I grin. 'I'm okay thanks, but would you mind taking the pianist another G&T with my compliments?'

The bartender delivers the drink on a silver tray. Jamie looks across at me and smiles. 'Thank you,' he mouths.

There's a long queue at the reception desk. I check my watch. These people can't all be ordering taxis. I should have booked one last night.

Someone taps me on the shoulder. I spin round.

'We could still share that cab?' Jamie grins. 'Mine's due in five minutes.'

The driver drops us at the entrance to Leeds Castle. Jamie insists on paying. As we approach the kiosk, I pull an auction pass from my handbag and glance at Jamie. 'Did you really plan to visit Leeds Castle today?'

'Sure.' He hands over the money for a ticket. 'I haven't been here in years. Mind if I tag along?'

We stroll through the entrance and make our way towards the cluster of marquees erected on the lawn.

'So,' Jamie asks, 'you're in antiques, but what exactly do you do?'

'I work at *The Emporium* in Brasted.'

'*The Emporium's* an antique store?'

'It's more than a store. We pride ourselves on tracking down specific items for discerning clients.' Jamie and I are entering the first marquee and, spotting an unusual piece, I move closer to examine it. 'Like this, for instance.'

'A sideboard?'

'*George III Chiffonier*.' I run my hand across the top. 'Satinwood cross banding with tulip wood. See these doors? Pleated silk with brass grills.'

Jamie examines the door panels. 'It's different I suppose, but not really my style.' He steps towards another piece of furniture. 'Now this one's nicer.'

'You've got good taste.' I examine the Art Deco side-board he's picked out. 'It's made by *Hille* - Burr Walnut veneer with ebonised detailing.'

Jamie looks for a price tag, but it's not labelled. 'So, what sort of money would this fetch?'

'I'd not want to pay more than a thousand for either piece, although Jacint could retail them for more.'

'Jacint?'

'My boss and mentor.'

'And how long have you worked at *The Emporium*?'

'Four years.'

Jamie raises an eyebrow. 'Surely you're not old enough to have worked anywhere for four years?' He shakes his head. 'No, I take that back, you've proved how knowledgeable you are.'

I laugh. 'Thanks, I think... Jacint is encouraging me to build my own collection. In fact, he's investing in me.'

We browse for another hour before heading to the refreshments tent. I grab a table, while Jamie queues for tea.

As he transfers tea and scones from the tray to the table, he's grinning.

'What?'

He takes a seat. 'I was just wondering what you're doing next weekend?'

'Why?'

'I've got another gig at the *White Bear* in Sevenoaks.'

I glance anxiously around the crowded bar until I spot Jamie over by a small stage.

Seeming to sense my gaze, he turns round smiling. 'Ilona.' He beckons me forward. 'I've saved you a seat.'

Sitting near the front in my new top and black jeans, I tap my feet to the music, feeling like I'm someone special.

I've just taken a sip of beer when Jamie speaks into the mic. 'You all know the next one, made popular in *Lion King*. Tonight, I dedicate it to my friend, Ilona.'

I splutter. Everyone cranes their necks to stare. I feel my cheeks burning up.

Jamie smiles at me as he sings, *'Can you feel the love tonight…'*

I lower my head, trying to stifle giggles.

Finishing the set, Jamie jumps down from the stage. His eyes sparkle as he steps towards me.

'Unbelievable.' I thump him on the chest. 'I can't believe you did that.'

He laughs. 'You looked so lovely, I wanted everyone else to know you were with me. That colour really suits you. Is it turquoise?' He takes my arm and steers me to a quiet corner.

'Great set,' says the landlord, depositing two bottles of Budweisser on our table.

'Cheers, mate.' Jamie passes me a beer before taking a long drink from his own. He tilts his head to one side as he looks at me. 'Am I forgiven?'

'I suppose so.' I sip my drink. 'Actually, you were great.'

Jamie winks. 'Great enough to earn a second date?'

I grin. 'Isn't this our second?'

'How about next weekend? I try to get uni work done during the week so I have time for a social life.'

'I forgot I was dating a college boy,' I tease.

'Hey.' Jamie reaches across to tickle me.

'Stop it.' I giggle. 'Actually, I've already got something planned for next weekend and I doubt it's your cup of tea.'

He takes another swig of beer. 'Try me.'

'I'm up in London. I'm going to the *National Museum of Childhood.*'

'A day in London sounds good. And speaking of tea, perhaps we might fit that in too?'

After battling through the crowds at Bethnal Green tube station, I take a breath of relief as I step out into brilliant sunshine. I glance right and left before spotting him across the road. My pulse races. I wave and he crosses the road to join me.

'I can't believe you agreed to come,' I say, as we walk along Cambridge Heath Road.

Jamie grins. 'Why?'

'Well, dolls and teddies are probably not your thing.'

'I guess we might have time to look at a few other things.' He nudges me. 'Everyone likes the odd train set.'

'You didn't tell me you were a bit of an anorak on the quiet?'

Jamie makes to grab me as we enter the venue.

'Now look, we're here, so behave,' I scold. 'You'll get us chucked out.'

The red brick entrance gives way to a vast light space. 'Wow.' I stare up at the two terraces above us.

Jamie gapes. 'It's like the Tardis.'

I gaze up at the glass ceiling encased in an iron framework. 'More like a train terminal than a museum.'

'So,' says Jamie. 'Are we looking for anything in particular?'

I pull a leaflet from my bag. 'The *Amy Miles Dolls' House.* She made it herself. It features all sorts of household items from 1850 onwards. There's even a sponge wedding cake.'

Jamie pats his stomach. 'Hmm, I'm not sure dolls' house cake is enough to keep me going.'

I nudge him playfully before making a beeline for the teddy bear section, where I stare in wonder. 'Aren't they fabulous? Look at this Chiltern teddy. I want to take him home.'

'Bit bald in parts.'

'So would you be if you were nearly eighty.'

'Robots.' Jamie tugs me towards a nearby display. 'I had one just like this.'

Further on, I stop to peruse a display card and read: '*Japanese crawling doll believed to be 1930s*. I saw one once at an auction. Wish I'd had the money to buy it.'

'Well, now your boss is investing in you, next time you'll be able to.'

'I know, it's so good of him.' Spotting another display, I grab Jamie's arm. 'Come on, I want to look at doll parts.'

He makes a horrified face. 'Sounds a bit macabre.'

'Can you bear it if I make a few notes?' I take a notebook from my shoulder bag. 'It will be helpful when I'm estimating and doing valuations. I don't often get the chance to see the real thing.'

After dragging Jamie around the museum for two hours, we retreat to a little café we'd spotted on our walk from the tube.

I take off my coat and lay it over the back of my chair. 'Was it awful?'

'Not enough train sets, but I enjoyed playing with the magnets and iron filings.' Jamie reaches across and touches my hand. 'I'm sorry we couldn't get a table in *The Garden Café*.'

'Don't worry.' I lift a bone china teacup from its mismatched saucer. '*Miss Daisy's Café* is quaint.'

An elderly waitress bustles over with a laden tray. 'Lemon drizzle and coffee walnut.' She sets scones and cake down on the table. 'I'll top up the hot water when you're ready.'

As she moves away, Jamie and I catch each other's eye. 'Mrs Overall,' we mouth in unison.

I start to giggle.

'Stop it.' Jamie's face is stern. 'You'll get us chucked out.'

'You out tonight?' I ask, thumbing through *Delia's Complete Cookery Course*.

Emmy pulls another section of hair through her straighteners. 'Yes, meeting the girls. I'll probably crash at Rachel's. Why?'

'Thought I might cook a meal for Jamie.'

'*Oh là là.* This is getting serious.'

'It's just a meal.' I close the book and sigh. 'There's something old fashioned about him. Something solid and dependable.'

She laughs. 'Sounds like you're describing one of your antiques.'

I poke out my tongue. 'You know what I mean. With Jamie it's easy. It just feels right.'

Emmy holds up a mirror to check her hair at the back. 'So, will he stop over, do you think?'

I snort. 'I shouldn't think so.'

'Why not? You said he's nice.'

'I like him, but it's too soon. I've only known him three weeks.'

'I doubt Jamie thinks it's too soon.' Emmy squirts a blob of gel on her hands and rubs them together before running fingers through her hair. 'If you've invited him for a meal, he might expect you *pour le dessert*.'

'Oh hell, do you think so?'

'Relax. Don't be pressured. Make an excuse. Say you have an early start or something, but tell him early so he doesn't get the wrong idea. It'll be fine. What're you cooking?'

I open the book again. 'There's a recipe here for chicken with tarragon and grapes. And probably new potatoes.'

'*Bien.*'

'I'll grab something from *Marks & Spencer* for pudding.'

'Good, keep it simple. Well, enjoy yourself. You've got the place to yourselves.' Emmy does one last check in the mirror before grabbing her wheelie suitcase. She turns back at the door. 'Jamie sounds fit. If it was me,' she winks, 'I'd shave my legs.'

I hurry home to clear through the flat. Emmy's room is a mess compared to my own, but at least her clutter is behind closed doors. I put on my *Spiceworld* CD, singing along as I give the whole place a once-over.

After completing the chores, I tackle the food. Potatoes scrapped and in the pan on the hob. As the chicken is precooked, I only need to add tarragon to the mayo and stir everything together. When the mixture's ready, I pour it onto a bed of lettuce and turn the potatoes off. *There, all looking good.*

I take a quick shower and, on impulse, shave my legs. I dry myself with a fluffy towel and sit down at the mirror to do my make-up and straighten my hair. My hand is shaking as I apply mascara. *Just butterflies.* Afterwards, I step into my new blue dress and glance at my reflection in the mirror. *Not too shabby.*

I'm putting finishing touches to the table when the doorbell rings.

Jamie kisses my cheek. 'You look gorgeous.' He hands me a bunch of flowers.

'Thank you, they're lovely. Come in.'

Jamie steps inside and I close the door. The flat feels suddenly small.

'Anything I can do to help?' he asks.

'Fix the drinks?' I fill a vase with water and plonk the flowers in. 'Mine's a Malibu and coke.'

Jamie mixes my drink and hands me the glass.

'Thanks. What are you having?'

'Might have a beer for now.' As he opens the fridge to help himself to a Budweisser, Emma and Mel launch into *Hasta Mañana.* Jamie grimaces. 'Mind if I change the music?'

'Sure.' I tip the potatoes into a dish and garnish with parsley, while Jamie goes through my CDs. He swaps *The Spice Girls* for *Beautiful South.*

After we've eaten, Jamie sits back, patting his stomach. 'I'm stuffed. That treacle pudding was amazing.'

'I didn't make it, I'm afraid. A *Marks & Spencer* special.'

'The chicken dish was great and that was your creation.'

'Thanks.' I wave the half empty bottle of Pinot Grigio. 'Shall we finish this?'

'Actually, I'd prefer another Bud if that's okay?' Jamie grabs a beer before easing himself down on the sofa. I top up my wine glass and join him.

'So.' He slides closer. 'Have you got work tomorrow?'

'Yes. *The Emporium's* really busy…'

He takes the wine glass from my hand and places it on the coffee table beside his beer. 'You pretty much run things, from what I hear.'

'Jacint does rather leave me to it lately.'

'And he wouldn't do that if he didn't trust your judgement.' He lifts a strand of hair from my face and kisses my forehead. 'You've become indispensable.'

'Oh, I don't know about that.'

'I don't mean to your boss…'

CHAPTER THIRTY-TWO

'I thought I might do dinner again Friday night,' I say, buoyed by the success of *Tarragon Chicken*.

'Fine by me.' Jamie looks up from his *Bernard Cornwell* novel. 'It'll be a change from takeaway.'

'Hey.' I throw a cushion at him. 'Like you're such a great chef. I'll have you know, my repertoire has expanded greatly since Rowena got me the Delia cookbook.' I flop down on the sofa beside him. 'I was thinking I might invite Emmy? She starts her course at *The London College of Fashion* at the end of the month and I've kind of abandoned her lately.'

Jamie closes his book and places it on the coffee table. 'From what you've told me, she's pretty busy herself.'

'Work experience at the fashion house certainly keeps her occupied, but I feel bad we haven't done anything together for ages.'

He reaches for me. 'Since you met me, you mean?'

I push him away playfully. 'You haven't even got to meet her properly. Emmy's been living here six months and Jacint has made sure I'm not out of pocket. Without his contribution I'd have had to find a new flatmate.'

Jamie grimaces. 'Wish I could find new flatmates.'

I laugh. 'Yours is definitely a boys' pad.' Jamie shares with two other guys, a teacher and a sports coach. All three leave their clothes strewn about the floor. 'The place reeks of old socks and sweat.'

He puts his arms around me again. 'I could always move in here.'

'We've only been seeing each other a few weeks.' I wriggle away and stand up. 'So, dinner Friday?'

He picks up his book. 'Sure. I'll bring wine.'

Chicken Chasseur is not as easy as Delia makes out. I've been slaving away for a couple of hours. Emmy emerges from her room looking chic in a little black dress. Expensive but understated, it fits all the right places, emphasising her curves and tiny waist. 'You look amazing,' I say, sweeping frizzy curls back from my face.

'So do you. That top is pretty.'

'Hmm.' I touch the underarm of my new lime green blouse. 'It's showing sweat marks already. Have I got time to change?' The doorbell rings and I sigh. 'Too late.'

Throughout dinner, conversation is animated and, as the wine flows, it becomes apparent Jamie and Emmy share an interest in French architecture. Their discussion on the merits of Romanesque versus Flamboyant arches goes way over my head.

As I clear plates from the main course, Emmy fetches a box from the fridge, placing it on the table with a flourish. '*Voila! Millefeuilles aux framboises.*'

Jamie lifts the lid. 'Wow. These look amazing.'

'From *Maison Angelic.*' Emmy smiles. 'Can you believe it? French *pâtisserie* in London.'

This is the extent of her contribution to the meal. I slump back down on my chair. 'They put my *Chicken Chasseur* to shame.'

Over dessert, Emmy describes life in Paris – gliding down the Seine on *Bateaux Mouches*, lingering meals in the *Place du Tertre.*

Jamie shakes his head. 'I can't believe you actually lived in *Montmartre.*'

'*Mais oui,* like all best artisans of Paris, *j'avais un petit appartement.*' She pushes her dessert plate aside to lean one elbow casually on the table as she smokes her *Gauloises*. It's funny how she becomes more French with each glass of wine.

I get up and stomp over to flick the switch on the kettle.

'I'd love to spend time in Paris.' Jamie's voice is husky. 'The museums, the galleries…'

'*La vie nocturne.*' Emmy flutters her eyelashes.

I'd like to show you bloody night life, I mutter. I fill the cafetière with boiling water and carry the coffee tray over to the table.

'*Pardon,*' Emmy offers Jamie a cigarette.

I've never seen Jamie smoke, but tonight he takes one. 'Thank you.'

She offers her own cigarette to light it.

I reach across them and plunge down the knob on the cafetière.

Jamie takes a drag before slowly exhaling. 'You studied there, too?'

'*Mais oui,* until *l'indiscrétion.*'

He raises an eyebrow.

I pour the coffee. 'What indiscretion?'

'*Mon professeur.*' Emmy waves a hand as if it's nothing. 'Did I not mention? He had quite the reputation…'

As she recounts a story of amorous advances from her university tutor, Jamie's eyes don't leave her face. It's like I'm invisible.

'*Ciel, il se fait tard!*' Emmy turns to me. 'I must help you to clear away.'

'No, it's fine,' I say. 'You've got work experience tomorrow.'

'Are you sure? *D'accord.*' She air-kisses me before giving Jamie the customary French three kisses on alternate cheeks. 'Then I'll love you and leave you, for I have an early start.'

She tiptoes across the room. Jamie follows her every move. How does Emmy make stockinged feet look so sexy?

I stand up and move across to switch on the main light before carrying the dishes to the sink. I turn on the tap and let water cascade noisily into the bowl.

Jamie follows me. His arms encircle my waist. 'What a great evening.' He kisses the back of my neck. 'Do you have to do those now?' he murmurs.

'Yes,' I snap, 'they won't wash themselves.'

'Let me help then.' Jamie picks up a tea towel.

I stare at him. 'Hadn't you better be going?'

He screws up his eyes. 'Thought I was staying over?'

'Best not, with Emmy in the next room.'

Jamie pulls his phone from his jeans pocket. 'I'll call a cab then.'

While lying alone in bed, I can't stop playing the evening over in my head. Bloody bitch. Emmy knew exactly what she was doing. Perhaps it's no bad thing she's leaving soon.

I wake feeling thirsty. I pad into the bathroom, cup my

hands under the tap and gulp down cool water. But when I raise my head and look in the mirror, I realise I have no face. I have no eyes, but I stare. I have no mouth, but I scream.

Waking for real, I lay gasping for breath, my bedsheets soaked in sweat. I check the time. Can't be seven-thirty already? I stumble into the kitchen to make coffee. Propped against the kettle is a note from Emmy: *I take it back. Definitely NOT an antique. Jamie's gorgeous, you lucky cow. Thanks for a lovely evening. Ciao.*

Am I overreacting? Perhaps their flirting was down to too much alcohol?

———

Three weeks later, Emmy leaves. The flat seems quiet without her.

Jamie and I are cuddling on the sofa. It's hard maintaining a sulk when the person you're directing it at fails to notice.

'You going to be okay?' he asks.

'Yeah.' I get up and flick the switch on the kettle. 'It'll be easier for Emmy, living nearer to Uni. But I'll miss her. She's been my closest friend since school. We shared some great times.'

He follows me and gives me a squeeze. 'You'll stay in touch. And anyway, now you've got me.' Jamie takes two mugs from the cupboard. 'Will you manage the mortgage without her?'

'Yes. I don't fancy starting over with a new flatmate. And my collection's coming along nicely. It'll be reassuring to know I have a safety net.' I pour boiling water onto coffee granules. 'And when you're here, you can do your marking in the spare room. Saves having my room cluttered up with schoolbooks.'

'There is that other solution I mentioned…' Jamie carries the biscuit tin over to the coffee table and flops back down on the sofa. 'We could share costs.'

Jamie and I have been sleeping together for a couple of months now. It would make sense, but I'm not sure I'm ready for a live-in boyfriend. I pass Jamie his coffee. 'There's no rush. I kind of like things the way they are.'

⁘

'My God,' shouts Jamie as they replay the collapse of the second tower. We've been watching the attack on the World Trade Centre for an hour. Like the worse kind of rubber-neckers gawping at an accident.

Now footage from CNN – flames and black smoke as the planes hit the towers; smoke pluming and flowing like an erupting volcano; the twin towers collapsing as if constructed from cards. It's like the worst disaster movie ever. This can't be happening.

My mobile phone rings. I tear my eyes away from the TV and answer. 'Hello?'

'It's Jacint,' says the voice on the line. 'Are you watching?'

'Yes.' I stare back at the screen. People on the ground running as a cloud of dust engulfs them. Jacint had closed *The Emporium* and sent me home as soon as we heard the news. He'd wanted to be with Francine. 'It's unbelievable,' I whisper.

'We've managed to contact Francine's sister, Monique,' he says. 'She works in New York, but she's fine.'

'You've spoken to her?'

'Yes. Francine's relieved, although she'll be happier still when Monique's back in the UK.'

'Thanks for letting me know.' I hang up. 'Francine's sister is safe,' I tell Jamie.

'That's a relief at least,' he says.

It's as if, like Hermione in *The Chamber of Secrets,* I've been petrified by the Basilisk. 'I'm worried about Maya.' My voice sounds robotic.

'There's no reason to think Maya's in the States.'

'I don't know where she is. I've not heard from her in months.'

'I think we need a drink.' Jamie gets up, heading for the fridge. 'How about a glass of wine?'

'Oh God.' I gasp. 'Look at that.'

Jamie turns back to see. High up in the towers, people wave t-shirts from windows.

I'm mesmerised. 'What's that falling?' I ask.

'Fuck, they're jumping,' says Jamie.

'Oh no.' I put a hand over my mouth. I'm going to be sick. Those poor people. What a choice. Burn alive or leap from a window ninety storeys high. What would I do?

CHAPTER THIRTY-THREE

As I walk up the stairs to my flat. I'm looking forward to relaxing on the sofa. Jacint and I have been sorting lists for the next auction and I'm shattered. I can't wait to take my shoes off. When I get to my door, I find Maya sitting crossed legged on her velvet jacket. She's listening to her iPod. Or rather, my iPod. So that's where it went. I wondered why I hadn't been able to find it since last time she was here.

'Mind out the way.' I lean over her to unlock the door.

Maya yanks off her headphones. 'Hi you. I've been waiting.'

'I can see that.'

'You don't keep a spare key under the flowerpot anymore.'

'No.'

'I thought your flatmate might be here.'

'You'd better come in.' I don't tell her Emmy's moved out.

Maya follows me inside. 'Why are you always so cold?'

I spin around towards her. 'What do you expect? I didn't know if you were alive or dead.'

'The terrorist attack? I wasn't even in the States.'

'And how was I supposed to know that?'

'Point taken.' Maya hops from one foot to the other. 'Sorry, you've been ages and I need a pee.' She trots off to the bathroom.

I make my way to the kitchen and flick the switch on the kettle.

The loo flushes and Maya stands in the bathroom door with Jamie's shaving gel and aftershave in her hands. 'Don't tell me you've finally let a man move in?'

'No, he just leaves stuff here.'

'He?'

I sigh. 'Jamie.'

'And who's Jamie?'

'Just a guy.'

Maya lifts Jamie's copy of *Sharpe's Tiger* from the coffee table. 'Just a guy who seems to have his feet firmly under the table.' She wanders through to my bedroom.

Shit, some of his clothes are in there...

'So, what does this guy do?' Maya calls.

I drop tea bags into mugs. 'Teaches, at Canterbury University.'

She returns from my room, thankfully empty handed. 'Nice. Solid, respectable. Just your type.'

'So, what have you been doing since I saw you last?' I pour boiling water and prod the teabags, expecting to be regaled with a list of exotic places Maya's visited. When she doesn't answer right away, I turn around.

She blinks.

'Maya?'

Tears flow down her cheeks.

'Maya.' I take her in my arms. We stand like that for ages.

I rub her back like she used to do for me when we were little. I'm crying too. I can't help myself.

Maya pulls away and looks at me. 'Do you even know why we're crying?'

'No.' I grab a piece of kitchen roll and blow my nose. 'You always did start me off.'

Maya takes a seat at the table.

I place the mugs down and sit opposite. 'Here.' I pass her the kitchen roll.

'Things haven't been so good.' She sniffs. 'You remember that guy I went travelling with?'

'The bloke with a Harley?'

'Yep.' Maya sips her tea. 'When we came back, he told me he had stuff to sort out. I moved up to Glasgow to be near him. Turns out the "stuff" was a wife and child.'

'Oh, Maya.'

'You know me. Always did pick wrong 'uns.'

I rest my hand on her arm. 'You really cared about him.'

She stares into my eyes. 'I had to have an abortion.'

I feel a rip through my heart. How could I not have known?

'Don't judge me.'

'I'm not. It's just... I always thought I'd know about the big stuff. I thought if something bad happened to you, I'd feel it. But while you've been gone, we've become...'

'Distant?'

'Yes.' I take hold of her hand. 'It must have been a tough decision.'

Maya tosses her hair. 'Not really. After all, what sort of mother would I make? Now you, you'd have been great.'

I wonder at her use of past tense. 'Does he know?'

'The father?' Maya shakes her head.

'When was this?'

'Six weeks ago.'

Not long then. About the time I was getting closer to Jamie, my heart experiencing new emotions. Is that why I didn't know? 'So, it's over?'

'Oh yes. Completely. I didn't want anything long term anyway. To tell you the truth, he might not have even been the father.' She looks at me defiantly, before taking another sip of tea. 'So, what happened to that other guy you were seeing?'

'Nate? It didn't work out.'

Maya nods. 'Yeah, he's not worth fretting over. I'm glad you've found someone new. So, tell me about Jamie.'

'I don't know.' My face flushes with heat.

Maya studies me and I'm sure she knows we've done it. 'I'm pleased for you.'

It's late morning when Maya emerges from the bedroom rubbing her eyes. 'What're we doing today?'

'Sit down.' I pass her the Cornflakes. 'I thought we'd have a quiet weekend. Watch box sets, order in takeaway…'

Jamie isn't best pleased when I call him. 'But why can't I come over?'

'I told you, my sister's here. She's in a bad way.'

'Okay. Of course. Family comes first.'

'So, I'll call you tomorrow?'

'Oh shit. Sorry.'

'It's okay.' I grab kitchen roll and mop up the milk Maya's spilled.

'So,' – she speaks with her mouth full – 'it's all right if I stay for a bit?'

Maybe it would be good? I shrug. 'Actually, Emmy's moved out, so the spare room's free.'

'Cool.' She munches a few more spoonfuls. 'No bad thing, that.'

'What? Emmy moving out?'

'Yeah.'

'What do you mean?'

'Boyfriends and flatmates don't exactly mix.' Maya sips her orange juice.

My tummy flips. 'What are you trying to say?'

She helps herself to more Cornflakes. 'I didn't tell you at the time, but I caught the last one and Nate together.'

'Courtney and Nate?' I set down my coffee mug. 'When?'

'I called around one evening. Courtney was being dead evasive. She wouldn't even open the door. I heard Nate's voice, so I barged my way in. You should have seen them, guilty as hell. Definitely doing it, or about to.'

I press my fingers into my forehead. My brain's a fog. 'Are you sure? I can't believe they'd do that to me.'

'Yes, I'm sure. I knew it would upset you.' She swallows another mouthful of cereal. 'That's why I didn't say anything before. But it's okay. I dealt with that scheming tart.'

I stare at her. 'Let me get this straight. You spoke to Courtney?'

Maya pushes her bowl away. 'Told the slag if she didn't move out, she'd have me to deal with. Come on, Ilona. You must have known.'

'Oh my God.' I leap up. 'Courtney was always funny about me seeing Nate. She must have been jealous.' I put a hand to my mouth. 'Shit, shit.'

'What?' says Maya.

I pace the rug. 'That weekend Nate stood me up…'

'He stood you up?'

'We were supposed to be going to the Cotswolds. Courtney was away that weekend.'

'I told you.' Maya gets up too. 'What a bitch. Don't worry, I'm here now.' She pulls me into a hug.

I switch off the TV and carry our dirty cups to the sink. I yawn. Don't know why I'm so tired. All we've done for two days is laze about and eat… Oh shit, I didn't call Jamie. I wipe my hands on the tea towel and pick up my mobile. 'Hi babe.'

'How's your sister?' he asks.

'Okay.'

'Has she told you what's wrong?'

'Kind of…'

'Right.'

He's still narked. 'Look, I can't say any more. It's not my secret to share.'

'I get it.'

'Don't be like that.'

'Sorry. I miss you, that's all.'

'I know. I miss you too.'

'What about this week? Shall I come over Wednesday night?'

'I'm not sure…'

'Okay. Well, ring me when you can.' He hangs up a bit abruptly.

Maya wanders back through to the kitchen. 'That Jamie?'

'Yes.'

She fills a glass with water. 'You don't have to babysit me you know?'

I can't stop fidgeting. *The Sixth Day* had been Jamie's suggestion, but the film isn't grabbing me.

Jamie turns to me. 'Do you want to get out of here?'

'Sure.'

'Come on.' He takes my hand as he stands up. 'Excuse us…'

The other cinema goers move their legs to one side, tutting as we squeeze past.

Jamie scans the menu in *Pizza Express.*

'Sorry,' I yawn. 'I guess I wasn't in the mood.'

'It was a bit far-fetched, even for Arnie. Shall we share a pizza?'

'Yeah, that's fine.'

Jamie reaches across and takes my hand. 'Where are we, Ilona?'

'What do you mean?'

The waiter comes to take our order.

'One Margherita and two plates,' says Jamie. 'Oh, and a side salad.'

'Certainly, sir,' says the waiter. 'And to drink?'

'A couple of Buds. Thanks.' Jamie holds my hand again.

'Look, I'm not sure where we are. You've been distant since your sister came back.'

'Sorry.'

'I don't know where I stand.'

I pull my hand away. 'You know I've got stuff to sort out.'

The waiter brings our drinks.

Jamie stares at me. 'So, that's it?'

I gulp a mouthful of beer from the bottle.

'I really care about you, Ilona.'

'I know.'

'Really?' Jamie slams his hand down on the table. 'I tell you that I care, and you say I know?' He rubs his face. 'Before your sister came back, I thought we were on the point of moving in together.'

I don't need this tonight... 'I'm sorry.'

'You don't need to keep apologising.' He sighs. 'I'm worried about you, that's all.'

I take another sip of beer.

'Fuck's sake.' Jamie snatches the bottle from my hand. 'Ilona, talk to me.'

───────

The phone rings. I pick up the receiver. '*The Emporium*. Can I help you?'

'Ilona? It's me.'

'Emmy. How's the course going?'

'Good so far. Listen, *S Club 7* are playing Wembley Arena on Tuesday. I was going with my mate, but she's bailed. Her grandad's funeral or something... Do you fancy it?'

'You joking? Of course.'

'Okay, great.'

'I don't suppose we can get another ticket?'

Emmy snorts. 'It won't be Jamie's thing.'

'No, for Maya. She's staying with me for a couple of days.'

'I doubt it. The gig's a sell out.'

'Okay, don't worry.'

'I'll meet you at Embankment and we'll grab the Bakerloo line together.'

The Organic café is busy and I have to queue. I set down two cappuccinos on the table Maya's holding for us. 'We're lucky to get somewhere to sit at lunchtime.' I slide into my seat. 'How are you feeling?'

'Better, thanks.' Maya adds sugar to her coffee.

'Will you be all right if I go out Monday night?'

'I told you, I don't need a babysitter.'

'Emmy's got tickets for *S Club 7*. I don't know whether we could still get you one…'

Maya pulls a face. 'Not really my thing.'

Thank goodness for that. I sip my coffee.

She purses her lips. 'You're pretty tight with Emmy.'

'Yes, I told you. We were flatmates for a while until she started her course at the *London College of Fashion*.'

Maya nods her head. 'Mmm.'

'Why?'

Maya fiddles with the menus.

I reach across to take them from her, replacing them in the holder. 'What?'

'She left some photos tucked around the dressing table mirror in her room. Pretty, isn't she? I bet Jamie likes her.'

'Course he does. Emmy's my best friend.'

'I shouldn't let them get too close. I mean, your track record isn't great.'

I glare at her. 'Thanks a bunch.'

'Well, I mean, I'd keep an eye on them if I were you.'

CHAPTER THIRTY-FOUR

'Where are you Ems?' I text. No reply. I check the time again. Ten to seven. We'll miss the start... My mobile phone rings. 'Em? Where are you?'

'Ilona?'

'Jacint?'

'Ilona, can you hear me?'

'Yes. Why are you calling me on Emmy's phone?'

'Ilona, there's been an accident.'

'What?'

'Can you get across to University College Hospital?'

'What's happened? Is Emmy okay?'

'I'll meet you in A & E.'

My heart pounds as I dive into the tube station and consult the map. Exiting forty minutes later at Euston Square, I run the rest of the way, arriving in A & E panting.

'I'm looking for Emmeline Perez.' I gulp for air. 'She's been in an accident.'

The woman behind the reception desk consults her screen. 'Emmeline Perez, let me see...'

'Ilona?' Jacint's behind me, a coffee cup in each hand.

'What happened?' I ask.

He shakes his head.

I follow him through to a side room. Emmy's laying so still with an oxygen mask over her mouth and nose. She looks like a doll. Her eyes are closed. Wires connect her to a machine making low, intermittent beeps.

'*Si je perdais ma fille…*' murmurs Francine, her eyes not leaving Emmy's face.

Jacint passes his wife a cup of coffee, but Francine waves it away, continuing to stroke Emmy's hand.

When he offers it to me, I take it, although it's the last thing I want. 'What happened?' I repeat.

Jacint answers in a hushed tone. 'We don't know yet. A young man found Emmeline like this and called an ambulance.'

'*Dieu merci il l'a fait,*' whispers Francine.

'The doctor says she sustained a blow to the back of her head,' Jacint continues. 'The police think it might have been a mugging but, if it was, they didn't take anything. Her handbag and phone were with her when she was found.'

'Where was that?'

'An alleyway near Covent Garden. Was she meeting you? I saw you'd rung her mobile a few times.'

'Yes, we were going to a gig at Wembley.'

Jacint wipes his brow. 'She must have been taking a short cut.'

Placing the full coffee cup on the windowsill, I stand beside Jacint feeling helpless.

It's twenty minutes before Emmy's eyes flicker. *Is she dreaming?*

Francine squeezes her daughter's hand. 'Emmeline?'

'I'll call the nurse.' Jacint rushes from the room.

Seconds later, a nurse hurries in with Jacint, followed by a doctor.

Emmy frowns. *'Maman?'* She starts to retch.

'Easy,' says the nurse, grabbing a sick bowl from a side cabinet.

The doctor checks the monitor.

Emmy coughs a couple of times before opening her eyes. 'What… what happened?' She holds her head. 'Ow.'

'Try not to move.' The nurse takes Emmy's pulse.

The doctor shines a light into Emmy's eyes. 'Follow my finger. All right, good.' He drops the torch into his jacket pocket. 'Perhaps I could have a word with the parents outside?'

Francine holds back.

'It's okay.' The nurse touches Francine's arm. 'Doctor just wants a quick word.'

'I'll stay with Emmy,' I say.

Francine follows the doctor and Jacint into the corridor, while the nurse straightens Emmy's sheets.

Emmy blinks. 'Sorry about the gig.'

'It doesn't matter. As long as you're okay. What happened?'

She winces. 'I don't know. One minute I was on my way to meet you. The next I'm waking up to the three of you around me and attached to that thing.' She gestures to the monitor.

'I feel really bad. If only I'd known…'

'Don't feel bad. It's not your fault.'

Jacint returns. *'Nos has dado un buen susto, cariño.* Do you know who attacked you?'

Emmy shakes her head.

He strokes Emmy's forehead. 'I've told the police they can't interview you until tomorrow. Now try to sleep.'

'Are they keeping me in?' Emmy asks her father.

'Just for the night, *cariño*. They need to make sure you're not concussed.' He picks up his raincoat. 'Ilona, can I offer you a lift home? Emmy needs to rest.'

'No, you're okay thanks, Jacint. I'll get the train.' I kiss my friend on the forehead before leaving her room and making my way downstairs and out of the hospital. I ring Jamie as I walk back towards the tube. 'Jamie, hi.'

'Hello you. I thought you were out with Emmy tonight?'

'She's been attacked. She's okay, but has to stay in hospital overnight.'

'Are you okay?'

'Yes. It happened before we met up.'

'That's not what I meant. Where are you now?'

'Catching a train back to Sevenoaks.'

'I'll meet you at the station.'

'No. Maya's home. I'll grab a cab.'

Lucas opens his office door. He looks me up and down. 'Come in. You look as if you need a coffee.' He punches buttons on the new espresso machine. It emits a cacophony of whirs and hisses.

I slump down on the designer couch. 'My flatmate was attacked.'

Lucas sets two tiny cups on the table. 'What happened?'

'No one knows for sure. Probably a mugging gone wrong.'

He eases himself into his armchair. 'Is she all right?'

'She'll be okay. She's staying with her mum and dad so they can look after her.'

'And what about you? It must have shaken you up.'

I pick up one of the coffee cups and take a sip. 'I'm all right.'

Lucas strums his fingers on the arm of his chair. 'So, you have your flat to yourself again? Or has the boyfriend moved in?'

'No, my sister's back.'

He picks up his cup and takes a mouthful as he waits for me to continue.

I sigh. 'Maya's not in the best of places. She's had a few issues to deal with.'

'Such as?'

'Two-timing boyfriend and an abortion.'

'And, as usual, you take it all on?'

I frown. 'It's not Emmy's fault she got attacked, and it's not Maya's fault her boyfriend turned out to be married.'

'I'm not saying it is, but it's you we're here to focus on.'

I stare at my fingers before looking up defiantly. 'Okay, but I have another question for you. Do you know anything about the meaning of dreams?'

'Try me,' says Lucas, sitting forward.

'A couple of weeks ago, I had this weird dream that I woke in the night and went to the bathroom. When I looked in the mirror, I had no face.'

He grins. 'Ahh, the faceless person.'

'What does it mean?'

'I'm no expert, but I'd imagine it suggests your subconscious mind is searching for true identity.'

I snort. 'I know who I am.'

'Do any of us really know who we are inside? We all feel a little lost at times. It may be that you're struggling with something. Trying to understand someone's reactions towards you. Seeking resolution.'

'Huh,' I say.

He strums his fingers again. 'I wonder if we might try something?'

'What?'

'I'd like you to create a spider diagram showing all the demands everyone places on you – Emmy, Maya, work, your boyfriend. Bring it along next time and we'll try to organise it into some sort of priority.'

———

'Maya?' I close the front door. *She must have gone out.* My stomach rumbles. I go to the kitchen and stick a jacket potato in the oven. I open the fridge, take out lettuce and tomatoes, and quickly prepare a salad to go with it. The potato will be a while, so I find a notepad and tear out a page. I write *Ilona* in the middle and draw a circle around it, before adding lines and other names – *Maya, Emmy, Jacint, Jamie, Rowena…* I keep drawing more lines and adding more names. When I've run out of names I go back and add words. Beside Maya's name I write, *Beautiful but high maintenance.* Alongside Emmy's, *Confident, life and soul.* My pen hovers over my name. *Ugly.*

'That's not true,' I say out loud. 'I have a boyfriend.'

For how long? When he discovers what you're really like he'll be off, just like the others.

'Jamie loves me.'

Ah, but he hasn't met Maya yet. Once he meets Maya, it's game over.

The timer beeps. I screw up the paper and toss it in the pedal bin before pouring myself a large glass of wine.

———

'Sit down,' says Maya as I wander into the kitchen. She sets a cafetière on the table.

I take a seat and she pushes a plate of toast my way, along with butter and a jar of marmite.

'What's all this?' I ask.

'You're always looking after me. I decided it's time for me to return the favour.' She sits beside me and spreads peanut butter on her toast before pouring us both a coffee. 'So.' She slides a sheet of paper towards me. 'Want to tell me about this?' She's flattened it out, but it still has creases from being screwed up.

I push the paper away. 'I threw that in the bin.'

'I know. It was me who retrieved it. What's this about?'

'Something my therapist asked me to do.'

'I didn't know you were seeing a therapist.'

I shrug. 'Lately I've needed someone to talk to.'

'Er, hello.' Maya waves her hand in front of my face. 'I'm right here.'

'I know, but it's not the same.'

'So, you still see Helen?'

'No, a new guy.'

'A man. Interesting. And what's he going to make of this?' She pushes the sheet of paper my way again.

I turn it around and read the words scrawled across the page: *Ilona – disaster at relationships, no one likes you, ugly, ugly, ugly…* 'I didn't write that.'

Maya stares at me. 'Course you didn't.'

I glance again at the untidy block lettering. I might have thought it, but I didn't write it.

CHAPTER THIRTY-FIVE

After unlocking the shop door, I attempt to hustle Maya through. Jacint isn't in today, but I'm still uneasy about taking her into work.

Maya's busy checking out the other shopfronts in the parade and comparing them to *The Emporium.* 'Yours isn't very festive, is it?'

'You're right, we're missing the season.' I hang up our coats, turn on the till and fill the coffee maker.

Maya stares vacantly at the circular *William IV* table in the window.

I touch her arm. 'Come on, you're the artistic one.'

'Shhh, I'm trying to visualise.'

'Well, let's stick with the same era.' I go through to the back of the store and return with a box. Setting it down on one of the dining chairs, I lift out a bubble-wrapped parcel and unwrap it with care. A beautiful wine glass catches the light, reflecting rainbow colours onto the polished walnut tabletop. 'Hand blown and facet cut,' I tell Maya.

'Fab,' she answers,' but what about knives and forks?'

'Ah.' I let myself into Jacint's office to fetch a wooden

cutlery case. 'Can't do better than silver *Fiddle Thread & Shell*.'

We clear the old window display away and Maya lays three place settings while I locate some matching dining room chairs.

'It's missing something…' Maya wanders about the store until she spots a pair of *Queen Anne* candlesticks. 'How about these?'

'Great, but I don't have any candles.'

Maya grabs her Afghan coat. 'Leave it to me.' Thirty minutes later, she returns with a pack of red candles and two chicken sandwiches from the deli. 'My treat,' she announces, her eyes sparkling.

While she adds finishing touches to the table, I make coffee. We sit at the desk to eat lunch.

'Have you heard how Emmy is?' asks Maya.

I sip my drink. 'She's doing okay.'

'Is she coming back to the flat?'

'No, she's staying with her parents for a while. I don't think Francine will let her out of her sight.'

'So, it's okay if I stay longer?'

'Of course.' The shop door chimes. I jump away from our impromptu picnic. 'Can I help you?' I ask the man who's looking nervously about the store.

'There was a necklace,' he says. 'My fiancée spotted it in the window yesterday. Sort of yellowy brown colour?'

I lift a jewellery box from under the counter. 'This one?'

He moves closer.

'Art Deco.' I lift the necklace, holding it against my neck so he can see where it sits. 'Two drop citrines, honey orange, set in a diamond shaped drop. The chain's nine carat.'

He smiles. 'That's the one. Is it genuine?'

'Of course. We deal frequently with the owner, so I can

vouch for its provenance. A tiny bit of wear and tear…' I turn the pendant over and point out a small chip. 'Age-related. It's reflected in the price, £120.'

'Mmm.' He takes the necklace from me, weighs it in his hands and checks the clasp.

'I could do it for a hundred,' I say. 'Gift wrapped.'

'Perfect.' He pulls a credit card from his wallet.

While I'm wrapping the gift, I sense Maya watching me.

'Happy Christmas,' the man calls as he leaves the store.

'What?' I ask Maya.

'Impressive,' she says.

I clear away the sandwich wrappers and sit down at reception. 'Jacint's asked me to update the client list.' I open a desk drawer and take out the customer receipts book. 'He wants to digitalise things in the New Year.'

Maya sighs. She wanders across to a box of military hats and tries them on. 'What do you think?' She moves her head from side to side.

'The Officer's tricorn suits you best.'

She picks up a WW2 medal. 'I reckon I deserve one of these for putting up with the boredom in this place. How do you stand it? Don't you get stir crazy?'

'No. I like it when it's quiet.'

'But we've not had a customer except that man who bought the Art Deco necklace.'

'It goes like that. It's not Claire's Accessories.' I look up. 'I have other stuff, like this paperwork for example, and research. By the way, did I tell you Jacint's letting me build my own collection?'

Maya spins around from the cheval mirror. 'No?'

'He's investing in me. I only buy small stuff, of course. Have to start at the bottom.'

'That's great.' She unpins the medal ribbon from her blouse.

'Next year I'll be a millionaire, eh?' I laugh.

Maya returns the hats to the box. 'Is it here?'

'Is what here?'

'Your collection.'

Damn, I shouldn't have said anything. 'Yes.'

'Where?'

'In the basement, but I can't leave the shop.'

'We didn't take a proper lunch break and it's dead in here.' Maya runs to the door, slides the bolt and turns the sign to *Sorry, we're closed*. 'There, sorted.' She heads for the basement stairs. 'Where's the light?'

'Hang on.' I press the switch, hearing the familiar click of the timer.

Maya charges down the steps. 'In here?' She's already at the bottom, pushing open the door to the lower storeroom.

'Yes.' I turn on the strip lights, which flicker a couple of times before lighting up the space.

'Crikey.' Maya stares in awe at the racks of shelving. 'Even your basement's tidy. I've never seen such organised storage.'

'Jacint had it fitted out years ago. As stock grows, he adds extra shelving from *B&Q.*'

'I bet you know exactly where everything is.'

I turn around to a shelf unit. 'Yes, it's the small leather trunk at the top.'

Maya stretches to reach it, but can't quite make it.

'Wait.' I fetch the little two-step stool. 'Here.'

She hops on the steps, grabs the trunk and pulls it towards her.

I reach up and help her. 'Let's carry it over to the worktop.'

We set the trunk down on the surface used to inspect and package bigger items. Unbuckling the straps, I flip the lid.

Maya pulls out a wad of bubble wrap, tossing it to the floor. She hesitates before diving in. The first item she unwraps is a Victorian porcelain doll with chestnut wavy hair and eyes the brightest of blue.

'Sweet.' Maya gives the doll a cursory glance and lays her down. She moves on to a *Steiff* teddy bear, ripping tissue paper from it like an excited child.

'He's a little worn, but his ear button is intact,' I say. 'Don't you love his red velvet collar?'

Maya prods him. 'Reminds me of Brown Bear. Look, same expression.'

'Hmm.' I bet teddy bears all look the same to Maya. I swallow, unable to predict her reaction as she gets to the last item.

Maya lifts the tissue. The doll's sleeping face peeks out from her bonnet. Maya gasps. 'Is this…?'

'Yep. The doll that used to scare us.'

'How come you've got her?'

'She was in that box of personal effects stored with the solicitor.'

Maya reaches for the knob on the doll's head and turns it slowly, revealing the crying face, followed by the manic grin. 'Still scares the daylights out of me. Ugly thing.'

Ugly thing, ugly thing…

I twist the knob and restore the doll's sleeping face.

'Is she valuable?' asks Maya.

'Not really. I found out she's made by *Carl Bergner*. She's rare, but not in great condition. See how faded her clothes are? Her limbs are damaged too, but her head still turns, so she'd probably fetch a few hundred if the right people were bidding.'

'A few hundred?' Maya's eyes shine. 'That would cover flights to Europe, plus a hotel for a few nights.'

I take the doll from Maya and rewrap her in tissue.

'We could do with a week in the sun,' says Maya.

'I'm not looking to sell.'

'I thought that was the whole point. Buy antiques and sell them to make profit.'

'It is, but not her. This is my personal collection. She may only be worth a few hundred, but to me she's priceless.'

'By rights…' Maya reaches forward to place a possessive hand on the doll. 'She's ours, not yours.'

My heart thumps. 'You never wanted her.'

'I could do with the cash. Tell you what, slip me a couple of hundred and I'll say no more.'

I place the toys back in the trunk, close the lid and carry it back to the shelf. When I step onto the stool, I momentarily lose my balance.

'Careful.' Maya reaches out to steady me as I slide the trunk back on the shelf.

'Thanks.' After returning the steps I move towards the door. 'I need to open up again. Do you want another coffee?'

She follows me upstairs. 'Actually, I've had enough of being cooped up. I think I'll pop out for a while.'

———

Maya opens the passenger window of the Citroën. 'So, where are we going?'

'I told you,' I say. 'A little trip.'

'Not sure I'm good with surprises.' She rubs her belly. 'I'm a bit peckish.'

'You've got to be kidding! After that massive all-day breakfast?' We'd stopped at a *Little Chef* on the way.

She fiddles with the dials on the dashboard. 'Why haven't we done this before?'

'Because I don't have my own car. Close that window. It's bloody freezing.'

'You should borrow Jacint's more often.'

I check my mirror as I pull out onto the M20. 'Jacint's asked me to check out some furniture. It's the other side of Canterbury. He said expenses would run to a B & B.'

'Cool.'

The *Art Deco Epstein* dining suite is lovely, but enormous. Where on earth would we store it? There's no room at *The Emporium*. I write down the measurements in my notebook and take a couple of shots with my camera. If Jacint's client wants to go ahead, he'll have to commit. I head back to the car, where Maya's waiting.

'Sorry I've been so long.' I start up the engine. 'Now we can relax.' The afternoon sun blinds me and I adjust the sun visor. 'Sunset already.'

Maya shivers and cranks up the heating.

The road to Whitstable is busy, but twenty minutes later I pull into the hotel car park.

Maya glances up at the ivy-covered façade. 'Afternoon tea?'

'No, this is where we're staying.'

'Neat.' She unbuckles her seatbelt and climbs out.

I grab our overnight bag and follow her into the foyer. 'Ilona Parrish,' I tell the young man at the reception desk. 'I've booked a room.'

He taps into the computer. 'Twin with ensuite. That's £80.

Would you like to pay now, or I can swipe your card and you can settle when you leave?'

'Swipe the card,' whispers Maya. 'Then we can add drinks.'

I hand the guy my card.

He runs it through the machine. 'Okay. Room 14. It's on the first floor. Do you need help with luggage?'

'No.' I hold up the bag. 'Travelling light.'

I glance around the room. The twin beds have matching blue throws. I lay down on mine. 'Not bad. I could go to sleep here right now.'

Maya grabs a towel from the pile at the end of her bed. 'I'm gonna take a shower before we hit the bar.'

I close my eyes. The unpacking can wait. Moments later, I'm giggling as Maya belts out the lyrics from The Prodigy's *Firestarter*.

Emerging from the bathroom, hair dripping wet, she tweaks my toe. 'Come on, lazy bones.' She saunters over to the dressing table rubbing her hair dry. 'Any sign of a hair dryer?'

'Try the top drawer.'

She pulls it open. 'Oh yeah.'

The dryer disturbs my peace. I get up and head into the bathroom. Maya's discarded clothes sit in a pool of water. She can't have closed the shower door properly, because the bathmat is sodden. Plastic bottles lay in the base of the shower. Shampoo and body wash trickles down the drain. I lean over and wipe the steamed-up mirror, revealing my reflection.

Be careful, Ilona.

I can't be bothered to shower. I refresh my makeup and tidy my hair.

I stroll out of the bathroom. Maya's put on the top I intended wearing. 'Hope you don't mind?' she says.

I bite my tongue as I rummage through the bag for my chiffon scarf. I arrange it around my neck.

We slam the door shut and head downstairs.

In the bar area, two other couples are already seated at small tables. The waiter approaches us. 'I'm afraid the restaurant's undergoing refurbishment.'

I let out a slow breath. 'I rang to check there'd be food available.'

'It was supposed to be finished in time for Christmas,' he explains, 'but I can accommodate you in here?'

'That's fine,' I say.

We follow him over to a table in front of the inglenook and pick up the bar snacks menu.

'Why don't we have tapas?' says Maya. 'Then we can share.'

'Good idea.'

'Are you ready to order?' asks the waiter.

'Yes, *chorizo a la sidra, gambas al ajillo* and *alitas de pollo*. And a bottle of house red. Thank you.'

'So, what's this about really?' Maya asks.

'It was you who said we could do with a break.'

'I meant somewhere warm.' Despite the log fire, she shivers.

The waiter returns with our wine.

I pour. 'I thought it would be nice to spend time together.'

Maya raises her glass. 'It's a start I suppose.'

I sleep badly. The chocolate fudge cake we shared for dessert gave me indigestion. Or perhaps it was the *Baileys*? I check my phone and find a missed message from Jamie. *When are you getting back?*

Maya's still asleep, so I take advantage of the empty bathroom with a dry floor. I manage to salvage a little shampoo from the spilled bottle.

By the time I return to the bedroom, Maya's up. 'Mind if I borrow your toothbrush?'

'If you must.' I'll buy a new one when we get home.

Neither of us fancy a cooked breakfast, so we make do with coffee and croissants. I head to reception to settle the bill while Maya thumbs through tourist leaflets on the rack.

'That'll be £147.50,' says the girl. 'I hope you enjoyed your stay.'

'Thank you.' I hand over my card.

CHAPTER THIRTY-SIX

I pick up the letter from the mat. I don't recognise the hand-writing. I tear it open.

Dear Ilona,
I've wanted to write for so long, but they said I
shouldn't. They told me it would be too disruptive for
you. Better to have a clean break. And Jack thought it
wasn't a good idea. He was always a little concerned
about you.
Anyway, Jack and I broke up last year and I moved
down to the West Country with my son, Michael. He's
all I need in my life right now. He's fifteen, can you
believe it? I look at him sometimes and remember how
much you wanted a brother...
Please forgive me, Ilona, for not being there for you.
I think about you often.
Love Fiona.

She's sorry, but not sorry enough to have stayed in touch. I cast the letter aside.

A few days later, I search for it everywhere. I'm sure I left it by the spice jars where I keep all the opened post. I root through every cupboard and every kitchen drawer, but it's nowhere to be found. Later, as I'm throwing out vegetable peelings, I discover the letter torn to bits in the bin.

I glare at Maya. 'Did you do this?'

Maya stares down into the rubbish bin. 'No, what is it?'

'A letter from Fiona.'

'Fiona? Fiona and Jack?'

'Yes.' I reach in and retrieve the shreds of paper.

'Why's she writing to us?'

'She's not writing to us. She's writing to me.'

'Huh.'

I lay the shreds of paper on the table and attempt to piece them together. 'She says she's sorry for not being there for me.'

'Bit late now.'

I rummage frantically among the peelings and old tea bags. 'It's not all here.'

'You read it though, didn't you?'

'Yes, but I wanted to write back. I need the address.'

'Why do you want to write back?'

'You'll never understand.' I sigh. 'Fiona could have been our mum.'

'You only get one mum.'

'It's not here.' I kick the pedal bin in frustration.

Maya peers at the bits of the letter. '*Moved down to the West Country…* That's Cornwall isn't it?'

'Or Devon. I wish I could remember where.'

'Perhaps she left a forwarding address with the neighbours?'

'Two return tickets for Wateringbury.' I pass my card to the man in the ticket office.

The whole journey takes less than thirty minutes. 'I hadn't realised it was so easy,' I say to Maya, as we walk from the station to Fiona and Jack's cottage. We pass the primary school on the way.

Maya points. 'St Mark's.'

'Yeah.' I stop to read the sign. *School roll 120 pupils.* 'I wonder what our lives would have been like if we'd stayed with Fiona and Jack?'

'We'd have a brother or sister for starters,' says Maya.

'A brother. Fiona told me his name is Michael.'

'A brother. Wow, wonder what that would have been like.'

Although it's winter and the garden sparse, a festive wreath adorns the door adding colour.

'What's the plan?' asks Maya.

'What you said. Ask if Fiona left a forwarding address.' I march up the path and tap the brass knocker. There's no reply.

'Perhaps they're away?' says Maya.

I lean across the flower border to peer in through the sitting room window. 'No sign of anyone.'

'Do you think Old Mr Simpson still lives next door?' Maya asks.

'I doubt it. Probably died years ago.'

We wander down the lane, craning our necks to see over the fence into Old Mr Simpson's allotment. Maya nudges me. 'Look.'

Could it be? 'Mr Simpson?' I call to the figure crouching down among the Brussels sprouts.

Leaning against a spade, he hauls himself slowly from the ground before staggering towards the fence.

'It's us,' I say, 'Ilona and Maya. We used to live next door.'

He pulls the cap from his head. 'I remember you right enough. Prayed for you, lass. Prayed for the both of yer.'

'Jack and Fiona moved away?'

'Aye. They split up. It's a pity, but can't say as I were surprised.'

'Do you know where Fiona lives now? I don't suppose she left a forwarding address?'

'Not wi' me.' He shifts his gaze to Maya. 'Turn ye not unto them that have familiar spirits,' he murmurs. 'We do best not to meddle in things we can't explain.' He replaces his cap and addresses me again. 'You take care now, lass.'

Maya laughs as Old Mr Simpson stumbles back across his vegetable patch. 'Always was a funny old boy. Let's go and see if the park's still there.'

I lean against the gate, staring at the rusty swings in the deserted playground. 'It's so small.'

'Look at the football pitch.' Maya points. 'Just a scrappy patch of worn grass.'

'Yeah. It's all changed. Come on. Let's go.'

We make our way back up the lane. 'Remember that cat?' asks Maya. 'What was his name?'

'Boris.'

'I wonder what happened to him.'

I turn to stare. 'You know what happened.'

CHAPTER THIRTY-SEVEN

It's unusual for Jamie and I to go out midweek. I wonder if he picked the wine bar as neutral territory?

He drones on and on about a theatre trip he's planning for his students. '…to the *New Globe Theatre*… like experiencing plays in Shakespeare's own time…'

I zone out to *Fairytale of New York* playing in the background.

'…a really authentic experience. What do you think?'

'Sorry.' I blink. 'What did you say?'

Jamie smiles. 'I'm boring you.'

'No, you're not.'

'You're still thinking about Fiona.'

'I wish I could remember her address.' I sigh.

'Perhaps she'll write again?' He takes a swig of Bud.

'Maybe.' I sip my glass of pinot grigio. 'I always wanted a brother. Now I'll never get to meet him.'

'Talking about family, Mum asked about Christmas again.'

'Mmm?' I discreetly check my watch.

'Christmas lunch, remember? Mum asked if we'd go to hers.'

'I don't know, it depends…'

'On Maya,' he finishes. 'Yes, I thought it might.'

'You know I worry about her.' I glance at my watch again. 'I shouldn't have left her on her own.'

'You said she's been better lately.'

'She has. It's just… she can be a bit unpredictable.'

'You two are so different.'

'What are you saying?'

Jamie holds up his hands defensively. 'Nothing, sorry. Come on, drink up and I'll get another round in.'

'Look, would you mind if we headed back? I've got this funny feeling…'

Jamie drains his bottle. 'Okay.'

We arrive home to find the flat in darkness.

'That's odd. Maya didn't say she was going out.' I turn on small lamps and flick the switch on the kettle. 'I'm just going to check.' As I ease open the door to Courtney's old room, I hear Maya breathing heavily. Closing the door softly, I turn back to Jamie who's already made himself comfortable on the sofa. 'We'll have to be quiet,' I whisper. 'She's asleep.'

Jamie's bouncing my latest acquisition on his lap. 'Who's this little fellow?'

'A Sun Bear by *Gerald Kirby*.' I take the teddy from Jamie, stroke the plush yellow fur and give the bear's black snout an affectionate tap. 'I haven't given him a name yet.'

Jamie pouts. 'He gets more attention than me.'

'Seriously?'

Jamie pulls me down beside him. 'Ilona, talk to me.'

'What about?'

He runs a finger down my arm, tracing the freckles. 'Christmas for one. I need to give Mum an answer.'

'Then tell her I've promised to spend Christmas with Nigel and Rowena.'

'And what about us?'

I stare at my hands. 'I don't know.'

'Right.' He grabs his jacket and storms out of the flat.

I wince as the door slams. I'm surprised it didn't wake Maya. Opening her door again, I peer into the gloom. She's awfully still. As I move towards the bed, I stub my toe on something. I turn on the bedside lamp and spot an empty gin bottle lying on the carpet. 'Maya?' I say. 'Are you all right?'

She shoots upright, blinking. 'Turn off the light.'

'What's happened?' I ask as I switch off the light.

'Nothing,' – her words are slurred – 'bloody men…'

Lowering myself down on the bed, I notice Maya's fully clothed. 'I didn't know you were seeing anyone?'

'Not seeing anyone…'

'Come on then. Let's get you undressed.'

She allows me to pull off her jeans before lying back down in her t-shirt and knickers. She waggles a finger at me. 'Nate, he was the one…'

I place a blanket over her. 'I'll get you some water.'

She pushes the blanket away, tugging her t-shirt down from her left shoulder. 'Right here…' She giggles. 'Not even your name.'

I feel a sudden chill. 'How do you know about that?'

'Wasn't good enuff…' Her eyes roll before closing. Moments later she's snoring.

I fetch a glass of water and a bucket, and set them beside her bed. I leave the door ajar so I'll hear if she's sick. Wandering back to the living room, I pick up the bear and examine the stitching on his paws, the maker's label sewn into one pad. I've never mentioned Nate's tattoo to Maya. It wasn't something you could see, not unless he took his shirt off. He'd shown it to me one evening when we were playing a silly game of truth or dare. He told me the tattoo originally said Ally, the name of his ex. He'd regretted it almost immediately and had it covered with a Celtic cross, but it remained a bodge-up. How did Maya know about it? I curl up on the sofa, close my eyes and finger the bear's label.

The next morning, I tackle Maya. 'Last night you were going on about Nate.'

She teeters across the kitchen and lowers herself onto a chair. 'Nate?'

I run the tap, fill a glass of water and place it on the table in front of her, feeling like I'm conducting an interrogation. 'Nate, my ex. Unless there's another Nate with a tattoo on his shoulder like my Nate.'

'Oh, he's your Nate again now?'

'No, not anymore, but how come you know about his tattoo?'

Maya groans.

'What?' I ask.

She looks at me with pleading eyes.

My heart sinks. 'What did you do?'

'Oh God. It wasn't planned.' She lets her head drop onto her arms.

'What wasn't?'

'He rang.'

'When?'

'Ages ago, I don't know...' She sits up, rubbing her eyes.

'I was staying over and the phone rang. I answered and it was Nate, asking you to meet him for a picnic in the park. It sounded kind of fun and…' She took a deep breath. 'Anyway, I needed to check him out to see if he was good enough for my sister.'

'And?'

'And that's it. I met him.'

'You pretended to be me?'

'Come on. You know how much fun that used to be.'

'Not for me.'

Maya sighs. 'What can I say?'

'So, you met him?'

'Yeah.'

'And?'

'And nothing. He seemed okay. Kinda fit, actually.'

'And his tattoo?'

'I guess we got talking…'

'In the park?'

'Yes, in the park. So, shoot me.'

Nate and Maya sharing a picnic in the park. I couldn't imagine Nate stripping his shirt off in broad daylight. But he wasn't with me, he was with Maya. I feel sick. 'Did you see him again?'

'No.' She glares at me. 'What do you take me for?'

'That time he stood me up. Did you have anything to do with that?'

'No, course not.' She sips her water. 'You know, I feel a bit better. I might shower and take a walk to the shops.'

'You promise nothing else happened?'

'Oh, grow up, Ilona. He dumped you, that's all. Get over it.'

CHAPTER THIRTY-EIGHT

After locking the back door, I work my way through *The Emporium,* turning off lights and checking the display cabinets are secure. I'm pleased Jacint trusts me to lock up as he and Francine are having a chat with Emmy about her future plans. I wonder how it's going. Halfway across the shop floor a crash comes from the basement.

I stop dead. Creeping to the top of the stairs, I peer down. A flicker of light. Is someone down there with a torch?

My heart thumps. I grab a stout walking cane from the jardinière, switch on the security light and tiptoe down the steps. As I round the corner, I spot her. 'What are you doing?' I yell.

Maya jumps. 'Keep your hair on.' She steps away from my trunk. 'It's not like I'm stealing or anything.'

'Then what are you doing?'

'Look, I need money. I gave you a chance. Told you if you gave me my share, we'd call it quits, but you wouldn't play ball. This doll is as much mine as yours.'

'And the *Steiff?*' I recognise the shape of the bundle under her arm.

'Oh God. How many teddy bears do you have? Didn't you buy another the other day?'

'Not a *Steiff.*'

'Don't make such a fuss. You'll find another.'

Call the police, Ilona. Call Jacint.

The walking cane feels heavy in my hand. 'Put them down.'

Tell them you had an intruder, you were protecting Jacint's property.

Maya steps towards me. Bubble wrap strewn across the floor pops like tiny firecrackers. 'No.'

Take her out, Ilona. She's a burglar. You've every right to protect the stock.

My hand tightens around the cane. 'I won't tell you again.'

'Ooh, should I be scared?'

I imagine myself lifting the cane, swinging it like a cheer-leader's baton, striking her silly head.

Maya stands there, smirking. 'Thought not.' She pushes past me and runs upstairs.

I don't recognise the caller number on my phone. 'Hello?'

'Ilona?'

'Courtney?'

'How are you?'

'I'm okay. How's the job going?'

'It's okay.' She takes a deep breath. 'Look, Ilona, I need to talk with you. Can you meet me for coffee?'

'Are you somewhere local then?'

'Yes, visiting friends. How about that organic café near *The Emporium?* Eleven-ish?'

'Okay.'

Courtney's sitting in the window seat. As I walk into the café, she stands as if to hug me. I hold back and we air kiss instead. I order a cappuccino before sitting down.

'How are you?' she asks again.

'I'm good. Where have you been? I haven't heard from you in months.'

'I know, I'm sorry.' She twists and untwists the wrapper from her sweetener. 'I should have got in touch before, but it was difficult.'

'Why?'

She stares at me. 'Maya.'

The waitress brings my drink. 'Thank you.' I turn my attention back to Courtney. 'Yes, she told me about you and Nate.'

'Me and Nate?'

'Anyway, it doesn't matter now.' I stir my coffee. 'I'm with someone new.'

'And Maya? Is she still around?'

'Off and on.' I sip my drink.

'I need to tell you something.' She exhales. 'I'm not sure Maya has your best interests at heart.'

'Of course she does. She's my sister. We always look out for each other.' *But do we?*

'We had our work Christmas party at *The Donnington,'* Courtney continues. 'I bumped into Nate.'

'Well, that was nice for you both.' I glance around at the other customers. 'So, is that what you wanted to tell me?'

'Ilona, nothing ever happened between Nate and me. It was Maya who broke the two of you up.'

'Don't be ridiculous. Look, if you've come here to get back at Maya because she dobbed you in, forget it. Me and Maya are tight,' I lie. 'Closer than we've ever been.' I get up. 'Have a nice life.'

'Ilona.' Courtney grabs my wrist. 'Please, sit down and hear me out.'

I sit back down. 'Five minutes.'

She takes a deep breath. 'That weekend when you thought Nate stood you up…'

'Yes, you were with him.' I glare at her. 'I know. Maya told me.'

'It wasn't me. It was Maya.'

There's a flutter in my tummy. I'm light-headed. Perhaps I've had too much caffeine? I push my cup away. 'No. Maya said she caught you and Nate together. You were both away that weekend. He took you instead of me.'

'I was in Deal, visiting my dad. There was nothing going on between me and Nate. I told you, I bumped into him at *The Donnington* last week. We had a drink together and I challenged him about why you two broke up. He told me what happened. It must have been Maya.'

'What do you mean, it must have been Maya?'

'Maya pretending to be you. Nate said when he pulled up in the Morgan that night, you were standing outside. You just had a small bag, he'd told you to pack light. You were in a great mood. Top form.'

I tap my fingers on the table and glance at my watch.

'He drove to the cottage and you both went in to change. He'd booked a nearby pub for dinner. Over the meal you didn't say much, but after a few drinks you livened up again. Nate put your mood swings down to nerves. He wasn't planning for anything to happen but, back at the cottage, as soon as he closed the front door, you pretty much jumped him.'

'This is ridiculous.' I try to stand up again, but Courtney puts a hand on my arm.

'Nate said it was like you were someone else. You were all over him, calling the shots like you had loads of experience. He was uncomfortable talking about it, but I asked him straight out if you had sex…' Courtney squirms. 'He said yes, twice. He said you were gagging for it. Afterwards you went into the bathroom. When you came out you started acting crazy, accusing him of raping you, saying he got you drunk and…'

'That didn't happen. He's making this up.'

'Why would he do that?'

People are staring. I realise we're shouting.

Courtney lowers her voice. 'Nate said he was scared. You were all over the place. You told him you were getting a train home. He tried to reason with you, but when you insisted on leaving, he called a cab. He gave the driver a hundred quid and told him to take you wherever you wanted to go. Nate was sure you'd go straight to the police. He stayed at the cottage overnight, expecting the cops to knock on the door at any minute. Next morning, he drove back to Sevenoaks. He didn't hear from you again and wasn't going to risk rocking the boat by contacting you.'

I stare at her. 'Well, that's quite a story. Still, you've had plenty of time to come up with it.'

Courtney slides a slip of paper across the table. 'Ring Nate. Ask him if it's true.'

I snatch the paper and tear it up. 'Have a nice life, Courtney.' I get up and don't look back as I walk out of the door.

I march along the street, my heart thumping. My phone beeps and I pull it from my bag. *Ring him,* reads the text. Courtney's added Nate's phone number.

It's ridiculous. She's made the whole thing up. But why

would she do that? Nate's made it up then, to make himself look less of a heel. But that seems a bit extreme. And anyway, if Nate made it up, that means Courtney's telling the truth because she seems to believe him. But Maya told me she caught Nate and Courtney together? None of this makes sense.

———

Maya's in the kitchen cooking when I let myself in. She glances over her shoulder. 'You're home nice and early.'

I slip off my coat and hang it on the peg. 'What have you done with my collection?'

She carries on stirring something on the hob. 'I'm having a dealer take a look at them.'

I dump my bag on the sofa. 'You didn't need to take them to someone else. I could have given you the money if you're so desperate.'

'You've changed your tune.' A pan of water comes to the boil and Maya turns down the heat. 'Anyway, I'm only getting a valuation.' She adds spaghetti to the pan. 'Once we know what the doll's worth, we can decide what to do.'

I drum my fingertips on the worktop. 'I saw Courtney today.'

'Did you?' Maya pushes the spaghetti under the water. 'Thought she was living in Dover now?'

'Deal, but she's back visiting friends.'

'Lay the table if you like.'

'We had coffee together,' I say, taking knives and forks from the drawer.

Maya sets a bowl of salad on the table. 'How is she?'

'She's okay.' I fetch a bottle of wine from the fridge. 'She told me she bumped into Nate.'

'Nate?'

'The guy who stood me up that time. You remember, you met him for a picnic in the park.'

'I do know who Nate is.'

'You told me you caught Nate and Courtney together.'

Maya stirs the Bolognese sauce. 'Exactly. You were way too good for him.'

'Nate told Courtney this weird story about how I went with him to the Cotswolds.' I pour wine into two glasses. 'Apparently, I wasn't myself.'

'He probably took someone else. Courtney perhaps? I don't know what you ever saw in him. Jamie sounds much nicer.'

'Yeah.'

Once we've eaten, Maya disappears into her bedroom. After I've cleared away, I take out my mobile and call the number that Courtney had texted me. 'Hi, is this Nate?'

'Yes, who is this?'

'Ilona.'

'Ilona, fuck. Has Courtney spoken to you?'

'Yes. She told me what you said.' The line goes quiet and I wonder if he's hung up. 'Hello?'

'I'm still here. Are you better now?'

'I haven't been ill.'

'Ilona, you were out of your fucking mind that weekend. I kept expecting you to ring and apologise. You put me through hell. I thought the police would come to the school and arrest me, cart me off to a cell. Jesus, I could have lost my job, or worse…'

'It wasn't me,' I say.

Nate goes silent again.

'Could you meet me?' I ask. 'To talk about it?'

'No, I don't think so. Look, I'm glad you're better now, but I'm seeing someone. She's nice. Normal. I don't want to talk about what happened. I want to draw a line under the whole fucking episode.'

'Okay.'

'Bye, Ilona.'

When Jamie arrives the next evening, there's an awkward moment when I don't know what to say.

He kisses my cheek and breezes past, carrying a brown paper bag through to the kitchen. 'I've brought us a takeaway. Is Maya in? I got enough for all of us.'

'No.' I get two plates from the cupboard. 'She's out tonight.'

He peels the cardboard lids from the tinfoil trays and dishes up the rice. 'I'm glad you said yes.'

'I thought we should clear the air.' I set the poppadoms and chutney on the table.

Jamie takes two Buds from the fridge and uncaps them. 'Are you okay?'

I help myself to a portion of chicken madras. 'Yes, why?'

He swigs his beer. 'You don't seem yourself.'

My pulse quickens. 'In what way?'

'Nothing, it doesn't matter.' He spoons some of the curry onto his plate.

'But it does matter.'

'Let's eat.' He picks up his fork.

I lay mine down. 'Perhaps I am myself tonight. Perhaps this is me. Perhaps you don't know me at all.'

'Ilona, calm down.'

I jump up. 'I won't calm down. What are you saying? You don't like my mood swings? Perhaps you should fuck off then.'

'Ilona…'

'Get out.' I throw his jacket at him.

'I can't leave you in this state.'

'Get out!' I'm screaming now, shoving and pushing him towards the door.

'All right, all right. I'm going.'

I slam the door and lean against it.

CHAPTER THIRTY-NINE

The pavement below Lucas Trent's office is heaving with Christmas shoppers and the traffic's building up. I don't recall my journey here. That happens sometimes when I'm travelling. It's like I go on remote. I remember being at home and putting on my lipstick, picking up my handbag and keys. The next moment, I'm staring out of Lucas's window. Did I catch the bus, or was it a train?

'You seem unsettled.' In the window's reflection I spot Lucas behind me in the armchair.

I shrug.

'Are you cross about something?' Lucas steeples his fingers.

'I don't know what I'm doing here.'

'You asked for a session.'

'Well, I don't need it now.' I remain staring out of the window. Did I make this appointment? I must have, otherwise I wouldn't be here.

'Where were you?'

I turn around. 'When?'

'Just now. You seemed far away.'

'I don't know, a lapse of concentration.'

'Does that happen often?'

'What?'

'These lapses of concentration.'

'No more than anyone else, I suppose. We can't be present all the time, can we? I mean, I know they say, "Live in the now," but that gets exhausting, right?'

Lucas watches me.

I sigh. 'Do you ever feel you've missed whole sections of your life?'

'I don't think so. Do you?'

I shrug. I don't tell Lucas about the chunks of time I've missed. Weeks and months when I suddenly woke to find I'd missed half a term of maths lessons. I'd look through my exercise books and couldn't remember writing those equations and proofs, and yet I understood them.

'Is it scary?' Lucas asks, as if I've spoken aloud.

'Sometimes.' I move away from the window and sink down on the couch. 'Sometimes I feel like everyone's lying to me.'

'When you say everyone…'

I stare at him. 'I don't trust anybody.'

'Do you trust me, Ilona?'

I shrug. 'Kind of…'

'What about your boyfriend?'

You can't talk to Jamie, Ilona.

'I don't know.'

'And what about your friends?'

I examine my hands. 'I should never have trusted Courtney. Sometimes I'm not even sure about Emmy.'

'Where is she now?'

'In London, sharing a place with three other students.'

'And Maya?'

You can't trust anything Maya tells you.

His eyes search my face. 'Do you want to talk about Maya?'

'Not really.' I get up and slope back to the window.

'Is Maya someone you don't trust?'

'You see that seat down there, right beside the car park?' I point across the road. 'That's where I was last time.'

'You sat on that seat after your appointment?'

'No, last time. When I didn't come in.'

Lucas waits.

'Didn't you wonder where I was?'

He doesn't reply.

'I wondered if perhaps you wouldn't give me another appointment, seeing as I skipped the last one. It's a waste of your time, isn't it?' I look at him, daring him to have a go at me.

He continues to watch me.

'What?' I ask.

'You haven't missed an appointment, Ilona.'

'I have. Last time. I made an appointment and didn't come in.'

Lucas shakes his head. 'You mean last month?'

He's annoying me now. 'Yes.'

'When I met with Maya.'

'What?'

'The time Maya came instead of you.'

'How did Maya know I had an appointment? Oh, yes.' I smile. 'It was on the calendar in the kitchen. Well, at least it didn't get wasted.' But I'm angry with Maya for taking my place, even if I didn't want to come. 'So, have you seen Maya before?'

'Of course,' he answers. 'I'm available to both of you.'

I inspect my nails. 'I did wonder if you were meeting with her, too.'

Lucas nods.

'I guess you can't talk about it? Patient confidentiality and stuff…' What I really want to ask is whether he talks to Maya about me.

'I never reveal anything my client hasn't agreed for me to share.'

Maya waltzes into the living room in my best jeans. I don't remember buying that top, but it's probably mine too. She has hardly anything of her own. I grudgingly pour her a glass of wine.

'Thanks.' She sinks down on the sofa.

I lean against the kitchen worktop and say, 'You attended my therapy session with Lucas?'

'Well, you weren't going.' She sips her wine.

'How do you know? I might have done.'

'Ilona, I know everything. It was silly to waste it. Anyway, I wanted to check him out. I must say, he's a substantial improvement on Helen.'

I place the wine bottle and a plate of cheese and biscuits on the coffee table before taking a seat beside her. 'So, you've been having sessions with him?'

'Did he tell you that? He's not supposed to. Isn't it an abuse of client confidentiality?'

'He only admitted it because I asked. So, did you go as me or as you?'

'Don't you think Lucas would know the difference?' Maya laughs. 'He's not much of a psychotherapist if he doesn't.'

A thought occurs to me. 'Have you done it before? With Helen?'

'Don't you remember?'

Have I missed other appointments? It's all a blur. I visualise myself in Helen's office, but it's like I'm looking down from somewhere above. Was that real, or a dream?

Maya reaches for the bottle and tops up my glass. 'Here. You look as if you need it.' She finishes her wine and gets up. 'Well, I'd better be going.'

'Where are you off to?'

'Out.' She slams the door.

I stare at the sweating cheese and push the plate away. I've only had two bites of a sandwich and a mouthful of coffee since lunchtime. Picking up my wine, I wander through to the bathroom. I stand my glass on the back of the basin and stare in the mirror. I'm so ugly. Christ, whatever did Jamie see in me?

No idea, Ilona.

As I reach for my toothbrush, I knock over the glass. Red wine runs off the sink and pools on the floor tiles.

Clumsy too.

I bend down and pick up the larger pieces of glass. When I stand up again, the girl in the mirror is speaking.

Nice and sharp, she says.

I watch in fascination as the girl lifts a piece of jagged glass towards my face and presses it against my cheek. A droplet of blood breaks the skin.

That's it, she says. *Won't even hurt…*

'No!' I yell, dropping the glass into the basin. Shaking, I stumble into my bedroom, climb into bed and cover my head with the duvet.

Someone knocks at the door. It can't be Maya; she has a key. I reach for my mobile to check the time – quarter past two. There's a bottle of gin on the bedside table. How did that get there? It seems I've missed a few calls from Jamie. It's probably him at the door. Maybe if I keep quiet, he'll think I'm out. I turn off my phone and burrow back down under the duvet.

I awake to darkness with a vague recollection I was supposed to meet Jamie, but I can't remember where. He probably came round to see where I'd got to. How long have I been lying here? Too long. I sit up. My head throbs. That bottle. Who put it there?

I climb out of bed and stagger to the kitchen. I fill a glass with water and rifle through the cupboard for headache pills. None there. I glance at my reflection in the kitchen window. Look at the state of me. I can't go to the corner shop. Perhaps Maya has some pain killers?

Although I'm pretty sure she's not in, I knock before going into her room. What a fucking mess. No wonder I can't find any clothes, they're all in here. The bed and the floor are littered, and I can't tell what's clean and what's dirty. I make a half-hearted attempt to gather up a few tops before dropping them in a heap on the bed.

I open the drawer of the bedside cabinet and find a packet of prescription pills. I can't read the instructions, the font's too small. They must be what Maya was prescribed after the abortion. As long as they're for pain, they'll do. I'd happily put a shotgun to my head, the way it's aching.

I swallow two pills, then take the packet and a glass of water back to my room.

'Ilona, what have you done?'

Is that Maya? Her face is fuzzy. No, it's Emmy. Of course. She still has a key.

Another voice. 'I've called an ambulance.' Is that Jamie?

'Thank God you rang me.' Emmy leans over me. 'Ilona. Open your eyes. Wake up.'

'We should get her walking.' Jamie yanks me from the bed.

Emmy takes my other arm, and they drag me backwards and forwards through the flat. My legs won't work and my head lolls to the side, but they don't give up. Soon I figure it's easier to go with them rather than fight. My limbs make stumbling attempts to co-operate.

Other voices now. 'What's her name?'

What is my name?

'Ilona,' someone answers.

Ilona? Is that me?

'Ilona, we're taking you to hospital.'

I open my eyes to a blur of green uniform. The light. My eyes hurt.

'Can you tell me what you've taken?' A woman waves a packet in front of me. 'These? Ilona, how many?'

I wrinkle my nose. What's that disgusting smell? Did someone puke?

'There's a bottle of gin, too,' says Emmy.

Jamie grimaces.

'I'm sorry,' I say. 'I'm sorry.' I close my eyes again.

———

I'm in a strange room. Everything's white – walls, bed, window. 'Too bright…' I blink a few times.

'Ilona, it's Emmy.'

'Where…? what…?'

'You're okay.' She squeezes my hand. 'You're in hospital.'

'Why can't I move?' I look at my arm and see it's connected by a tube to a clear bag. 'I need to…'

'You don't need to do anything. Just rest.'

'How's the patient?' Jamie places a punnet of grapes on my bedside table. 'They wouldn't let me bring flowers.'

'I'll leave you two alone.' Emmy pats my arm. 'Want a coffee, Jamie?'

'Yes please.' Jamie takes a seat on the plastic chair beside me and takes my hand.

I'm so ugly, I can't bear him to see me like this. 'I'm sorry.'

He kisses my forehead like I'm a little girl and lifts my chin with his finger. 'Don't,' he says.

We sit in silence until Emmy comes back. 'Bloody machine. Only has black. Is that okay?'

'Thanks.' Jamie takes a sip from the cup.

'Was the car park busy?'

'Not too bad…'

I close my eyes while they discuss ordinary things as though I'm not here. I hear the door open. A voice, a nurse? 'Perhaps you should let her rest?'

Two more kisses on my forehead and they're gone.

The door closes and once again the voices start inside my head.

That went well.

Can't do anything right.

One bloody mess…
'Shut up,' I murmur.
Try to get it right next time.
First opportunity you get.
May as well die…

CHAPTER FORTY

It's strange to be back in Lucas's office. Almost as if I'm not here at all. I pinch the skin on the back of my hand and give a half laugh.

'What?' Lucas asks.

'It's like I've been sent to see the headmaster.'

He gets up, walks around his desk and seats himself in the armchair. 'How are you feeling now?'

'Okay.'

'Do you still feel like you want to kill yourself?'

'No.' I swallow. 'That was an accident.'

Lucas looks at me, waiting.

'I had a bad head and got confused. Took too many tablets.'

'Where did you get the tablets?'

'They were Maya's.'

'Okay, where did Maya get the tablets?'

I run my palm over the arm of the couch.

He scans a sheet of paper. 'Your hospital notes say the pills were purchased on the internet.'

'That's possible. It's the sort of thing Maya would do.'

Lucas looks like he expects me to say more.

'I don't know why I'm here.' I sigh. 'I don't know why I ever come.'

He waits.

'It doesn't help. It's like I'm on remote control with someone else pushing the buttons.' I rub my forehead. 'I remember playing this computer game once, running through a strange world killing people. Courtney's friend explained the characters in the game were avatars. Sometimes my life feels like that. Like I'm an avatar and someone else is holding the controls.'

'Who is holding the controls?'

'I don't know.' Why do I feel like he's waiting for me to trip myself up?

Don't trust him.

I don't. I didn't trust Helen either. She never heard me. All she did was watch. I see a little girl wandering around a playroom. Not this room. Messier than this and filled with toys. There's a doll she likes. She carries it, feeds it, burps it before laying it down. Where did she learn to do that? Didn't she always want a little brother?

He's still watching. Why doesn't he speak?

Don't trust him.

'Who said that?' I glance from side to side. 'Who are you?'

'Who are you talking to, Ilona?' asks Lucas.

'No-one.' I won't tell him. I won't betray you. At first, they pretended to be my friends, helping me through lonely times. Then they became mean and sarcastic, telling me how ugly I am, draining my confidence. You're not like them. They came together, whispering things, making me feel bad, but your voice is clear. Distinct from my own and yet familiar. Khalu, is it you? It is you, isn't it? I can tell because you're on my side. Not like Maya. I can't trust Maya.

She'll hurt you.

'I know,' I say. 'It was Maya's fault. Everything is Maya's fault.'

'Where is Maya?' says Lucas.

'I don't know.'

'Does she do this often?'

'What?'

'Turn up, wreak havoc and disappear.'

I shake my head, but I know he's right.

'Have you ever tried to get Maya out of your life?'

———

I push my breakfast plate away. 'Have you moved back in?'

Emmy smiles. 'Only for a couple of weeks. Just to make sure you're okay.'

'Where's Maya?'

'Who knows? I haven't seen her.'

'Didn't she visit me in hospital?'

'Perhaps she doesn't know what happened? If you've got her number, I could give her a call?'

'No, it's okay.'

'Oh, I meant to say,' – she gets up, returning almost straight away with something behind her back – 'these arrived. She holds up a massive bouquet of flowers.

'They're gorgeous. Are they from Jamie?'

Emmy points at the card. *Get well soon. We love you, Ilona. Nigel and Rowena xx*

'That's nice,' I say. 'Nothing from Jamie?'

'He says to call him as soon as you're feeling up to it.'

Has he bumped into Maya at the hospital? 'Hi, Jamie,'

she'd say, giving him one of her looks. 'Wow, you're so alike,'
Jamie would say. 'Wanna grab a coffee?'

Emmy's speaking and I miss what she says. 'Sorry?'
I ask.

'I wondered if you fancied a coffee?'

'No thanks.'

Twenty minute is all Maya needs. 'Why am I with the
crazy one?' Jamie would think, 'when Maya has all the good
bits and more…'

I clutch my tummy. 'I need the loo.' I run into the bathroom and lock the door.

Stand up for yourself. Fight for him. Why do you always
let Maya get her way? You're a chicken. You're such a wimp.
Might as well be dead…

'Shut up!' I yell. 'Shut up.'

———————————

I draw back the curtains. Ice has created fern-like patterns on
the glass, but there's no sign of snow.

'You're looking chirpier,' says Emmy, as I emerge from
my room. She's been so good. Hasn't complained once about
the mess Maya made of her room. While I was in hospital,
Emmy went right through the flat tidying everything up.

'I think I might take a walk,' I say.

'Want me to come?' she asks.

'No, I've got some thinking to do.'

'Wrap up warmly then. It's icy out there.'

I layer up with coat, hat and scarf, before pulling on my
boots and heading out in the crisp December air. Making my
way to the local park, I complete two circuits of the frozen
pond.

Time to sort yourself out, girl. Time to fight back. What

was it Lucas said? Have you tried to get Maya out of your life?

I slide out of bed and pull on my dressing gown. It's strange to be back in my old bedroom at Rowena and Nigel's house.

I slope downstairs and find Rowena in the kitchen. 'Happy Christmas. How did Midnight Mass go?'

'Oh, it was beautiful.' Rowena clasps her hands together as if in prayer. 'And the choir were heavenly. I wish you could have joined us.'

'I'm pacing myself.'

Rowena gestures towards the filter coffee machine. 'There's coffee. Freshly made.'

'Thanks.' I fill a mug from the glass jug and perch on a kitchen stool. 'Anything I can do to help?'

She puts on a pair of oven gloves and lifts the turkey from the oven. 'No, you're okay,' she answers, setting the roasting tray on the worktop. 'Everything's in hand.'

'At least let me set the table.'

'Erm...' She bastes the turkey. 'All right, but get dressed first. Use the anniversary cutlery from the box in the dresser. Oh, and you'll need to bring the best linen tablecloth down from the airing cupboard.'

After lunch, we retire to the lounge. Nigel puffs on his after-dinner pipe. 'It's a shame you and Jamie couldn't spend Christmas together.'

I drain my wine glass. 'Jamie's mum expects him to spend Christmas with her and the family.'

'...six, seven, eight.' Rowena counts as she moves the

Scottie dog around the Monopoly board. 'Electric Company. Now, what does that mean?'

Nigel adjusts his glasses and scrutinises the card. 'I've got both so that's... ten times eight.' He rubs his hands together gleefully. 'Eighty pounds please.'

Rowena counts out notes. '...seventy, eighty. So, when are we going to meet Jamie?'

'Leave the girl alone, Rowena,' says Nigel. 'She'll introduce us when she's ready.'

Smiling gratefully, I haul myself up from the rug. 'Anyone want a top up?'

'I'll have another sherry, dear.' Rowena studies the board before pointing at the top hat. 'Did you land on my hotel, Nigel? Bother, I missed it.'

'Too late now, old girl. You need to keep your eye on the board.' Nigel winks at me. 'Didn't we have a tin of Quality Street somewhere?'

My New Year's Resolution for 2002 is to walk every day. While we walk, we plot and scheme.

It's funny how I always thought I was in control, when all along you controlled me. First, you echoed Lucas's words. *Is Maya a positive influence? Have you ever tried to get rid of her?* Lately, I've realised your power. Your voice has become your own. *You'll never manage to get rid of Maya on your own but together, you and I can do it.*

Don't listen to her, Ilona, the others say. *You're a nice person, and anyway, you're too weak.*

But your voice is determined. *I will help.* When you speak, strong and vengeful, you shut the others out. *Let's think about this rationally. Remember what Lucas inferred?*

Maya comes into your life when things are going well and disrupts everything.

'He's got a point,' I say.

Exactly. Now we need to work out what to do about her.

'She's gone for now.'

She'll be back. We need to entice her.

'I can't.'

With my help, you can.

CHAPTER FORTY-ONE

Emmy places a sheet of tissue paper over her blouse and folds it carefully. 'I'm worried about leaving you.'

'Don't be daft.' I pass her toiletries bag. 'I'll be fine.'

She tucks undies and socks around the edge of her suitcase. 'I'll only be gone a week. Honestly, I don't know why my cousin's chosen to get married in January.'

'You don't need to worry about me.' I perch on her bed. 'I've rung Jamie. He's coming to dinner tonight.'

Her eyes shine and for a moment I think she's going to cry. 'Ilona, that's great.' She pulls me into a hug.

'New year, fresh start…' I pull away. 'Don't forget hair straighteners.'

'Oh yes. I left them cooling down.' She winds the lead around the wands. 'Jamie's been dying for you to get in touch. I'm so pleased you're feeling up to it.'

The doorbell rings.

'That'll be *Papa*.' Emmy zips up her case and drags it off the bed. 'Hope this isn't too heavy.'

Jamie's punctual, arriving with flowers in one hand and a box of Ferrero Rocher in the other. He stands hesitantly on the doorstep. When I smile, he sets the flowers and chocolates down and takes me in his arms. 'You're back,' he murmurs into my hair.

Despite the doorstep hug, there's a distance, like we're on a first date. I keep things easy, sourcing both meal and wine from *Marks & Spencer*. Jamie is lavish with his compliments and works hard to make me smile.

We finish dessert. Jamie picks up the bowls and carries them to the sink. 'I'll wash up.'

'No, let's sit down.'

We move across to the sofa, leaving a space between us.

'So,' says Jamie. 'This Lucas guy. He's good?'

'Yes. He's helping me to see things more clearly.'

'I'm pleased, Ilona.'

I don't mention Maya, although I know we're both thinking about her. Jamie's probably comparing me with her. I wonder if I'm holding my own.

At the end of the evening, Jamie kisses me and it feels almost like it did before. He doesn't ask to stay. That's fine. We can take things slow.

After he's gone, I stack the dishes and squirt washing-up liquid into the sink. The tap's running when I hear the key in the door. I turn off the water and spin around. 'I've been expecting you.'

'I waited until Jamie left.'

'I thought you might.'

'You two are back together then?'

'We were never apart.'

Maya sticks a fork into the remains of the pavlova. 'How are you now?'

'Good.'

'You seem good. Kind of different.'

'The counselling sessions help.'

'With that Lucas guy?'

'Yes.'

'Perhaps I should see him again?'

I laugh.

'What?' she says.

'The idea of you taking therapy seriously...'

Maya grins. 'I know, right? But you know what? Since the abortion I've thought a few times that it might be good to speak with someone.'

'Someone other than me?'

She smiles. 'You were right. I'm not sure we're always the best people to speak to. So, where's Emmy?'

'Away with her parents. A family wedding in Barcelona.'

'Can I stay over then?'

'Of course.'

———

'Good of Jacint to let you have the car again,' says Maya.

'Yes.' I keep my eyes on the road. 'I told you, they're away in Spain.'

'So, where are we going?'

'I thought it would be nice to spend some time together.'

She fiddles with the car radio. 'No Jamie?'

'I cleared the decks.'

'But you didn't know I'd be here?' She twists the tuning dial.

'Yes, I did.' I reach across and slap her hand. 'Leave that, you'll break it.'

'I can't find anything decent... Ah.' *Someday* by The Strokes, blares from the speakers. Maya headbangs along to the music.

'I thought we'd take the scenic route.' As I turn off the A21, remnants of slush and ice line the edges of country lanes. The air is crisp and bright. Birds sing. Maya dangles her arm from the window and I resist telling her it's dangerous.

Twenty minutes later, we pass a sign to *Hever Castle*.

Maya sits forward. 'Is that where we went with Mum and Dad?'

'No, that was *Bodiam Castle*, but we can stop here if you want? There's plenty of time.'

I turn the Citroën around in the next driveway and head back fifty yards to park at the castle. We cross over and stroll down the lane.

'Is the castle open?' I ask the man in the kiosk.

'No, miss. Only the garden for winter walks.'

We wander through the formal gardens. Most of the bushes are bare, pruned to within an inch of their life. We giggle over naked statues in the Rose Garden before following a sign towards the lake. Apart from a man walking his dog, the trail is deserted. Maya runs ahead and stops at the water's edge. The wind whips hair across her face as she turns back to face me. 'This was a good idea.'

Arm in arm, we meander back towards the castle. The gift shop is closed, but Maya spots a kiosk selling coffee. 'Shall we get an ice cream?' she asks.

The woman serving gives us a funny look, but digs out two Magnums from the bottom of the freezer.

I point at a metal seat. 'Let's sit down.'

Maya holds her hair back with one hand as she nibbles away the chocolate outer layer. 'Have we got much further to go?'

'Not far.'

CHAPTER FORTY-TWO

It's another thirty minutes before we arrive. We sit in the car staring at the *For Sale* sign.

'Did you know it had closed down?' Maya asks.

'Nigel told me. He's a bit obsessed, spends half his life looking at properties for sale. Rowena says he must have been an estate agent in a former life. Anyway, he got the details. Said it's going for a song.'

'It would be weird if he bought it.'

I shake my head. 'He won't. It's only a hobby.'

We get out of the car. The building is surrounded by heavy wire fence panels set in concrete bases.

I spot another sign: *Danger. Keep Out. This site is managed by Wreck-Clamation of Rochester.* I rattle the fence. 'I wonder what's to become of it?'

'Flats, I expect. If they don't decide to pull it down and start again.' Maya roams around until she finds a panel out of line with the rest. Leaning against it, she creates a gap and steps over the concrete base to gain access.

I squeeze through after her.

She approaches the front door and presses the bell. We

hear it ringing inside. 'Sounds the same,' says Maya, 'although no-one's coming to answer it.'

'Come on,' I say. 'Let's have a look around the back.' This time I take the lead, scrambling over fallen bricks and tiles.

Maya follows. 'You're getting daring.'

I stare at the lean-to where Robbie kept his motorbike, remembering how Dwayne attacked me. It's as if I'm watching him attack someone else.

The back door is locked. Maya thumps and pushes, but it won't give.

'Here,' I call to Maya, spotting a broken window. Sliding my hand through the metal pane, I turn the catch and tug the window open. 'Give me a leg-up.' I tie my scarf so it doesn't catch on anything, and clamber in. Moments later I'm unbolting the back door. Maya stares at me.

We step into the kitchen. I glance around. It's empty apart from the old units and work tops thick with dust. Someone has ripped out all the white goods, leaving pipes and wires exposed. Years of grease cover the wall where the huge double oven once stood.

I scream as a mouse – or maybe a rat – scurries across the floor. With no skirting board, he has his pick of holes to squeeze through.

'Probably a whole city of rodents living behind these walls,' says Maya.

I shudder.

Go home.

Maya tugs me thorough the doorway into the old canteen. The chairs are still there, although the tables look worse for wear. An abandoned mop and bucket clutter the corner, as if someone making a half-hearted attempt to clean the floor was interrupted.

We cross the hallway to the games room. The snooker and pool tables are gone, the shelves are bare and the TV's been ripped from the wall, leaving twisted and bent brackets. I stoop to pick up a small red man from the game Halma. 'I wonder what happened to all the toys?'

'In a skip I should think,' says Maya. 'Although they probably sold the games tables. Worth a bit, even if they were old.'

The quiet room reeks of damp. We find a few original chairs. Perhaps they weren't worth moving.

'The old settee!' shrieks Maya.

'Minus one arm.' I rummage through a stack of magazines on the floor and pull out a copy of *OK!* '15th March 1999. When did you leave?'

'September 97.' She winces. 'They chucked me out when I hit sixteen.'

'You didn't go to Sycamore House?'

'No, got digs in London. Took an art course in Islington.'

'Do you know when they closed this place?'

'Probably a couple of years later.' Maya takes the magazine from me. 'Yeah, that's about right. Shall we check upstairs?'

We head up the main staircase. The carpet's missing, making our footsteps echo on the bare floorboards. I tiptoe.

Maya spins around. 'There's no one here. You don't need to be so timid.'

We peer into abandoned bedrooms. Most of the carpets have been taken up. They must have used newspapers for underlay, because the floors are littered with old newspaper pages.

A photo of Princess Diana in her wedding dress catches my eye. '1981, the year we were born.'

Those rooms that still have carpets bear marks where

furniture once stood, along with stains from spills and accidents. In the centre of one room is a hole the size of a dinner plate. It looks like a burn.

Maya sniffs. 'You can still smell it.'

'What?'

She laughs. 'Did you never do that? Light a canister of aerosol and watch it go off like a bomb.'

Up we go, until we reach our old room. The bunks are gone and the curtains different to when we were here – faded gold replacing faded green. I wander across to peer out of the window. A pigeon shelters near a chimney cowl.

Maya follows me over and yanks open the sash window. Rummaging in her bag, she pulls out a packet of cigarettes.

'I didn't know you still smoked,' I say.

'I don't, not really, but they're handy to offer to others when you're out and about. Come on, for old times' sake.' She grabs the sides of the window and hooks one leg over.

It's dangerous, Ilona.

'No,' I say.

'Chicken.' Maya climbs out. Extending her arms for balance, she moves slowly across the roof. When she reaches a dormer, she slides down, resting her back against the tiles.

I watch for a moment.

You're such a wimp.

I climb out to join her. It's blowy up here. I glance over the edge and feel myself wobble.

'Don't look down, idiot. Here.' Maya shuffles closer. She reaches out a hand and helps me over to where she's perched.

I lean against the roof and close my eyes, feeling sick.

Maya lights a cigarette, takes a couple of drags and holds it out to me.

I shake my head.

She grins. 'First time for everything?'

I take the cigarette, bring it to my lips and inhale. It makes me cough.

Maya laughs. 'An acquired taste. Try again.'

I do as she says. This time the smoke enters my blood stream, making me a bit woozy. It's not wholly unpleasant. I exhale. 'So, this is why people do this.'

The sun comes from behind a cloud and warms my face. I look down again, this time not directly, but towards the town. Shops and houses; buses and cars trundling along the main road to the bypass. 'What a great view.'

When we've shared the rest of the fag, Maya drops the stub, grinding it with her foot. Dozens of old fag ends are wedged in cracks between the tiles. I stare at Maya.

'Busted.' She grins. 'Wanna go back in?'

I nod.

'This is a real trip down memory lane,' she says, as we clamber back into the bedroom.

Once inside, I feel wobbly, like I'm trying to get my sea legs.

Aren't you supposed to be running this thing?

'Okay,' I say.

'Okay what?' says Maya.

'Okay, let's do something else.'

We retrace our steps along the corridor to the door marked, *Staff only.*

'Did you ever go through?' asks Maya.

'Not from here.' I push the door. It opens onto an identical corridor the other side. We amble along, opening doors and peering in. The rooms this side of the house are similar to those our side, although there are only three bedrooms, each with a single bed – spring base, no mattress. The other rooms, also strewn with old newspapers, are bare except for the odd item of furniture.

I walk into one of the larger rooms. Stepping over a broken chair, I stare out of the window.

You haven't thought this through. You won't be able to do it.

Maya comes to stand next to me. 'What's the matter? You're quiet.'

I shake my head.

Maya fumbles in her shoulder bag for her cigarettes. 'Only two left. Now I've corrupted you, we may as well finish them.' She lights both cigarettes and hands one to me.

I take a deep drag.

'Wow, steady,' she says, 'you'll be addicted. I don't want that on my conscience.'

I snigger. 'You mean you couldn't live with something on your conscience?'

'What?'

I drop my cigarette and grind it under my toe. 'You don't have anything bad on your conscience, do you Maya? Not Robbie? Not Boris? Not Khalu?'

'What on earth are you talking about?' says Maya.

'I'm talking about living with things on your conscience.' I reach down and pick up the top rail from the broken chair.

Maya's eyes widen. 'What are you doing?' There's a flicker of something in her eyes. Is it fear?

I swing the wood like it's a baseball bat.

'Stop it, Ilona!' she yells. 'What's all this about?'

'Oh – just – things – on – my – conscience.' I swing between each word. 'Things I live with every day of my life. But you wouldn't know about that, would you? I don't think you've even got a conscience.'

'I have,' says Maya.

'Tell me,' I say. 'How do you sleep at night? How do you go on breathing knowing you destroyed our lives?'

'I don't know what you're going on about.' Maya ducks and shoots past me, out into the corridor.

'Our whole lives, Maya.' I follow her. 'You messed up all our lives. Khalu, Mum, Dad…'

'I didn't do that.' Maya backs up against the *Staff only* door.

'You pushed Khalu.'

Her nostrils flare. 'I did not! You pushed Khalu off the climbing frame that day.'

My head spins. I hear Khalu taunting, feel the rush of air, see Khalu go flying and land on the ground below. Was it Maya or was it me?

Taking advantage of my hesitation, Maya grabs the end of the timber. I try to pull it back, but it's impossible with her hanging on. Our eyes lock. I twist the wood, yanking it hard. Maya's wrist makes a cracking sound and she lets go. Lifting the rail over my head, I bring it down with a thwack.

Maya falls to the floor. She doesn't move. A small pool of blood seeps out onto the floorboards. My eyes alight on the littered newspaper.

Destroy the evidence, Ilona.

Leaving Maya where she fell, I go back down the way we came in. I run around to the front of the building and, checking no one's about, approach the car. The can of petrol is hidden under a blanket in the boot. I lift it out, close the boot and head back inside.

Upstairs, I kneel beside Maya, feeling for a pulse. It's weak, but she's not dead. Her breathing is laboured. I guess she's stunned by the blow.

You don't have much time.

The strap of her shoulder bag is tangled about her from when she fell. I tug it free. Unscrewing the lid of the can, I pour the petrol over her. Grabbing pages of newspaper from the floor, I screw them into balls and tuck them around her body. I open her bag and retrieve the matches, before sliding the bag over my shoulder.

What are you doing, Ilona?

Just building a fire in the grate… I kneel down to strike a match. When I hold it against the makeshift firelighters, the edge of the paper curls and spits. There's a whoosh as it catches. I jump away as the petrol ignites. In moments, Maya's clothes are aflame. I watch, mesmerised.

I'd figured without the wallpaper, torn and hanging from the walls. Perhaps it's the wallpaper paste, but suddenly the whole corridor is ablaze. How will I get past this flaming, fiery fiend?

Stupid, stupid, girl. Go down the staff staircase.

I run along the corridor and across the landing. At the top of the stairwell, I come to an abrupt halt. The space below resembles newsreel footage of a war-torn country. All that remains of the House Manager's office are remnants of its plasterboard shell. There's a gaping hole where the staircase should be. I remember running my fingers down the carved spindles, across the beautiful *Fleur de Lys* carvings. The staircase was probably the only thing worth salvaging.

You have to jump, Ilona.

I look down. It must be a three-metre drop. Am I brave enough?

From below comes a sound like a gun shot, before something collapses. Falling masonry. The way may be blocked anyway.

I turn and scoot back across the landing. The corridor is obscured by thick smoke. Pulling my scarf from my neck, I tie it around my mouth and nose. My eyes sting, so I close them, feeling my way forward, the walls hot to my touch. My eyebrows are burning. I risk opening my eyes. The smoke ahead has turned from grey to amber, but I've found a door. My fingertips search blindly for the handle. 'Ow.' I snatch my hand back, as if burned on a hot pan. Bunching up the end of my scarf, I use it to protect my fingers. I open the door and skid into the room. Slamming the door closed, I pull the scarf from my face and take deep gasps of sweet, clean air.

I stumble across to the window. No balcony and no trellis. The drop down to the concrete drive is risky, but I have no choice. Reaching up, I attempt to slide open the sash windows, but they've been nailed shut. I kick the scattered newspapers in frustration. Then I remember Maya's bag. I slide it from my shoulder, drop to my knees and tip the contents out onto the floor. Hairbrush, nail file, pen... Nothing suitable for extracting three-inch nails.

Smoke is seeping under the door. No point blocking the gap, I'm not safe in here.

Retying my scarf, I cross to the door. I take a deep breath, turn the handle and yank it open.

As I step into the corridor, an acrid smell, like burning rubber, hits my throat and nostrils. I cough and retch. Behind Maya, the doorway to the staircase is ablaze. The heat is intense – sparks spit while the paint blisters and bubbles. It would be suicide to try to get through. Perhaps someone will have seen the flames? Called the fire brigade?

I drop to the floor, crawling on hands and knees. My breath is shallow. I'm disorientated. The smoke is so dense, I can't tell which direction I'm moving in.

Get up, Ilona.

I ball my fists and rub my streaming eyes.

Maya raises a hand, turning her soot-blackened face towards me. 'Ilona.'

'I'm here.' I drag myself closer and wrap my arms around her. 'I'm not going anywhere.'

The floorboards, hot against our cheeks, vibrate with a ferocious rushing.

My throat burns. What will Jamie think when we're found together?

The old house roars like a dragon expelling fiery red butterflies from its jaws.

My skin peels, my hair crackles…

'All we need is Khalu,' murmurs Maya.

Khalu spoons herself around us. 'I'm right here.'

'Three peas in a pod,' whispers Mum.

Ash falls like snowflakes, clothing us in a blanket of white.

How will anyone know who is who?

CHAPTER FORTY-THREE

Everyone stands to sing *Lord of All Hopefulness*, but Jamie mouths the words. As he sits back down, he looks around the church. He doesn't recognise anyone. Perhaps he shouldn't have come?

The light oak coffin is processed down the aisle, followed by the vicar. As the rest of the congregation move into the graveyard for the committal, Jamie purposely lags behind. He stands under a nearby rowan tree while everyone else surrounds the grave. It's as if he's looking down on himself – a solitary figure, chewing his bottom lip, clenching and unclenching his fists. The vicar is speaking, but Jamie is too far away to hear his words.

It's finally over. The funeral party make their way to waiting cars. Jamie hangs back. There's a rustle in the trees, a light touch on his arm, sweet breath on his cheek…

'Jamie.'

He spins around to see Emmy waving from beside the

open door of a black limousine. 'Come back for tea at Rowena's,' she calls.

'Oh no, I don't want to intrude. It's not like I'm family…'

'Ilona really cared about you, and I know Rowena will want to meet you.'

Reluctantly he walks across the grass to join her.

The middle row of seats is already occupied. 'Mama, Papa,' says Emmy, clambering in behind them. 'This is Jamie.'

Emmy's father nods politely. 'Jacint Perez and my wife, Francine.'

'Pleased to meet you.' Jamie slides in beside Emmy. As the vehicle pulls slowly away, he fumbles for a seat belt.

Emmy shakes her head. 'You don't need to bother in a limo.'

He sits back, unsure what to do with his hands, his mind a churning mess.

While the convoy drive sedately along country lanes, Jamie senses the building frustration of regular car drivers stuck behind them. Eventually they pull into a quiet cul-de-sac. He stares out of the window at a well-presented chalet bungalow.

'Come on.' Emmy leads him to where a man is waiting in the porch to greet them. 'Ilona's foster father,' she whispers.

'Thank you for coming.' The man forces a smile as he extends his hand. 'I'm Nigel.'

'I'm so sorry for your loss,' says Jamie.

Nigel nods. 'Please, go on through.' He turns to embrace Emmy's parents.

Jamie steps inside. The entire carpet is covered in a thick layer of plastic. His shoes squeak as he follows Emmy into the lounge. She gestures towards a tray of drinks on the table. 'Help yourself.'

On autopilot, Jamie takes a glass. When he turns back, Emmy's disappeared.

He wonders why he's here. Trying to be inconspicuous, he sits down on one of several chairs lined up against the back wall.

An elderly woman shuffles sideways to make room.

'Thank you.' Jamie extends his right hand. 'I'm Jamie, Ilona's boyfriend.'

'Mrs Wilson, neighbour. Hadn't seen Ilona in years.' She dabs her eyes with a tissue. 'Terrible thing…'

'Yes.' Jamie sips his drink. It's sweet sherry and he screws up his nose. Inharmonious chatter fills the room. He rubs his brow, pondering how soon he can leave without appearing rude. Glancing up, he spots Emmy approaching, accompanied by a smartly dressed woman in her sixties. Jamie jumps to his feet.

'Rowena, this is Jamie. Jamie, meet Rowena.' Emmy smiles. 'Jamie and Ilona thought the world of each other.'

'Jamie.' Rowena hugs him. 'I'm so pleased you came. We were sorry not to have met you at Christmas.' She shakes her head. 'We didn't get to meet many of Ilona's friends. Well, apart from Emmy, of course, and Courtney over there, chatting with Nigel.' Rowena gestures towards a dark-haired girl talking to her husband. 'Come with me.' She takes Jamie's arm. 'Let me introduce you to a few people.' She guides him towards a woman with spiky hair the colour of an aubergine. 'This is Doctor Lewis.'

As the woman spins round, her long earrings jangle. 'Helen, please.'

'And this is Lucas Trent,' continues Rowena. 'Excuse me. I must go and check on the sausage rolls.'

'You must be Jamie.' Lucas Trent shakes Jamie's hand. 'Ilona often spoke of you.'

Jamie nods, wondering what Ilona said.

A waitress circulates with a tray of drinks. Having successfully abandoned the sherry, Jamie helps himself to a glass of wine. 'Thank you.' He turns back to Helen. 'You're Ilona's therapists. I knew she had counselling.'

Helen and Lucas exchange a glance. 'Ilona was our client, yes,' says Helen.

'Dreadful thing…' Lucas shakes his head. 'I'd only known Ilona a couple of years. Helen and Ilona's relationship was more established.'

Rowena returns carrying a plate loaded with sausage rolls. 'I got there just in time. Another moment and they'd have been burned… Oh.' She lifts a hand to her mouth, her eyes brimming with tears. The plate tilts and sausage rolls slide to the floor.

Helen crouches down to scoop them up. Lucas pulls a handkerchief from his pocket and offers it to Rowena.

'Thank you.' Rowena dabs her eyes. She glances at the floor. 'Oh, Helen, leave that.' She attempts a brave smile. 'Good job we covered the carpet.' She turns to Jamie. 'Sorry, will you excuse me?'

The remaining three stand in awkward silence. All around the mood seems far from sombre. Jamie gives Helen a wry smile.

'People cope with grief in different ways,' she says.

Jamie can bear it no longer. 'Excuse me. I need to find the loo.' Leaving the therapists, he heads out to the hallway where he's waylaid by Emmy. 'Who's the fit guy you were talking to?'

'Lucas Trent, Ilona's psychotherapist.'

Emmy drains her glass. 'Think I'll go and introduce myself.'

Jamie leans against the wall. He watches as Helen extends

her hand to Emmy while Lucas adjusts his glasses like he's Clark Kent. On the other side of the room, Rowena is engrossed in conversation with an attractive, middle-aged blonde. He drains his wine glass. He really could do with the loo. He tries the door at the end of the hallway, but it's a small study. Nigel is sitting at the desk, a glass of amber liquid in his hand.

'Oh, I didn't mean to intrude...' Jamie goes to close the door.

'No problem.' Nigel smiles. 'I can't abide that wretched sherry.'

Rowena has approached unheard. 'I might have known this is where you'd be hiding, Nigel.' She turns to Jamie. 'I want to introduce you to someone.'

Jamie feigns a smile as the blonde woman steps forward.

'This is Fiona Taylor, Ilona's previous foster mum,' says Rowena. 'Fiona, this is Jamie, Ilona's boyfriend.'

He shake's Fiona's hand. 'Nice to meet you, Mrs Taylor. Ilona spoke of you fondly.'

'Please,' – she fluffs her hair – 'call me Fiona. It's so good to hear that Ilona had someone nice looking out for her.'

Behind her, a sullen looking teenager is skulking. Fiona draws him forward. 'And this is my son, Michael.'

'Michael,' says Jamie. 'Ilona always wanted to meet you.'

'Hmm.' The boy scowls as though he'd rather be anywhere else.

'So, when did you foster Ilona?' Jamie asks Fiona.

'Just before Michael was born.' She smiles as if recollecting a fond memory. 'Ilona was such a delightful little thing.'

'And you looked after the two of them?' asks Jamie.

Fiona frowns. 'What?'

'Ilona and Maya.' He scans the lounge. 'But Maya's not here?'

Rowena stares at him. 'Maya?'

'Yes.' Jamie smiles. 'I've heard so much about her, but I've yet to meet her.'

Rowena and Fiona catch each other's eye.

'Oh dear,' says Fiona.

'Sorry,' says Jamie. 'Have I said something wrong?'

'Nigel, we're coming in.' Rowena marches Jamie into the study.

Fiona turns to Michael. 'Wait here,' she says, before following them into the room.

Jamie's heart is thumping. 'What's wrong?'

'Nigel, pour Jamie a brandy. I'm going to fetch Helen.' Rowena closes the door behind her.

'What is it?' Jamie stares at Fiona. 'What did I say?'

Fiona's face is pale. 'Let's wait for Rowena.'

Nigel's hand is on his arm. 'You'd better sit down, lad.'

Jamie takes the seat vacated by Nigel. The door opens as Rowena returns with Helen in tow. 'I'm not sure I should comment…' Spotting Jamie's face, Helen stops talking.

Fiona takes a deep breath. 'Jamie, there is no Maya.'

'Sorry?' Jamie frowns. 'Ilona's sister, Maya. Ilona was always talking about her.'

'Maya was Ilona's imaginary friend.' Fiona looks to Helen for confirmation.

Helen shakes her head.

Rowena touches Helen's arm. 'Oh, Helen, please,' she pleads.

Helen sighs. 'Well, I suppose there's no harm…' She moves forward. 'Jamie, Ilona had dissociative identity disorder.'

'Dissociative identity…' Jamie's head is swimming. 'Is that the same as multiple personality disorder?'

'Yes,' continues Helen. 'A person with DID feels the presence of other identities, each with their own names, voices, personal histories and mannerisms.'

Jamie grabs the arms of the chair. 'Ilona didn't have a sister?'

'Oh yes. Ilona has a sister,' says Rowena. 'Khalu was badly injured in the fatal accident that killed Ilona's parents.'

'No.' Jamie feels like he's about to throw up.

'Here, lad.' Nigel forces a glass into Jamie's hand.

'Khalu's in a nursing home.' Rowena retrieves a handkerchief from her sleeve and blows her nose. 'She's in a permanent coma.'

Jamie lifts the brandy glass to his lips. He takes a slug, coughing as the warm liquid hits the back of his throat. 'I don't understand. You're telling me there never was a Maya?'

'Oh yes,' says Fiona. 'There was a Maya. The sisters were triplets, but Maya was stillborn. Their parents encouraged Ilona and Khalu to believe that Maya lived on in spirit form. That's why they never discouraged Ilona's imaginary friend.' She sighs. 'Perhaps now Ilona and Maya can finally rest in peace.'

CHAPTER FORTY-FOUR

The mourners have gone. Most drifting off as soon as the committal was over. Apart from Jamie. I almost touched him... Then Emmy came and even he left.

I lean over the edge of the grave pit, staring down at my coffin. The roses have wilted and some of their petals have dropped. Perhaps I've withered, too?

I stand back to watch as the gravediggers return to fill the hole. It's not something you normally get to see, the filling of a grave. The men leave a mound on top. When I was little, I thought the mound was the body, like when you buried someone in sand on a beach. Years later, I discovered the mound allows the coffin lid to collapse under the weight of six feet of soil. I shudder. Why did they bury me? Most people are cremated nowadays. It's not as if I have hordes of people who'll come to pay their respects.

Mum and Dad's graves are nearby. They share a head-stone. *David and Annie Parrish. Together in Life, Together in Death.* I suppose there'll be sufficient funds for a headstone for me. What will it say? *Ilona, Beloved Daughter, Sister, Girlfriend...* I never made it to wife, never made it to motherhood. Perhaps we three should share an epitaph? *Three Peas in a Pod...*

Four of us already under the earth. How odd, Khalu, that you should be the last one standing. Although you're not exactly standing, are you? Still, despite that terrible accident, you outlived us all. I'm sorry I never came to visit. I guess I tucked you away in a secret place in my head. But you were there at the end. That was you, wasn't it? You came to find me when I needed you.

A robin flies down to perch on the edge of Mum and Dad's headstone. He tilts his head, regarding me with interest. It was always Maya. Never me. Right from the start it was Maya. She caused all our problems. Well, now she's gone and we're well rid of her.

I look up at the trees. The wind breezes through a silver birch. This is a peaceful place I suppose, but not somewhere I want to spend eternity.

I've missed you, Khalu. Have you missed me? It won't be long now. Your body soldiers on but I fear your spirit has already left. Soon you will join me, and we'll make our way together. Like we were always meant to do.

CHAPTER FORTY-FIVE

Jamie steps through the revolving doors of St Margaret's Nursing Home. He smiles as he approaches the reception desk. 'My name is Jamie Marshall and I've come to visit Khalu Parrish.'

The receptionist stares back at him.

'Is that all right?' he asks.

'Yes, yes of course.' She takes off her glasses and cleans them with the edge of her scarf. 'It's just... I don't think Khalu Parrish has had a visitor, other than her solicitor, for many years.'

Jamie exhales. 'Well, I'm here now.'

'Take a seat.' The woman lifts the hand receiver from a phone. 'I'll call someone to speak with you.'

Jamie makes his way to the waiting area. He perches on a chair and gazes around. It's like any other waiting room, with a water dispenser and magazines fanned out on the coffee table. Advice posters on the wall. *How to recognise dementia; How to treat a stroke; Remember to ask your GP about your flu jab.*

On the other side of the window, a man creates uniform

lines with a sit-on mower. Jamie wonders how many of the residents get to benefit from the pristine gardens.

A woman hurries into the foyer. A member of staff by the look of it, in black trousers and tunic top with the care home logo. Her high heels seem somewhat inappropriate. She and the receptionist huddle at the desk, conferring in hushed voices. They glance across at Jamie and whisper some more.

The woman totters towards him, holding out her hand. 'Mr Marshall, is it?'

'Yes. I've come to visit Khalu Parrish, if it's convenient.'

'I'm Doctor Morris. I'm in charge of long-term care.' Strands of blonde hair escape from her tight ponytail. 'Here at St Margaret's, we provide care for residents with permanent or chronic conditions. May I ask your relationship to Miss Parrish?'

'My relationship was actually with Khalu's sister, Ilona, who recently passed away. We were very close.'

Doctor Morris settles down beside him. 'I am very sorry for your loss.'

'Thank you.' Jamie stares down at his hands. 'I'd like to meet Khalu if that's possible.'

'You've been appraised of Khalu's condition?'

'I know she's in a coma.'

'We call it unresponsive wakefulness syndrome. It's highly unlikely she'll be aware of your visit.'

Jamie swallows. 'Yes, I know.'

Doctor Morris stands up. 'Please, come this way.'

Jamie follows the doctor through a door, along a corridor and into a lift up to the third floor.

Doctor Morris pauses outside a room, her hand on the door handle. 'Are you ready? It can be a bit of a shock when you're not used to it.'

He takes a deep breath and nods.

Doctor Morris opens the door.

He'd been preparing for a scene from *Holby City*, but this is more like a sparse hotel room. The bed has equipment either side, but nothing is connected. He exhales. 'I thought there'd be more tubes and stuff?'

Doctor Morris shakes her head. 'Khalu's able to breathe for herself, so there's no need for permanent respiration. We use a PEG tube for feeding, but detach it when not in use.'

Jamie takes a step closer. The figure on the bed is so small she could be mistaken for a child. Her hair, presumably once the same as Ilona's, is shorter with streaks of white. 'Is she asleep?'

'Khalu's not awake in the normal sense of the word, but sometimes she opens her eyes.'

He feels grateful her eyes are closed today.

'You can talk to her if you like. It is possible she will hear.' Doctor Morris moves a chair to place it beside the bed. 'I'll leave you alone for a while.' She closes the door softly as she leaves.

Jamie moves forward. A thin white blanket covers Khalu's legs. Her arms stretch out alongside her body. He recognises Ilona's features, although Khalu's cheekbones are more pronounced.

What if, like the prince in Sleeping Beauty, he bent down and kissed her lips? Would she smile and sit up? Pull yourself together, you idiot, he thinks. This is not Ilona.

As he sits down beside her, Khalu remains motionless; her skin as pale as a porcelain doll.

Jamie takes her hand, feeling its weight in his palm. He strokes the back of her hand with his fingertips, tracing the fine line of freckles leading up her wrist.

Finally, his tears flow.

EPILOGUE

'Lot 156. Ah now, this is an unusual item.' The auctioneer gestures to where a young man is holding up the lot. 'Doll with three faces, circa 1892, registered by German doll maker Carl Bergner and signed CB. Made of finest quality bisque with glass eyes, it has a crying, sleeping and smiling face, all revealed by turning the knob at the top of the bonnet. This lot is in excellent condition. May I start the bidding now at £800?'

He casts an expert eye around the room, spotting a raised hand. '£800... thank you.' He exchanges a glance with a man manning the telephone. 'And I have £900 on the phones... do I hear £1,000?' He jabs a finger towards the back of the room. 'Thank you.'

The man on the phone speaks rapidly into the receiver before looking up at the auctioneer and nodding.

'£1,100 on the phones... do I hear £1,200?' The auctioneer waits. 'No? £1,150 then? I have £1,150.' He turns his attention to the telephone desks.

The man on the phone shakes his head.

'All done on the phones? £1,150 then and mark my words, I'm going to sell.' The auctioneer makes one final sweep. 'The bid is in the room, young lady at the back with the red hair. All done at £1,150? Going, going,' – he bangs his gavel – 'gone.'

ACKNOWLEDGMENTS

With gratitude to my editor, Claire Chamberlain for feedback, copy editing and proof-reading. Thank you to my dear friend, Patricia M Osborne for developmental editing of my manuscript. Also, a big shout out to my beta readers - Jane Collins, Susan Morris, Sam Rumens and Maureen Utting.

Thanks to my friends and writing buddies at Hove Friday Writing Group who continue to chivvy me along.

I'm grateful to Andy Keylock for the beautiful and original cover design. Special thanks to Marketing Pace for marketing my books and their continued involvement with my social media platform.

Finally, thanks to my partner, Colin and family and friends for their encouragement, support and love.

ABOUT THE AUTHOR

Suzi Bamblett lives in Crowborough, East Sussex. In 2019 she graduated with a distinction for her MA in Creative Writing (University of Brighton).

Suzi writes psychological thrillers and suspense stories for adults and young adults and she's a huge fan of Daphne du Maurier. Her *Imagined Dialogue with Daphne* can be found on the Daphne du Maurier website. Suzi's writing has been published in literary magazines and anthologies. She was recently long-listed in the Canadian Amy Award for her memoir piece - *A Grandmother's Grief.*

Three Faced Doll is her second novel.

Suzi's third novel will be released in 2022. For more information please visit her website Broodleroo.com where you can sign up to receive news.

ALSO BY SUZI BAMBLETT

The Travelling Philanthropist

Printed in Great Britain
by Amazon